CYPRESS LAKE

CYPRESS LAKE

A Romance Thriller

BY
LINDA WELLS

Library of Congress Control Number:2019916328
Dublin, Ohio

ISBN-9781079494440

PROLOGUE

Friday, Midnight

The screaming was loud, and Kim realized she was the one screaming. Everyone had frozen on the dance floor, but the fucking song had kept playing. What was that song? Oh yeah. "Truly, Madly, Deeply." An oldie but goodie. Someone had grabbed her arm and tried to pull her away. But she couldn't stop herself. Alexa deserved to be told what she was. *Fuck her.* Rick was her husband, and he'd humiliated her. All their friends had seen him with that blonde bitch. *How could he have done this to me?*

Someone had pulled her into the bathroom; then she started crying. Some of her supposed girlfriends tried to talk to her. They said Rick was outside, asking her to come out. But she wouldn't talk to him. It had become a blur, a scene from one of those movies where the party turns into chaos with nothing making sense. They'd left her in one of the stalls. "Let her cry it out," she heard someone say. "She's so drunk, she won't remember anything in the morning." But they were wrong. She'd remember. And Rick would pay.

After several tries, Kim found the "Start" button, and the engine came to life. Shifting into reverse, Kim pressed the accelerator to the floor, slamming her silver Acura into the SUV parked behind her. Her body was whiplashed, her weight pulling hard against the shoulder restraint. But she didn't stop or care. She was oblivious to everything except the last thing she saw before she was dragged out of the banquet room. Rick dancing with Alexa, holding her close, his arms wrapped around her slim body, her face nestled against his neck, her blonde hair draped over his shoulder. The alcohol was having the needed effect; Kim was numb but not unconscious. She'd have another drink when she got home. Maybe that would erase the image of seeing the two of them together, but she doubted it. She would never forget how they looked, their bodies pressed together and barely moving. She wouldn't let Rick forget it either. Not in a thousand lifetimes.

She hit the gas, and the sleek sedan jumped forward as she raced out of the parking lot, tires screeching. She held tight to the steering wheel, concentrating on her driving, but everything appeared out of focus. *Goddamn him. Why did he have to do this?* Kim licked her dry lips. She knew there was a bottle of vodka on the top shelf in the bedroom closet. She'd hidden it behind a stack of shoeboxes—he never checked there. And if she was lucky, she'd have time for a drink before he got home. Maybe more than one.

Kim drove down the dark two-lane road, her eyes straining to see the reflectors that marked the driveway entrance. She barely made the turn, cutting across part of the lawn. *Who cares,* she thought. She pressed the opener on the visor, raising the garage door. She steered into the space, knocking over the plastic trash can that was sitting next to the back wall. *Dammit!* She felt out of breath. *This can't be happening. Why would he do this to me?* She sat there for a few minutes, trying to orient herself to what had just happened. Her head was spinning, and dizziness and nausea hit all at once. *Maybe I had too much to drink,* she thought as her head collapsed onto the steering wheel.

The opener lamp overhead clicked off. The garage was in total darkness now. The mysterious figure hiding in the shadows had been waiting. A quick look up and down the road to make sure no one was coming, and then it only took a few steps to get to the car. The door opened easily, and the figure slid into the back seat, directly behind Kim. Grabbed by the forehead, Kim was forced upright, her head tilted back in an unnatural pose, her mouth gaping. The smell of booze was overpowering. The small pillow was pressed against Kim's face. The struggle was minimal; hardly any effort was needed to keep Kim from pushing the pillow away. When Kim's arms fell lifeless next to her slack body, the pillow was removed, and Kim fell sideways across the console.

The final touch—splashing the clear liquid on the back seat, then placing the bottle where it would be easily found. The figure got out of the back seat, shut the car door quietly, and tucked the pillow under the oversize nylon jacket. No one saw the dark silhouette leave as it came. A few minutes later, the only sound that might be heard was the low hum of a car driving down the deserted street and the faint whimper of a baby starting to cry.

1

Friday

Alexa Lee Smith's hands shook with nervous energy as she threw the empty plastic glasses and vodka miniatures into the rear galley's recycling bin. Suddenly, the plane hit an air pocket and began to rock and bounce, and two of the minis slipped from her grasp, rolled across the sloping laminate floor, and rested against the stainless-steel bulkhead. She picked them up and dropped them into the bin, just as the captain announced that he was turning on the seatbelt sign. *Thank goodness*, she thought as she steadied herself in the turbulence. She looked down the aisle, relieved that all the passengers were seated. Just as suddenly, the plane was out of the choppy air and continued its smooth approach to Orlando International Airport. She couldn't believe it. The flight from Chicago to Orlando seemed to have only taken minutes, not two hours. Her heart began to race as she thought about the week ahead.

Alexa was wiping spilled coffee from the counter when Meghan Jamison joined her.

"I think that's the last of it," said Meghan, throwing a handful of coffee cups and napkins into the trash bin.

"I've never served so many Bloody Marys!" Alexa tucked a loose strand of blonde hair behind her ear, took a deep breath, and turned to look at her friend.

"I know! At least they were in a good mood." Meghan laughed. Then her eyes trailed to Alexa's necklace. "You're wearing that?" She raised her eyebrows.

Alexa touched the gold heart that hung around her neck. "Why not?" she asked defensively. "I always wear it."

"It's beautiful. I didn't mean that. But what if he sees it?"

"He probably won't even remember," she said, shrugging her shoulders.

"I think he will." Meghan nodded her head in a definite yes.

"You're a hopeless romantic, Meggie." Alexa slipped the necklace inside the neckline of her blouse, out of sight, and finished cleaning the counter.

"Maybe I am," she agreed, sliding the last of the serving trays into the storage units. "Are you getting excited?"

"Yes, but I'm a little nervous too. It's been a long time."

"You'll have fun, and who knows what will happen?" Meghan said, a twinkle in her eye.

"You never know." Alexa smiled half-heartedly.

But Alexa knew the answer: nothing was going to happen. Not with *him* anyway. Maybe she shouldn't have made the trip. But it was too late now.

Meghan gave her a reassuring hug. "Don't worry. Seeing him again might be the best thing that could ever happen. Life has a way of working out the way it's supposed to."

Not always, thought Alexa. She loved Meghan, but she just couldn't tell her that life didn't always work like that. She wished it did, but Alexa wasn't going to count on it.

"You always say the right thing." Alexa hugged her back, truly grateful to have such a good friend.

"Have you heard from John?" asked Meghan as she popped open a can of Diet Coke and took a drink, looking over the rim at Alexa.

"No. I don't expect him to call." Alexa shook her head, pouring some leftover coffee into the cup that she'd stashed at the back of the counter.

Alexa knew he wouldn't call. She hadn't heard from John since last weekend. They'd spent Saturday evening together, and it had started out perfectly. He'd taken her to their favorite Italian restaurant, and over wine and a candlelit dinner, he'd asked her if she'd made a decision. She hadn't been able to answer him. He hadn't pressed her, but she knew that was the end, especially when she'd told him she was going on a week's vacation back to her hometown. She'd left out the part about her high school reunion. He'd gotten very quiet, and when he'd taken her home, he'd kissed her tenderly and held her longer than a brief moment before he turned and walked away, leaving her standing alone on her doorstep. She'd felt the goodbye in his kiss.

When she and John Wesley had started dating, Alexa had become infatuated with the handsome airline captain, and they'd gotten involved quickly. He'd been flying for Century Air for ten years, and he was ready to settle down. When he'd asked Alexa to marry him, she was stunned. She cared deeply for John, but she realized she wasn't in love with him. She wanted to love him, but something was missing. That instant desire, the passion, spark—whatever you call it—was just not there. Alexa remembered exactly how that spark felt, and she wasn't going to settle for anything less. John was considerate and loving, and he had a maturity that made her feel secure. He was everything she could want in a husband. But when he proposed, she'd asked him for time to think about it. That was six months ago. Last weekend, she knew he'd given her an unspoken ultimatum. Marry him, or it was over. But she just couldn't tell him that her feelings for someone else were getting in the way. How could she explain to John when even she couldn't understand it? He was perfect for her in so many ways, and she'd miss him terribly, but she knew she couldn't marry him. She'd been honest with him and finally honest with herself.

"You don't seem upset," said Meghan, taking a sip from Alexa's coffee cup and handing it back to her.

"I'm sad, but in some ways, I feel relieved," answered Alexa.

"I'm sorry it didn't work out, Alexa." There was concern in Meghan's voice.

"So am I," said Alexa, finishing the last of the coffee, then tossing the cup in the trash. "I better check on the passengers. We'll be on the ground soon."

Alexa meant it. She was sorry, and she couldn't blame John. She'd felt an emptiness in her life for so long, and she'd hoped he was the one. But she couldn't commit to him when she had unresolved feelings for someone else. And the stupid thing was that she hadn't seen Rick in years.

Thank goodness she could talk to Meghan. They were as close as sisters, and they'd shared everything with each other. Meeting Meghan in flight attendant training seven years ago was the best thing that could have happened to Alexa. Neither had been to a big city before, much less lived in one. Then they learned they were both going to be based in Chicago. They found a small two-bedroom apartment near the airport and began their exciting careers, and Alexa knew that Meghan loved their new working-girl independence as much as she did. Every trip was an adventure, and Alexa couldn't imagine doing anything else. Since then, Meghan had moved in with her fiancé, a businessman she'd met on a flight, and Alexa had bought a newly renovated condominium in the O'Hare district. But the two had remained close, bidding on the same trips so that they could fly together as often as possible.

After one last pass through the cabin on the final seat belt check, Alexa grabbed an empty seat in the last row. She pressed her forehead against the oval window, and through the wispy white clouds, she saw it: Cypress Lake, the expanse of beautiful blue water that she and her friend Katie had paddled across in her dad's canoe when they were in junior high and just starting to have their schoolgirl crushes. Boys were all they'd talked about back then.

She smiled at the memory, but other memories came flooding back. She'd just started her junior year at Florida State College when she'd gotten the phone call that her dad was in the hospital. She rushed home, but it was too late. (She'd lost her mom when she was only six.) Suddenly without her dad, Alexa's whole world fell apart. She was in a daze at the funeral, and going back to school felt impossible. She scrambled, applied for a flight attendant's position on a whim, and to her surprise was hired on the spot. She loved her new job—the travel, the perks, and making new friends, especially Meghan. But more important than anything, she learned she could take care of herself.

Now she was coming home for her ten-year high school reunion. She'd gotten the invitation, and her first reaction had been, "No way!" She hadn't been back to Cypress Lake since her dad's funeral, and that had been on purpose. Some memories were too painful. But when she saw the names of those who were attending, she'd known she couldn't stay away. He was going to be there. She'd heard through the grapevine that he was married, but she still wanted to see him. Nothing could or would happen. She was sure of that. Maybe she just wanted to try to erase him permanently from her thoughts, and seeing him with his wife might do that. She hoped so. Nothing else had worked. And she'd tried. She'd also tried to forgive herself for walking away from him. But she never would. One foolish moment had changed her life forever.

Alexa took one last look at the lake, then hurried back to the rear jump seat and fastened her seat belt. She could feel her heart beating faster as the plane made its final approach, the familiar sound of the landing gear locking into position. Moments later, the wheels chirped; then there was the loud contact as the brakes slowed the huge jet on the runway. Alexa Lee Smith was back where it all had started. She was coming home.

She unfastened her seat belt, buttoned her uniform jacket, straightened her trim skirt, and joined Meghan in the forward cabin as she announced their arrival and connecting flights on the PA. As the passengers were leaving, Alexa and Meghan stood at the cabin door and thanked them for flying Century Air. But inwardly, Alexa's little voice was telling her this trip was a big mistake.

Stop it! thought Alexa. *Look forward, not back!* Her new mantra.

After the passengers had left, she gathered her purse and carry-on and stopped to talk to Meghan, who was finishing the flight report in the forward galley.

"Thanks for signing me out in crew scheduling," said Alexa.

"No problem, Alexa. Promise you'll call or text me when you get a chance?"

"I promise," said Alexa, giving Meghan one last hug. "Have a safe trip, and I'll see you next Saturday."

Suddenly she didn't want to leave. She wished she were flying back to Chicago with Meghan on the turnaround. *Too late now!* She waved goodbye to the captain and first officer, and while walking through the Jetway, Alexa checked her cell phone. One missed call. She didn't recognize the number. *Whoever it was will call back,* she thought.

She made her way through the bustling terminal, trying to ignore the uneasy feeling in the pit of her stomach. *The flight went perfectly,* thought Alexa. She couldn't understand why she felt so jittery. She decided she must be hungry; she hadn't had time to eat anything all morning. But the sense of foreboding stayed with her as she made her way to baggage claim, where she retrieved her rolling suitcase before picking up her rental car, thrilled to discover it was an orange Mustang convertible. After stowing her luggage, she climbed behind the wheel.

Already feeling the heat, Alexa took off her jacket, placed it on the back seat, and rolled up the sleeves of her blouse. She lowered the visor and checked herself in the mirror—she'd changed, but not that much. Her blonde hair was longer, falling several inches past her shoulders, and her face was thinner, accentuating her high cheekbones and blue eyes. She'd have to do something about the dark circles under her eyes. Too many all-night flights and not enough sleep. She grabbed the silver lipstick tube from her purse, applied the pink shade, and put on her sunglasses.

Alexa took a deep breath, pushed the Start button, and cranked the AC to Max. She tuned the radio to her favorite country station, then backed out of the parking lot, surprised at the excitement she was feeling. She wanted to get settled into the Gold Palm Resort, her splurge for her weeklong vacation, but first she had to make a detour. She couldn't stay away from all the memories of Cypress Lake, many that still brought tears to her eyes. *Maybe it's not too late,* she thought.

Alexa exited the rental car lot, drove to the stoplight, and eased the Mustang onto the four-lane highway, the main road that would take her back. Back to her home, her friends, and maybe to a life that she could only dream about. The one she'd run away from. She'd soon find out. She just wished she could shake the feeling that coming back to Cypress Lake was a big mistake. She hoped she was wrong. But she didn't think so.

2

The drive to Cypress Lake took about forty minutes. When Alexa made the turn into Coral Estates, her heart sank. As a little girl, she'd always loved the sign at the entrance, with its pastel-pink flamingo and colorful seashells, but now it was weathered and faded, the words barely visible. She drove down the quiet street where she'd grown up and past rundown houses she barely recognized.

She parked the Mustang in front of the tan Florida ranch with peeling white trim and weeds growing along the front porch. The circular rock garden looked burned out with a single blanched cactus remaining, but the two palm trees her dad had planted arched over the house, beautiful and stately. She wished she could see into the backyard, but a slatted redwood fence blocked her view. Alexa wondered if the kidney-shaped pool where she and Katie had spent hours of their summer vacation swimming and sunbathing was still there. Alexa felt a lump in her throat, longing for what used to be.

This was where she'd last seen her mother, wearing red lipstick, a flowered dress, and high heels. The scent of orange blossoms floating around her, she'd given Alexa a quick kiss on the cheek and said, "Love you, honey; be a good girl" before leaving for work. When Alexa got home from school, her dad was there; it was the first time she'd ever seen him cry. He'd put his arms around her, told her about the car accident, said that it wasn't her mother's fault. She'd been too young to understand everything her dad had told her, but it hadn't stopped Alexa's heart from breaking. Tears filled her eyes as the vivid memories of that day came rushing back.

She would always love this house for other reasons too. It was the summer before Rick left for college. They'd waited until almost midnight, when she was sure her dad was asleep, then quickly changed into their swimsuits. Sneaking out into the darkness, they'd slipped into the cool water. Rick went in first and held his arms open to Alexa. She'd gotten in slowly, her arms hugging her shoulders, shivering in her blue ruffled bikini. He'd pulled her close to him, and she'd giggled and turned away, splashing water in his face. He'd gathered her in his arms again; this time, she hadn't pulled away. He'd kissed her, and she'd kissed him back, the contact taking her breath away. He'd unfastened her top, the night air cold on her skin before his warm lips grazed her breasts. Rick lifted her, wrapping her legs around his waist, and they kissed as he carried her to the blue tiled steps in the shallow end. She hadn't said no. It was the first time for them both, and she knew she belonged only to him forever. Those were the memories that brought back the old feelings—the passionate kisses that no one else could give her, the gentle touches of their young innocence, the deep love she'd never found with anyone else. Even though she'd tried. She touched the gold heart necklace that she never took off. The one Rick had given to her as a promise.

She was lost in her thoughts, remembering, when a car turned into the driveway. Startled, Alexa put the Mustang in gear, and with one final glance at the house, she drove away. She had to stop longing for something that was gone. Forever. She had to stop longing for something that was only a dream.

3

Rick wiped the sweat off his forehead with the sleeve of his faded T-shirt. The midday sun was hotter than hell, and he couldn't quite get the mailbox post straight. He threw his weight against the thick wood and muscled it vertical before shoveling dirt into the narrow space around the base. *What the hell,* he thought. Someone had hit the mailbox going full tilt, knocking it almost to the ground. He suspected it was Kim, but he hadn't said anything. He'd replaced the splintered wood and painted it, and now he was at the final step. Tamping down the last of the soil, he heard the front door open. He tipped his baseball cap back and looked toward the sound, squinting.

"Hey, Rick." Kim stood in the doorway wearing a denim mini-skirt, pink T-shirt, and sandals. The lush waves of her auburn hair fell over her shoulders. "Are you almost finished? I need to go to the mall."

"Can't you take the baby with you?" he asked, wanting to finish the project.

"No, I can't! Don't you remember? The reunion is tonight, and I need something to wear."

The last thing he wanted was to see a bunch of old high school friends and hear them brag about their jobs, their cars, the old high school football days, whatever. It was always the same BS. And he knew Kim. She always drank too much, and she'd probably already had a beer. It was getting to be a habit, one he hated but tolerated. When he'd mention it, she'd bite his head off. So he kept his mouth shut most of the time. At first it hadn't mattered, but with the baby, it more than worried him.

"Shit," he mumbled, then asked in a louder voice, "Do we have to go?"

"Of course! Mama's going to babysit. We've been planning this for months."

She meant that she'd been planning it for months. Rick knew it was pointless to argue with her.

"Let me finish this post, then I'll be in."

He heard the door slam, but Kim didn't answer. Maybe the re-union would be fun after all. He wondered if *she* would come. He doubted it. Last he'd heard she was living up north, Chicago, New York, somewhere—a flight attendant. He hadn't seen her since he'd gone to her friend Katie's wedding. He'd just graduated from Florida State College, and Alexa had just finished her freshman year there. She didn't speak to him until the reception. Rick ran into Alexa by accident when she was leaving the banquet hall, walking toward the ladies' room. She'd looked beautiful, her long blonde hair pulled up off her neck, the neck he remembered kissing in the back seat of his dad's car. She'd whisper his name, her breath warm on his skin, his hands all over her, the hours they'd spent petting and making love. Their kisses were deep and wet with promises and plans for their future. Together forever.

Rick had grabbed her hand, and she let him. They walked down the long, carpeted hallway, and when he saw an open doorway, he pulled Alexa in and closed the door. They were suddenly alone in an empty conference room. She looked angry but didn't try to leave.

"What is it, Rick?"

12

Her tone was cool but not her eyes. Alexa pulled her hand away and crossed her arms in front of her chest, not in a defensive way, but in a way that seemed as though she was holding herself back. The air between them was electric, and he sensed that she was feeling what he was feeling. At least he hoped so. And he couldn't take his eyes off her. She looked beautiful in the pale-lavender bridesmaid dress that draped off her shoulders and clung to her slender figure. And she was still wearing the necklace. He looked at the gold heart, then into her eyes.

"I just wanted to tell you that you look really nice," he said tentatively.

"Is that all?" Her anger filled the room.

"I'm sorry, Alexa." He reached for her hand and held it tight, not letting her pull away.

"You don't have to apologize," Alexa said.

"I messed everything up." His voice was low, his blue eyes staring into hers.

"It's over, Rick. Maybe we both made mistakes."

"Please listen. I didn't even know that girl. It was a fraternity party. Everyone had too much to drink, and she came into my room. I didn't expect any of it to happen." His voice was almost pleading.

He'd been a sophomore at Florida State College. The fraternity was a big deal to him, and the parties were fun, sometimes wild. He couldn't deny it. Alexa was still in high school, and he didn't think she'd find out. But she did. One of his friends told one of her girlfriends. And Alexa had broken up with him. All he'd ever wanted was to graduate and marry her. But Rick had blown it. Big-time. Now he wanted another chance.

"I know, Rick. I didn't think it would happen either." Her voice softened, and she was still holding his hand. She glanced toward the closed door. "I better get back. They're probably wondering where I am."

13

"OK. Just tell me. Do you like this guy?" he asked, meaning Alexa's escort, one of the ushers.

"We're just friends, and quite honestly, it's none of your business," she said.

"I know." Neither one of them moved.

She was so close, Rick could smell the scent of her fragrance mixed with the intimate smell of her skin that drove him crazy anytime he was near her. He pulled her toward him, and she didn't pull away. He held her against him, his arms wrapped around her, and exhaled at the feeling. It was right. He could tell it was right for her too. She buried her face in his neck, and her lips brushed against his before she pulled away and ran out of the room. He stood there for—he couldn't remember how long. Then he left the hotel. He couldn't go back and see her again, dancing with that asshole. That was the last time he'd seen her.

Rick dropped the shovel and walked to the blue Ford F-150 parked in the shade in the driveway. His cell phone was on the console, charging. He reached in through the passenger side window, scrolled through the contacts, and found her number. He'd never called her, even though he'd wanted to. Many times.

He hit dial. The call went straight to voice mail. He ended the call and threw the phone on the seat. *Dammit,* he thought, regretting that he'd called her. He headed back to the mailbox, gathered the shovel and tools, and carried them to the garage. He didn't notice the silver flash mirrored against the blue sky, the plane that would be landing in about ten minutes. With Alexa on it, heading straight back into his life.

4

Alexa parked the Mustang under the portico at the entrance to the Gold Palm Resort. She shoved her sunglasses into her hair, grabbed her purse and jacket, and entered the cool lobby, relieved to be out of the hot, still air. The lobby was elegant and contemporary with its polished marble floors, marble pillars, and potted palm trees. A Chihuly fountain, with its swirls of turquoise, blue, and white blown glass, was the centerpiece, the sounds of rippling water echoing off the vaulted ceiling. A sitting area with a circular turquoise sofa and two matching barrel chairs was in an alcove across from the registration desk. Boutiques lined both sides of the lobby, with beautiful window displays of designer fashions, jewelry, and sportswear. At the far end, floor-to-ceiling glass doors were open to lush tropical gardens and an outdoor restaurant. Alexa's stomach reminded her that she hadn't eaten, so she'd definitely have to visit the restaurant later. After checking in, she handed the car key to the attendant, who offered assistance with her luggage.

The suite was even more beautiful than Alexa had imagined, with a pale-yellow sofa and loveseat, a round glass coffee table, a wet bar stocked with assorted liquors and wine, and crystal cocktail glasses etched with palm fronds. A bistro set with floral-print cushions sat next to the French doors that opened onto a green awning-covered balcony. A palm tree filled one corner of the living room. The bedroom held a king-size bed with a white duvet, green and white accent pillows, and sculpted bronze lamps on the night tables. A hand-painted mural of Florida blue herons feeding along the banks of Cypress Lake covered the wall behind the bed. The adjoining bathroom was white marble with gold fixtures, with a sunken Jacuzzi bathtub and a walk-in shower.

She hung her uniform jacket in the closet and returned to the living room, opened the double doors, and stepped onto the balcony. It was midafternoon, hot and humid, and she could see a handful of sunbathers in deck chairs, lounging by the swimming pool. A patio with a snack bar and colorful umbrella tables overlooked the pool. Alexa admired the palm trees and manicured gardens, carved with paved walkways that led to tennis courts, a golf course, and the Palms Spa and Health Club. Alexa felt a calmness sweep over her. All of her concerns about the trip faded away, and she was happy she'd decided to stay at this luxurious resort. She couldn't wait to visit the spa and perhaps splurge on a relaxing massage.

An insistent knock interrupted Alexa's thoughts. She stepped back into the cool room, grabbed some bills from her purse, and opened the door. Her heart dropped.

"Josh!" Alexa was startled to see the tall, muscular, and extremely handsome man standing at her door. "What are you doing here?" She was caught off balance by Josh's unexpected appearance.

"Hey, Alexa," he said, cocking his head and giving her a wry smile. "I heard you were in town, so I thought I'd come by to see you. So we could have a little one-on-one time to catch up before the party tonight."

"Great," said Alexa, hoping she'd kept the disappointment from showing on her face.

The valet arrived just at that moment, and with an "Excuse me," she showed him where to place her bags. It gave Alexa time to get her bearings. *What the hell is Josh doing here?* she wondered.

She thanked the attendant and gave him the folded bills she'd been holding. When she turned around, Josh was across the room, standing next to the French doors. She realized she felt uncomfortable being alone with him in her hotel room.

"It's nice to see you again, Lexie. And you're as pretty as ever." He smiled, obviously checking her out.

Alexa didn't like being called Lexie, and Josh knew it. She thought she'd smelled beer when he was standing at the door, and looking at his eyes, she was sure of it.

"What have you been up to? How's Stacy?" she asked. Her nervousness came out as chatter, as she was still thrown by his unexpected visit.

"I'm the general manager at my dad's car dealership. He always wanted me to follow in his footsteps."

"You've done well for yourself." Alexa felt awkward, not sure what to say next.

Josh had a too-polished look, from his perfect haircut to his crisp dress slacks, expensive white golf shirt, and shiny loafers.

"Yes, I got my MBA and thought, 'What the hell, make the old man happy.'" His voice had a cold tone.

She asked again. "How's Stacy? I heard you two were married."

"Yes. Stacy and I are married." He began looking around the suite, checking out the bedroom and then walking over to the bar. He picked up one of the bottles, studied the label before putting it back down.

She knew he wanted her to offer him a drink, but there was no way. "I hope I get to see her tonight at the country club. Are you going to the meet and greet?"

17

Alexa felt her radar go up. What was he doing here? She and Josh Logan had dated a few times, but he was often drinking, and Alexa didn't like it. He'd been a star quarterback on the football team, but he had a dangerous quality that scared her. He'd had too many beers the last night she'd gone out with him. It was a night she wouldn't forget. He'd gotten rough with her when they were parking at the lakefront. He'd tried to touch her, tearing her blouse before pulling her bra strap off her shoulder. She'd screamed for him to stop. And he did, but she knew he wouldn't have if a police patrol car hadn't driven by at that very moment. She tried to brush the thoughts away.

Josh looked at her, his eyes lingering too long, and finally answered. "Yes, we're going, but I wanted to see you alone."

"I'm glad to see you, but I'm a little tired, and I need to unpack and do a few things before tonight." She walked to the door and opened it.

Josh's face turned cruel and ugly, and he was beside her before she realized what was happening. He pushed the door shut and grabbed Alexa by the waist, forcing his mouth on hers, even though she tried to turn her head away. The smell of alcohol was overpowering.

"Stop it!" Alexa put both hands on his chest and shoved hard to break free from his tight grip.

"Hey, sorry, Lexie," he said as he held his hands up and backed away. "Welcome home, sweetheart." His voice was husky, and he laughed, but it wasn't genuine. "I'll see you again tonight." His words held a warning as he left her room.

"Sure," she said, locking the door behind him.

Alexa pressed her back against the door, catching her breath. She knew coming back to Cypress Lake would open some old wounds—some more painful than others. She went into the bathroom and rinsed her mouth, her lips red and smarting from the forceful kiss. *What a creep!* She grabbed her blue running shorts, peach tank top, and sports bra from her suitcase, then gathered her hair back into a ponytail. Maybe a workout would ease the nagging doubts about her surprise visitor. As she grabbed her cell phone and key card, the disappointment swept through her. She wished it had been another man standing there when she'd opened the door.

5

Josh hated that stuck-up bitch. He pulled his white Cadillac Escalade out of the hotel parking lot, swearing under his breath. She hadn't changed since high school. He knew she'd fucked Rick and who knows who else. He'd heard she'd dated some older guy, too, a doctor. She'd no doubt fucked him too. Rick had never talked about Alexa, but it was obvious. They had been all over each other at the school dances, his hands on her tight little ass. He'd even seen Rick slide his hands up under Alexa's short cheerleading skirt one night after the homecoming game. Thinking about it turned him on. He should go back to the hotel and give her what she deserved. He looked at his watch. Shit! He had to get home before Stacy started asking him questions. And she'd give him hell because he'd been drinking. He wasn't ready to deal with her. Not just yet.

He made a quick turn into the crowded convenience store and parked in the back near the air pumps. He pulled out his cell phone. She answered after one ring.

"Hey, Josh." Kim practically purred into the phone.

"Where are you, sweetheart?"

"I'm at the mall. Where are you?" Her voice was teasing.

"I want to be where you are."

Josh was getting turned on just talking to her. She was always ready for a good time, no questions asked.

"I'd like to be where you are too," she answered.

He knew what that meant. "I'll meet you there."

He drove toward the fringes of town, where no one would recognize his car. By the time Kim got there, he was in the dark motel room, the one that had become special to them both. She tapped on the door, and he opened it, grabbing her arm and pulling her inside. He shoved her back against the closed door, covered her mouth with his, and kissed her hard. Her response was always quick and eager. She never played cat and mouse with him the way Stacy did, and he never got tired of Kim.

His breathing was rapid, his voice low. "Come over here."

His words were a command. He pulled her to the end of the bed, and he sat down, with Kim standing in front of him. She lifted her arms, and he pulled her T-shirt over her head, unfastened her push-up bra, and began kissing each breast as he ran his hands up under her skirt, sliding her bikini panties down to her ankles. She moaned with the sudden pleasure, clasping her hands behind his head as he nuzzled her chest.

"You're in a hurry." She looked down at him, breathless.

He maneuvered Kim onto the bed, his eyes fixed on her as he undressed. She was waiting for him, legs slightly apart, when he climbed in next to her. Josh pulled her against him, rolled onto his back, and positioned her on top of him.

"Sorry, this has to be a quickie." His voice was gravelly.

"God, yes," she moaned.

Her legs straddled him, his hands guiding her hips as they began the rhythmic motion, neither of them thinking of anything but the exquisite sensation.

Afterward, Josh grabbed the half-empty beer bottle off the chipped lamp table next to the bed. Leaning back against the crumpled pillow, he took a long draw and handed it to Kim, who was half naked and leaning close to him, her breasts against his chest. She sat up, took several swallows of the cold brew, and handed the bottle back to him. She got out of bed, pulled her skirt down, and fastened her bra.

"Are you going to the party tonight?" she asked, slipping on her T-shirt.

"I don't have any choice." He stood up and began dressing. "Is Rick going?"

"I guess, but he doesn't want to go. He doesn't like to party, not the way you do."

"It would be more fun if he doesn't show up," said Josh, grabbing Kim as she bent over to retrieve her panties from the floor.

Kim turned around, and he kissed her, his tongue in her open mouth and his hands under her skirt, caressing her bare skin.

"Stop it, Josh. I have to go. I'm late as it is."

But she didn't pull away. After one more lingering kiss, she pulled the skimpy panties up over her hips, grabbed her purse, and took a moment to look in the mirror. She ran her fingers through her long, tousled hair.

"Hey, Kim, you're one good lay." He smiled.

She blew him a kiss as she left. *Damn!* He hated going home, but the afternoon hadn't turned out to be a total waste. And maybe the evening wouldn't be so bad after all. He started thinking about Alexa, her long blonde hair, the lacy bra outlined under her blouse. Too bad she hadn't been in the mood. But maybe she would be tonight. He hoped he got the chance to find out.

6

After thirty minutes on the treadmill, Alexa's outlook had vastly improved. She'd put the bad scene with Josh out of her mind, determined to avoid him at the party that evening. She'd learned plenty about handling unruly passengers, so Josh was the least of her problems. But how did he know where she was staying? And why did he want to see her? She didn't want to think about his motives; she was just glad she'd gotten rid of him.

Alexa was dripping with sweat when she returned to her room. She peeled off her damp running clothes, showered, then wrapped herself in a large bath towel and checked her cell phone. She was excited to see that she had a text from Katie, asking if Alexa was going to be at the reunion party this evening. Alexa texted back a quick reply that she was at the Gold Palm Resort and that she'd love to meet her. "What time?" she typed. She also texted Meghan to let her know she'd arrived at the hotel. She'd tell Meghan about her unpleasant encounter with Josh when they talked later. Alexa was still rattled by his surprise visit.

She plugged her phone into the charger, threw the towel on the chair next to the bed, and slid under the cool sheets. She'd rest for a few minutes before getting ready. She was so happy to hear from her friend. They'd always stayed in touch with birthday cards and yearly phone calls, but she and Katie hadn't seen each other in years. Alexa was really looking forward to seeing her as well as so many of her former classmates. *The evening might turn out to be fun after all,* she thought, just before drifting off to sleep.

The ringing of her cell phone awoke her with a start.

"Hey, Alexa," said Katie, her voice bubbly and excited.

"Katie, I'm so glad you called." Alexa sat up, gathered the blanket around her shoulders, and propped herself up on the pillow.

"It's been so long since we've talked. How are you?" asked Katie.

"I'm great! I've really missed you," she answered. "Maybe we could get together early, before the party?"

"Let's meet at the country club bar around six thirty. We can catch up before everyone else gets there."

"I'd love it," said Alexa. "I can't wait to hear all the news." She didn't mention the one person she was truly interested in hearing about. She glanced at the digital clock on the nightstand. "It's four thirty. I better get going. See you soon, Katie!"

"Can't wait!"

Alexa was so happy to hear from one of her best friends. Maybe the evening would turn out to be better than she expected. But she couldn't ignore her hunger pangs any longer. She called room service and ordered coffee, orange juice, and chicken salad on a buttery croissant. After putting on the white terrycloth bathrobe she found hanging in the bathroom, Alexa grabbed her tablet from her carry-on, set it on the desk, and plugged it in to charge. She'd check email later. Then she took her time applying her makeup, with extra cover-up on the dark circles under her eyes. She'd just finished blow-drying her hair when she heard the knock on the door. "Room service!"

The waiter placed the tray on the bistro table near the balcony. After he left, Alexa poured the aromatic coffee into the china cup and enjoyed the view while eating her late lunch. She picked up the remote and turned the television to CMT as she drank her coffee. Keith Urban's and Miranda Lambert's blended voices were singing "When We Were Us," and tears started falling down her cheeks. She and Rick had been an "us." She had loved him from the moment they met. He was a senior, mature and serious, and they had their future all planned out. Had she made a mistake leaving him? Trust was everything, and in that one brief moment, it was gone. *Some things are better gone,* she thought, wiping the tears away. She lived another life now, without him. And obviously he'd moved on too. She had tried not to think about him. But it was becoming more and more impossible.

Alexa checked the time on her phone. She'd better hurry. She gulped the rest of the coffee and started dressing. After brushing her teeth and reapplying her lipstick, she slipped on a simple black knit dress, black kitten heels, and pearl drop earrings to finish the look. She stood in front of the full-length mirror. Her blonde hair fell in a soft flip, just below her shoulders. One more thing: a spritz of her favorite perfume, Chance. *The perfect fragrance for tonight,* she thought. She glanced at the gold heart around her neck. Meghan was right. It might send the wrong message if he saw it. She began to unclasp the chain but stopped herself. *No.* She couldn't.

Alexa tucked her cell phone and room key in her black leather clutch just as Whitney Houston started singing "I Will Always Love you."

"Forget it, Whitney!" She turned off the set, and with one more check of her lipstick, Alexa left the room and walked to the elevator, humming softly and remembering.

7

Where the hell was Josh? Stacy had called the dealership, but his assistant said he'd left early. When she called his cell, it went straight to voice mail. She was tired of trying to keep track of Josh's whereabouts. He always had a reasonable excuse, whether it was taking the deposit to the bank, going on a test drive with a client, or being tied up in a sales meeting. If he smelled like he'd been drinking, it was always a business lunch. The perfume scent that clung to him was always a customer's perfume. If she pressed him about it, he'd get angry. Then it would get very bad. He usually grabbed her wrists and squeezed them hard. So hard that tears would well in her eyes, and if she tried to pull away, he'd squeeze tighter. Sometimes it went further than that. But the bruises never showed. He was careful.

What could she do anyway? Leave him? They had two young children, and he could be wonderful. In fact, she believed he loved her. She knew it. He'd given her beautiful gifts, sometimes expensive jewelry. She touched the two-carat diamond earrings she was wearing. They'd often go on romantic trips together, just the two of them. When they were alone, she knew Josh belonged to her. If he did look at other women, she knew he'd never leave her. He was just the kind of guy who was good-looking and used to having women fall all over him. She was lucky that he'd even paid attention to her. She couldn't believe the first time he'd asked her out. She knew she was attractive but not in the way that most men liked. She was too slender, not voluptuous like most of the girls who Josh found attractive. But she kept herself in shape, and she wore her hair long, just the way he liked it. And she'd put blonde streaks in it. She kept a perfect tan, everything to keep his attention. And she was always willing when he wanted sex. However he wanted it. But it wasn't enough. If it was, why did he keep doing what he was doing?

Stacy had tried to stop asking him where he'd been or what he was doing. But she couldn't resist. She could tell when he was lying. Maybe that was why she asked. It was proof. And she knew he didn't want a divorce. He would hate the scandal—besides the fact that she'd take everything he had. Everyone in town knew what he did. It wouldn't be hard to prove it in court. She could take every cent he had, especially if she'd threaten to tell everyone what he'd done to her.

But she never wanted to hurt their two beautiful children. She didn't want them to know the kind of man their father was. Joshua and Anna deserved a father and a mother. Even if their parents were living a lie.

She looked at the clock. She'd better get to the school and pick them up. Joshua had soccer practice, and Anna had a dance lesson, and they'd be waiting. And she had to have dinner ready when Josh got home. He expected—no, *demanded*—a perfect meal, ready and on time. Even if he was late. Plus, she had to get ready for the reunion at the country club. It wasn't even her high school reunion, but she'd play the game and pretend to be the happy little housewife. She hoped Josh liked her dress. It fit her perfectly, and she'd bought a pretty push-up bra. She knew he liked her in sexy underwear.

She'd try Josh once more. She grabbed her cell and hit dial—no answer. *Dammit!* She wondered who he was with now. Maybe she'd find out tonight. He used to talk about some of his friends from high school. Kimberly Langston was one. Stacy had looked her up on Facebook. She looked like a slut in her photo. She was married, but that wouldn't matter to Josh. Kim hadn't been married very long, only about a year. And the baby must have come soon after that. Josh hadn't mentioned her name lately; Stacy guessed he didn't want her to suspect. She was smarter than he realized. He really should be more careful where he left his cell phone. Sometimes people got what they deserved anyway. Karma could certainly be, as they say, a bitch.

8

Patrice Langston sat with the metal foils stacked in tiers around her head, wondering if she was ever going to get out of the high-priced salon. Her hairdresser was running late with so many coming in for special occasions, including the reunion this weekend. But the popular salon was always busy, the music too loud, and Patrice's nerves were on edge anyway. And she needed a cigarette. Her cell phone rang, and she put down the *People* magazine to answer. She saw from the caller ID that it was Kimmie.

"Hey, sweetie," Patrice answered.

"Mama, where are you? Are you still coming over tonight to babysit?" Kim's voice was sharp and impatient.

Patrice was upset and worried about her daughter's drinking. She could tell from the sound of Kim's voice that she'd already started, and it wasn't even four o'clock.

"Of course I'm coming. I told you I'd watch Bethany."

"I know, Mama. I just wanted to make sure. And I wanted to tell you that you can eat here at the house, if you want. And Bethany should go to sleep early."

"She's always a doll for me, Kimmie. Every time I see that sweet little baby, I swear she's grown another inch." Patrice smiled, thinking of her beautiful granddaughter. But her thoughts clouded over. "Kim, I hope you haven't been drinking."

"Why would you ask me that?" she snapped. "Of course not!"

Patrice knew she'd made a mistake as soon as she'd said the words. "I'm sorry, honey. But you know I don't like you drinking around the baby. She needs you to be clearheaded."

"I'm fine, and it's none of your business," she blurted out.

"You're wrong. It is my business when it comes to Bethany." Patrice didn't want to go down this road. It was going nowhere, so she changed the subject. "Did you find a dress to wear tonight?"

"I found a cute red halter dress and gold strappy heels."

"You always look pretty, no matter what you wear," said Patrice.

It was true. Kimmie was pretty, with her long auburn (almost red) hair and hazel eyes that flashed fire when she was mad. But she wore too much makeup, and Patrice hated the way her daughter dressed, always too revealing, but she tried to keep her mouth shut. The girl always wanted attention and usually got it. Often the wrong kind. How did Rick put up with it?

Tiffany, the hairdresser, came over to check on Patrice's hair. "I have to go, honey. I'll call you when I'm on my way."

"Don't be late."

Patrice felt sick to her stomach. Why did Kim act like this? That baby was the greatest joy in her life, a perfect angel, and she didn't deserve to have a mother who did the things Kimmie did. And Rick couldn't seem to stop her. Maybe he didn't know what she was doing. But how could he not? He had to know about her drinking. And the other things. Maybe he didn't want to know. She was smart, knew how to lie and cover up. She'd been like that in high school. But Patrice always knew. Discipline hadn't worked. Nothing had worked. But alcohol was like that. Patrice cared about only one thing, and that was taking care of Bethany. Whatever happened beyond that was not her concern. She would do whatever it took to keep her one beautiful grandchild safe, no matter what.

9

Rick held Bethany against him, inhaling her warm baby scent, then placed her on her back in the crib, trying not to awaken her. Her soft blonde, wispy hair was sticking up, her long eyelashes resting against her round cheeks. He stood and watched her small chest expand as she inhaled deeply, her eyelids flickering as she settled into a peaceful sleep. Rick checked the monitor, then tiptoed from the room and closed the door. He was glad to have quiet moments alone with his daughter. She was calm with him, sensing his strength and steady hand. He hadn't experienced a love like this before. Maybe one other time. But that was gone.

Rick carried the almost-empty bottle downstairs to the kitchen and placed it in the sink. He poured himself a cup of still-warm coffee and headed down the short hallway to his office. He set the mug on the white ceramic coaster with the blue logo, RICK YOUNG CONSTRUCTION, next to a framed photo of himself and three buddies from his unit, dressed in full gear, sitting on a rocky hill in God-knows-where, Iraq. They were all smiling, two weeks from coming home. They'd all made it—except for one. He touched the scar above his right eye. Rick would never forget that day. The sound of the IED exploding was deafening, followed by lots of smoke and gunfire. He didn't know he'd been hit until later, when he felt blood running down his face. At times, he wished he'd been the one who hadn't made it home.

He relaxed into the black leather chair and checked his cell phone. No calls that couldn't wait. He looked out of the window that filled most of the wall across from his desk. The apron of lawn made a gradual slope toward the lake; the tall cypress trees were scattered along the bank, some growing straight out of the shallow water, branches thick with moss. His boat rocked gently in the covered boathouse at the end of the thirty-foot dock. The sun was late-day bright, and he could see two fishing boats bobbing in the distant chop. A door to the right of the window led to a slate patio where he often sat alone at night, watching the stars and listening to the water's gentle lap against the shoreline. Rick had picked this lot to build the dream house he'd always imagined sharing with Alexa. But some things turn out to be just that—dreams.

Rick opened his laptop, and while waiting for it to boot up, he checked his cell phone again. He'd hoped she'd call, but why would she? He hadn't spoken to Alexa since that day at the wedding. So many years had passed since he'd seen her. It was stupid for him to think she'd call now. Too much had happened that had changed everything.

10

It began with Kim calling and texting Rick on his business number. He hadn't seen her since high school and barely knew who she was, so he didn't pick up her calls. Then, out of the blue, she showed up at one of his construction sites, wearing cutoff shorts and a revealing tank top. He'd told her he was busy and didn't have time to talk to her. She wouldn't leave until he'd promised to meet her later for a drink. Embarrassed in front of his crew, he'd agreed. He hadn't planned to get involved with her, but she had a sensuality that attracted him, overwhelming his judgment, and she threw herself at him.

He remembered too many drunken nights, the sweat-drenched sex, waking up hungover with Kim next to him, her body warm and desirable, then more sex—which was always followed by morning regret. He was trying to forget, and he didn't know what she was doing. Rick knew he should stop seeing her, but she filled that empty place inside of him.

Then one night after a few drinks, she blindsided him with the news that she was pregnant. They'd never even talked about a future together. For someone who'd prided himself on maintaining control, he couldn't understand how he'd let this happen. In fact, he couldn't understand how she'd gotten pregnant since he'd always used protection. But he wasn't the kind of guy to walk away, even though he didn't love her. And he didn't believe she ever loved him. He suspected she'd been seeing other guys when they were dating. But he never accused her of misleading him. He had a responsibility, if not to her, then to their baby. And now that they had Bethany, he was grateful. She was the one good thing in his life. He had Kim to thank for that. But he could never love her. It wasn't her fault. It was his. He could only blame himself for his wasted life.

Rick had tried to be a good husband, treating Kim with respect, wanting everything to be right for Bethany, but Kim wasn't what he expected. Rick had been drawn to her because she was impulsive and exciting, but those qualities didn't fit with the marriage and family life Rick had envisioned. Her sudden disappearances and unpredictability turned into reckless behavior that worried him. He thought she'd step up to motherhood, at least try to put on a good front, but she wouldn't. Her drinking, when she thought he wouldn't find out, disturbed him. He cared only for Bethany's sake. She deserved a mother. Patrice helped out and adored her granddaughter. Rick saw the disapproving looks that Patrice gave Kim, but he and Patrice never talked about it.

Rick used work as an escape, and he'd managed to grow his construction business into a successful venture. He was well respected in the building industry; his company had more jobs than it could handle. The housing developments he'd designed had sold out before the first foundation had been poured. He'd always wanted his own business, and after getting out of the army, Rick had been at the right place at the right time. And he was glad he could provide security for Bethany. She gave him a reason to get out of bed in the mornings. But Kim worried him, and he often wondered why he'd ever gone out with her. The simple answer was that he'd missed his chance to have the life he wanted with Alexa. Big-time.

Rick looked at his watch. Where was Kim? She'd said she was going shopping, but she should be home by now. They were supposed to be at the country club by seven o'clock, and her mother would be arriving any minute. But Rick didn't know what Kim did most of the time, and he didn't really care. As long as she took care of the baby. And he wasn't sure she was doing that. She avoided Rick as much as possible. Maybe she sensed his feelings, his disapproval of her drinking. That he didn't love her. They hadn't been together in a long time, sleeping in separate bedrooms. But she'd gotten the life she wanted. He still wondered what he'd ever seen in her. He couldn't answer. It was too late now. Rick was trapped, and he knew it.

11

"Where've you been?" asked Rick.

He was waiting in the kitchen when Kim came through the door from the garage. Her pink T-shirt was wrinkled, her hair tousled, and she seemed out of breath. She threw the two department store bags and her purse down on the kitchen table.

"I told you I was going shopping," she snapped. "Is there any coffee left?"

He pointed to the coffee maker. She took a mug from the cabinet, poured the remainder of the stale coffee into the cup, and opened the microwave, punching twenty seconds on the timer.

"I didn't know you'd be gone all day," he said. "Your mom will be here soon, and the baby will be awake any minute."

"The mall was packed, and traffic was backed up on the interstate."

She was facing away from him, staring at the microwave.

"I guess we're not having dinner."

Rick was pissed, and he didn't want to go to the reunion anyway. She was keeping her distance; he knew why, but it wasn't working. The scent of alcohol mixed with sweat had been strong when she walked through the door.

43

"You can fix yourself something. I'll get the baby's bottle ready so you don't have to take care of her," Kim said sarcastically.

She pulled the can of dried formula from the cupboard and slammed it down onto the counter. Powder and water spilled around the bottle as Kim put in the measured amounts of both and placed the bottle in the refrigerator.

"I love taking care of her," said Rick. "I'm just sorry you don't seem to enjoy caring for your own daughter."

"You're an asshole to talk to me like that." She spit the words out like venom, turning around to face him. "I take care of her all the time while you're at work." Kim emphasized the word *work*.

"I have to work, Kim. In case you haven't noticed," he said. "You and I both wanted Bethany. You wanted to stay home and take care of her, and it's my job to provide for you and our daughter." Rick was trying to control his temper. "You wanted to be a mother. Start acting like one."

"I'm a good mother, and I don't have to thank you for anything."

Kim grabbed her purse and the shopping bags and stormed out of the kitchen. A few moments later, Rick heard the bedroom door slam. Then Bethany started crying.

"Shit," he said. "What a bitch."

Rick went upstairs to the baby's room. He heard the shower in the master bathroom running. He opened Bethany's door and walked to the crib.

"Hush, little girl. Daddy's got you," he whispered, picking her up and holding her against his shoulder. She was whimpering now, rubbing her balled-up fists against her wet, sleepy eyes.

He placed her on the changing table, talking softly and kissing her cheek; she smiled that little dimpled smile that tugged at his heart. He changed her diaper, then put her over his shoulder and carried her downstairs. Going into the kitchen, he grabbed the cool bottle from the refrigerator, heated it, then fed her while rocking her gently in his arms. Rick sat in the quiet kitchen at the round oak table, daylight fading, staring into the blue eyes of his beautiful daughter, wondering where her mother had been all day.

Rick was sitting at the kitchen table holding the sleeping baby in his arms when Kim walked into the room. Ignoring him, she opened a cabinet and took out a clean glass. She took the iced tea pitcher out of the refrigerator, filled the glass, and placed the pitcher back in the refrigerator. She leaned back against the counter and brought the glass to her red lips. Rick was dismayed by her appearance.

The red halter dress hugged every curve and stopped three inches above Kim's knees. The knit fabric barely covered her full breasts, the thin straps crisscrossing over her chest and tying behind her neck. Gold ankle-strap heels accentuated Kim's long legs, and waves of auburn hair cascaded over her bare shoulders. Large gold hoops dangled from each ear.

"You're not wearing that." Rick kept his voice low, trying not to awaken the baby.

"What's wrong with what I'm wearing?" asked Kim, indignant.

"I don't like it."

"It's pretty, and I'm wearing it."

Angry, Kim set the nearly full glass on the table, spilling tea on the wooden surface before she tried to take Bethany from his arms.

"No, Kim. I'll put her in her crib," he whispered, standing up and heading for the stairs, clutching the sleeping baby against his chest. "I'll be back in a minute, and we'll finish this conversation."

"There's nothing else to talk about. Mom texted me that she's going to be late, so I'll meet you at the country club."

"No." He turned to face her. "We're going together. I don't want you driving home by yourself." He was emphatic.

"I'll be fine. Don't you worry." Her words were full of sarcasm.

"I said, wait."

"Why do you all of a sudden want to go to the reunion? Hoping to see an old girlfriend?" Kim glared at him through her heavily made-up eyes.

"I'm not interested in seeing anyone, Kim. I'm going because you asked me to go." She always managed to twist their arguments into attacks on him.

"Yeah, right."

Kim was standing in the kitchen when Rick took Bethany upstairs, placed her in the crib, and crept out of the room. As he quietly closed the door, he heard the whirring sound of the garage door raising.

"Shit!"

He raced down the staircase into the foyer and opened the front door. The silver Acura was already at the end of the driveway. He could have pulled his cell phone out of his pocket to call her, but he didn't. Rick watched her back the car onto the street and drive away. He knew he couldn't stop her even if he tried. He wondered if Patrice had texted to say she'd be late or if Kim had lied so that she could go to the reunion without him. He'd soon find out.

12

Rick had just stepped out of the shower when he heard the front door open. He wrapped the towel around his waist and checked the time on his cell phone. It was 7:30 p.m. *It must be Patrice,* he thought. He dressed quickly, putting on his newest jeans, a light-blue button-down dress shirt, and tan oxfords. He grabbed a navy sport coat from his closet and hurried down the stairs, trying not to awaken Bethany. Patrice was in the kitchen making fresh coffee.

"Hey, Patrice," he said, giving her a quick hug.

"You look sharp. Wow!" She gave him a motherly smile of approval.

"Thanks," he said. "And thanks for making coffee." The water was starting to drip through the coffee maker, the aroma filling the kitchen.

"Where's Kim?" asked Patrice. "Is that girl still getting ready?"

"She's not here."

He didn't want to tell her about the fight. He and Patrice had always gotten along, but he knew that she was aware that his and Kim's marriage was less than perfect. Far from it. He'd overheard Kim talking on the phone to her mother about him, how he was never home, that she had to do everything around the house. Patrice had never mentioned any of it to him, but Rick always felt embarrassed when he saw her. He knew Kim bad-mouthed him, and he wasn't sure whether Patrice believed the things Kim said about him. Maybe he was embarrassed because some of it was true. He was angry at Kim and tired of the endless fighting. And the truth was that he didn't want to come home. He wouldn't if it wasn't for Bethany.

"Why didn't Kim wait for you?" asked Patrice.

He shrugged his shoulders. "She said you'd texted that you were running late. She got dressed and left."

He didn't know what else to say without going into the ugly details—that she'd been gone most of the day and that they'd fought. That she'd been drinking and looked like a whore.

"The baby's in bed. I don't think she'll wake up for a while. Do you mind making yourself something to eat? Kim didn't have time to make dinner."

"That's OK, Rick. I can make something for you to eat if you like," she said, patting him on the arm.

"No, thanks. I better get to the country club," he said. "Thanks for coming over."

"I know how Kimmie is." Patrice looked upset.

He put his arm around her. "You just have fun with Bethany tonight. When she wakes up, she'll be happy to see you."

The unanswered questions hung in the air—the ones about why Kim had left without Rick and whether she'd been drinking. They both knew the answers.

13

Katie was perched on a barstool, hard to miss in the striking orange palazzo sleeveless jumpsuit, her shoulder-length dark-brown bob with long thick bangs, and a cluster of gold bangles on her wrist. The bartender was placing a glass of white wine in front of her.

"Katie, I hope I'm not late," said Alexa, as she gave her friend a hug and sat down on the adjoining leather stool.

"No, I'm early." Katie smiled and hugged Alexa, looking her up and down. "Oh, my gosh! You're as beautiful as ever."

The bartender interrupted. "Would you care for a drink, miss?" He placed a square cocktail napkin in front of Alexa.

"I'll have a merlot, thanks," she said, then turned to her friend.

"You look awesome," Alexa said, admiring the stunning jumpsuit that clung to Katie's voluptuous curves. "You haven't changed a bit."

But Katie had changed. Alexa had never seen her dressed in anything quite so flamboyant. And over-the-top, low-cut sexy. Alexa stared at them both in the mirror behind the bar. Was this her best friend whom she'd known since elementary school, the one who was always ready for any adventure, a twenty-mile bicycle ride, kayaking on the lake, talking on the phone until all hours? Alexa wasn't sure.

"You never know who you might run into at these things, right?" laughed Katie. "I may not be on the market, but I still want to look good."

"You're right," said Alexa, and now they both were laughing. They each took a sip of their wine.

"I'm so happy to see you again," said Katie. "It's been too long."

They began filling in the details of their lives for the last eight years. Katie was a teacher at Cypress Lake Middle School, still crazy in love with her husband, Tim Cavanaugh, a bank manager, and they had two children who kept them busy. Tim couldn't make it because they couldn't find a babysitter. She showed Alexa several photos on her cell phone, two little girls with large brown eyes and long, dark curls, both spitting images of their mother. Alexa talked about her job, what it was like living in Chicago, some of the trips she'd taken, and a few of the guys she'd dated. She talked about John but said only that it hadn't worked out. What she didn't tell Katie was that he'd proposed to her, but she couldn't marry him. He was a good guy, but he wasn't Rick.

"They're adorable! It sounds like a storybook marriage, Katie," said Alexa, looking at a photo of Katie and Tim, the ocean in the background. "You found one of the nice ones."

"I did, and he still makes me melt." She laughed. "What about you, Alexa? Have you heard from Rick?"

Alexa thought her friend must have been reading her mind. "No. I heard he was married to Kim Langston." She shook her head in disbelief. "That was a shock."

"Did you know she was pregnant when they got married?" asked Katie, raising her eyebrows while finishing her glass of wine. She gestured to the bartender for another one.

"No, I didn't," answered Alexa, genuinely surprised.

"They haven't been married that long, a little over a year."

"I guess he's happy," she said, taking a sip of her wine.

"The talk is that he's not happy," said Katie. "And Kim hasn't changed since high school."

Alexa felt her heart break again, if what Katie said was true. Not just for her unhappiness but for Rick's. They'd both screwed everything up.

"I'm sorry to hear that," said Alexa.

They both knew what Kim had been like in high school. She was one of those girls with a flashy personality, not someone she ever thought Rick would get involved with. But Alexa knew that people could change, and a lack of judgment in high school didn't make someone a bad person. Alexa knew that all too well. Rick must have seen something good in Kim.

"What's he doing now? I heard he had his own construction company."

"Yes, he's doing well, from what I hear. He builds custom homes, and he's working on some new housing development," she said. "He still helps his dad with the citrus groves too." Katie picked her cell phone up from the bar and tapped on the screen. "Check this out."

Alexa stared at the Facebook photo. Rick, looking serious, had his arm thrown casually around Kim, and they were obviously in a bar somewhere. Kim had a wide grin on her face, laughing hilariously at something. Alexa was amazed at Rick's appearance. He was even more handsome than she remembered. His features were rugged, with a square jaw, dark hair cropped short, and scruffy beard. The prominent scar above his eye was new. The T-shirt with a black and gold army emblem was stretched tight over his wide shoulders. He appeared to be taller and more muscular but was still the man she would always know and belong to.

The bartender placed another glass of wine in front of Katie. She took a long swallow.

"Kim has everything now, including Rick," said Alexa wistfully, handing the phone back to Katie. She wished she hadn't come, but it was too late now.

"Do you want to see some more photos?" asked Katie, scrolling through other postings on her phone. "I saw one of Kim holding their baby. I think they have a little girl."

"No, thanks." Alexa stared down into her glass. She hadn't even known he'd been in the army. She fought back tears.

Katie put the phone down on the bar. "Trust me, Alexa. Kim's a first-class bitch. And she somehow managed to get Rick to marry her. She's slept with most of the guys in town, married and single. I can't believe Rick married her. And who knows if he's the father of Kim's baby?"

"Maybe he was trying to do the right thing." She tried to hide her shock about the baby. "Things work out the way they're supposed to," said Alexa, repeating the words of her best friend and trying to believe them.

"Not always. I make things work out the way I want them to work out."

The sharp edge of Katie's voice drowned out the soft background music, and others sitting at the bar turned to stare. Alexa had never heard her friend talk like this before. They weren't as close as they had been in high school, but this didn't sound like the Katie she once knew. It must be the alcohol talking.

"Look, just stick with me tonight. We'll have fun, and maybe we'll reconnect with someone we knew from high school," said Katie.

"Be careful, Katie; someone might take you seriously," said Alexa, trying to lessen the tension.

"You don't know me, and you're not me." Her anger came out of nowhere.

"This wine has gone straight to my head," said Alexa. "I haven't had much to eat. Maybe you haven't either."

"You're right. I'm sorry. It must be the wine." Katie looked uncomfortable.

Alexa changed the subject. "You won't believe this. I already re-connected with someone. Josh Logan."

"You're kidding."

Katie was shocked when she heard that he'd shown up at Alexa's hotel room.

"It's a small town. It was easy enough for him to track me down," she said. "But he's married, right?"

"Stacy's married, but I don't think Josh thinks he is. He's still the spoiled rich kid who thinks he's God's gift." Katie's tone was bitter.

"I'll do my best to avoid him tonight. Some guys never change." Alexa looked down at her watch, realizing the bar was starting to get noisy. "It's almost seven. We should probably go."

Katie said, "Let's stick together, the way we used to at the school dances."

"That sounds like fun," said Alexa, feeling the relaxing effects of the wine. "Here's to old friends."

She and Katie raised their glasses, clinking a toast before finishing their drinks. But her friend's abrupt anger had caught Alexa off guard. What had happened to Katie? She sensed that something might be wrong, but she hoped not. This evening could be full of surprises—but not necessarily good ones.

14

A banner reading "WELCOME CYPRESS LAKE WARRIORS, CLASS OF 2008" in brilliant blue and gold hung above the Oak Room doors, with the upbeat sounds of a well-known pop song spilling out into the hallway. Katie and Alexa picked up their name tags from the reception table. Alexa took a quick look to see if Rick's name tag was missing. His was still there, along with Kim's. She felt disappointed, but it was early. *Maybe he'll still come,* she thought.

She and Katie walked into the dimly lit banquet room. The music was blaring, and Katie started to do a few dance moves as they made their way to one of the round tables with seating for eight not far from the entrance.

"Let's sit here." She spoke loudly into Alexa's ear. "We'll be able to see everyone as they arrive."

Alexa nodded, sitting down next to Katie. She looked around the large banquet room, and she couldn't believe it—the room looked just like the high school gym when it was decorated for the school dances. A wave of nostalgia came over her.

"Katie, look. I think these are the same design as the centerpieces that were used when we were in high school," exclaimed Alexa, pointing to the blue and yellow paper carnations in the glittery gold vases. "There are twinkling lights over the dance floor too."

"You're right," said Katie, touching one of the carnations. "And look at the candles. It's like déjà vu." White floating candles were at each place setting.

Alexa had loved those dances. That's how she had met Rick. He was a senior, and she was in ninth grade. She'd always known who he was. He was the quarterback on the football team and the student body president. Everyone knew Rick Young. When he'd asked her to dance, she had almost fainted. He didn't even ask, really. He just walked up to her, took her hand, and led her onto the dance floor. He'd bent down, put his arms around her, and held her close against him. She'd had to stand on tiptoes to put her arms around his neck. He'd taken her breath away. They'd danced every dance together the rest of the night. When he'd said good night, he promised to call her the next day. And he did. From that moment on, they became inseparable, and she fell deeply in love. She knew he loved her too.

Alexa was lost in thought when Katie said something to her. "What did you say?"

"I said, I don't see any of the girls we hung out with; do you?"

Alexa looked around. Most of the tables were starting to fill, and in the candlelight, she couldn't recognize anyone. The room was noisy, everyone trying to talk over the loud music. A stage, with huge speakers on each end and blue and gold balloons floating overhead, had been set up next to the windows overlooking the golf course. A locally known deejay, Robbie Rox, the "Rock Jock," was playing one dance song after another, setting a festive mood. Several couples were already on the dance floor, moving to the upbeat rhythm of the B-52s' "Love Shack."

"This is going to be so much fun," said Katie, scanning the room. "Let's check out the bar, and I think I see the buffet table."

She pointed toward the far end of the room, where there was a long table with covered serving dishes.

"Wait a minute," said Alexa, grabbing Katie's arm. "Look over there."

"Where?" Katie turned her head to follow Alexa's gaze.

They saw Josh and Stacy standing at the edge of the dance floor, his head swiveling as he surveyed the crowd. He was tall, with his hair perfectly combed, wearing khaki slacks and a white dress shirt. He seemed to be ignoring his wife, who wore a sleeveless purple A-line dress, her streaked hair falling straight to her shoulders. She was dancing in place, her hips swaying to the beat.

"I hope I don't run into him tonight," said Alexa, uncomfortable at seeing Josh again.

"He won't want to face you after the stunt he pulled at your hotel," reassured Katie. "He's probably scared to death that you'll tell Stacy."

"You're right," agreed Alexa, determined to not let Josh ruin her evening.

Alexa and Katie made their way to the bar, saying hello to a few friends along the way. After they got their drinks, they stopped at the buffet table, which held a wide variety of delicious-looking food. After filling their plates, they went back to their table. They were sipping their drinks and enjoying the delectable meal when several former classmates joined them. They all began talking at once, reminiscing about the old days—their boyfriends, prom night, school dances, and their favorite teachers. Several were married, and they passed around their cell phones, sharing photos of their husbands and children. Katie was deep in conversation with a friend sitting next to her when Alexa touched Katie's arm to get her attention, whispering so that no one else could hear her.

"Look," said Alexa, gesturing toward the doorway.

Katie looked as two couples entered the banquet room, followed by a woman wearing a skintight dress.

"Do you think that's Kim? She doesn't look at all like she did in high school. Is Rick with her?"

"I haven't seen him. Maybe he's not coming," said Alexa, trying to hide her disappointment.

They couldn't stop staring at the young woman with the long, flowing hair, wearing a vibrant red halter dress and gold heels.

"Is she for real?" Katie's eyes widened.

"She's very attractive," said Alexa, trying to visualize Rick with Kim but finding it impossible.

They watched Kim walk toward the bar, talking to a few people along the way before disappearing into the crowd. Alexa kept staring at the entrance, but Rick never appeared. *Just as well*, she thought. Seeing Kim was the wake-up call she needed.

"Let's dance," said Katie to Alexa, putting her wineglass down on the table.

"No, I don't think so," said Alexa, shaking her head and smiling. She couldn't tell Katie that seeing Rick's wife had affected her more deeply than she anticipated.

"Come on!" She laughed. "Let's have some fun." Katie was on her feet, dancing and waving both arms in the air to the upbeat rhythm of a popular Bruno Mars song.

Reluctantly, Alexa followed Katie onto the dance floor. The deejay played a medley of playlist party songs, from "Let's Get It Started" to "Rock Your Body." Bodies were crushed together, moving to the high decibel beat. Alexa's mood lightened as she got caught up in the revelry, and all thoughts of Kim, Josh, and Rick began to disappear. The room pulsed with energy as friends reunited, hugging and laughing, on the crowded dance floor.

Alexa motioned to Katie that she was going to get something to drink, and while walking to the bar, she stopped to talk to two friends from her cheerleading squad. They exchanged hugs, happy to reconnect after so many years. The three young women talked about the fun times on the bus, the after-school practices, and the parties after the games. Both of Alexa's friends were married; one was in technical sales, and the other was a stay-at-home mom. One asked about her career as a flight attendant. Alexa said she loved her job, but it wasn't always as glamorous as it sounded, sharing some of the funny and not-so-funny incidents that had happened on her flights. She left out the part about how often she felt lonely, not having that special someone in her life. Seeing her hometown friends made her realize how different her life might have been if she'd married Rick and stayed in Cypress Lake. But Alexa was grateful for the life she'd made for herself, and she accepted the reality that some things just weren't meant to be.

Alexa took her glass of wine back to the table, and because Katie was still dancing, Alexa grabbed her purse and left the stuffy and crowded banquet hall to get some fresh air. The ladies' lounge was cool and quiet, with recessed lighting, an ivory leather sofa against one wall, and a marble vanity table with crystal vases of fresh flowers at each end.

Alexa sat on one of the vanity stools, opened her purse, and searched for her comb and lipstick. When she looked up into the mirror, she froze. She saw the reflection of the woman with the long hair and tight red dress standing directly behind her.

15

"I know who you came here to see, Alexa."

Alexa stood up and turned around, surprised at the confrontation. "What are you talking about, Kim?"

"He's at home with our baby, his and mine." She put her index finger on her chest and held it there for emphasis.

Kim was swaying slightly, her eyes unfocused and her words slurred. She was holding a glass filled with a clear liquid, a lime slice, and a few ice cubes.

"I don't know what you're implying, but I think you've had too much to drink." Alexa picked up her purse to leave, but Kim blocked her path.

"Sure you do. You always had a thing for Rick. Now he's my husband, and you'd better stay away from him," she stated. "You always thought you were better than anyone else, you and your stuck-up friends. Well, you're not!"

Her voice was getting louder and louder. She laughed as she tipped the glass back, some of the liquid dribbling down her chin.

Several women came into the bathroom and saw Kim and Alexa facing each other. Alexa didn't wait for another verbal attack. She shoved past Kim and left the lounge, but she could hear Kim's laughter as the door closed. Alexa walked back to the Oak Room as quickly as she could. She wanted to leave, but she had to find Katie first and tell her what had happened. She went to their table, but Katie wasn't there. She left the banquet hall, almost running to the country club entrance. She had to get as far away from Kim as possible. She pushed through the glass doors and stepped outside, took a deep breath of the fresh, warm air, and tried to decide what to do. She pulled her phone out to text Katie.

Then she saw him.

16

Rick drove around the crowded parking lot at the Lakeview Country Club until he spotted Kim's Acura. *At least she made it*, he thought.

The lot was nearly full, and Rick finally found an empty space in the last row. He parked the truck, grabbed his sport coat, and began walking toward the club entrance when he saw a slender blonde woman run out of the front doors. She began walking in his direction and then slowed her pace, looking directly at him. When Rick got closer, he was stunned to see who it was.

"Alexa?" he asked.

She was only ten feet from him, but he couldn't believe it. Seeing Alexa again felt almost like a physical blow; he was overwhelmed with emotions.

"Rick?" It was a question.

"What are you doing out here?" Rick asked. It appeared that she'd been running, as though she was trying to get away from someone or something.

She didn't answer him. She just bit her lower lip and shook her head as tears started falling down her cheeks.

"What's happened? What's wrong?" He rushed to her side, wrapped his arms around her, and held her close against him.

"Oh, Rick," she cried, leaning against him, her forehead on his chest, until she pulled away abruptly.

He stared at her face, the one he'd been imagining for ten years. The blue eyes, high cheekbones, and full lips were still there, but the young teenage girl was gone. Her face was slender, her cheekbones more prominent, but she was the same girl he'd fallen in love with in high school. The only girl he'd ever loved. And he couldn't believe he'd just held her in his arms.

"You have to tell me." He put his hands on her slender arms, reaching for her, not wanting to lose the connection.

"It's Kim," she said in a calmer voice. "She followed me into the ladies' lounge and said some pretty terrible things. I guess it really doesn't matter now."

Rick let go of Alexa. He couldn't believe Kim could do this. But why not? She was probably drunk, and although he never talked about his past, Kim knew how he felt about Alexa. Everyone knew about Alexa and Rick in high school. She was the unspoken threat to their marriage. One of many, but Alexa was the big one.

"I'm so sorry," said Rick. "She's probably had too much to drink."

Alexa's face was streaked with tears when she touched the scar above his eye. "What happened?" Worry clouded her face.

"I enlisted in the army after graduation." He didn't want to tell her that he was looking for some kind of meaning in his life. After he'd lost her, everything had seemed pointless.

"I wish we'd been together then," she said, her voice so low he barely heard her.

"Then I wouldn't be married to Kim." He laughed bitterly. "None of this would be happening."

"How did you get involved with her?" she asked. "You must have loved her."

"She came on to me. I went out with her, we got drunk, and she got pregnant. End of story." He looked away.

But that wasn't the whole story. He didn't tell her that when he was drunk, he could almost forget. When he was kissing Kim with his eyes closed, he was imagining she was Alexa. But why humiliate himself? Nothing could change what he'd done.

"You have a baby girl," said Alexa.

"She's beautiful, Alexa. Like you." His eyes were penetrating hers. He reached out and touched her face lightly with the tips of his fingers.

"Rick, I better go."

He took his hand away. "I know."

He stared at her. He wished she had called him. But she'd never do that. He remembered the last time they were together. How he'd screwed everything up. At times he'd hated her for leaving him. But then he'd remember what he'd done. He was the one who'd fucked up. Not Alexa.

Walk away now, he kept telling himself. *Don't make an even bigger mistake. You can't change the past.*

"Talk to me, Rick," she said.

She grabbed his hand. Words she always said to him that never needed to be explained. He knew what she wanted to know. Words that he needed to say and that she needed to hear. She let go of his hand and took several steps away, then turned back to face him. The moment was gone.

"But you're married now." People were starting to wander outside. "We'd better go inside separately," said Alexa.

"I don't care who sees us together."

He was upset and didn't want her to leave. There was so much more that he had to say to her. But he knew it was too late.

"Goodbye, Rick."

She turned and walked back toward the country club. But he'd seen the gold heart around her neck. The one he'd given to her. It was still there.

17

Rick watched Alexa walk away. He didn't try to stop her. She was right about everything. He was married, and it was too late. He had to find Kim and take her home. He sure as hell didn't need any more scenes. Kim had no reason to confront Alexa. That was a long time ago, too long for it to matter now, and he hadn't made any attempt to see Alexa in years. He'd had enough of Kim's out-of-control behavior. He'd had enough of her, period. How do you hold a marriage together by yourself? The answer was simple: you can't.

Rick went into the Oak Room and said hello to a few of the guys he recognized standing near the entrance. He made his way to the bar but didn't see Kim. He ordered a beer, paid the bartender, and looked around the room for his wife. Small groups were scattered throughout the spacious banquet hall, talking and laughing, the dance floor overflowing.

"Hey, Rick, how's it going?" Sean had played on the high school football team with Rick.

"Sean, how're you doing?" asked Rick, distracted.

"I'm doing well," he said, leaning toward Rick and raising his voice to be heard above the noise. "I hear you have your own business."

"Yes, I'm doing all right," he said. "What have you been up to?" Rick kept eyeing the crowd, trying to spot Kim.

"I work for a start-up IT company. Let me know if there's anything I can help you with." Sean reached in his pocket for a business card and handed it to Rick.

"Thanks." Rick nodded, sticking the card in his pocket. "I'll give you a call."

"Good. Maybe we can get together. Do you remember Lori? Lori Sellers? She was in Kim's class in school. We're married now."

Rick didn't answer. "You haven't seen Kim, have you?"

Sean hesitated. "I saw her dancing a little while ago. Man, she looks hot."

Rick felt his face flush with anger. Kim was making a fool of herself. And him. "If you see her, tell her I'm looking for her."

"Will do," said Sean. "Give me a call. Maybe we can all get together for dinner sometime."

Rick had stopped listening. He knew he'd better find Kim fast and take her home. He set his unfinished beer down on a nearby table and began walking around, his eyes searching the room. He'd had it with her shit! Where the fuck was she?

18

There was no sign of Kim anywhere; he'd circled the room several times but with no luck. Maybe she was in the country club bar, or she'd gone outside to smoke a cigarette. Rick left the sweltering banquet hall, passing some people he recognized, but he didn't stop to talk. He opened the heavy oak doors and checked out the bar, but she wasn't there. Maybe she'd decided to go home. He'd check the parking lot to see if her car was still there. Several people were standing outside smoking, and they said hello to Rick. He asked them if they'd seen Kim, but no one had noticed her come outside.

It was hot, and Rick took off his sport coat as he walked down the rows of cars, looking for Kim's Acura. He was in the farthest corner of the lot when he heard people talking; one was the deep rumble of a man, the other was a woman's voice. They were speaking in hushed tones before he heard a burst of female laughter. Then they stopped talking. He saw a white Escalade, the windows open. A woman's voice he recognized said, "Hurry up."

He walked over to the Cadillac and looked into the open rear window. Kim was lying on the back seat, the red halter dress untied, exposing her breasts. A man was positioned between her legs, his pants pulled down below his hips. Neither saw Rick standing outside the car, watching his wife getting ready to fuck someone else.

Enraged, Rick jerked the door open. "What the fuck do you think you're doing?"

He threw his jacket down, leaned in, grabbed the man by the shirt, yanked him out of the car, and spun him around. The man stumbled while trying to figure out what was happening.

"Jesus Christ," Josh mumbled as he bent down to pull up his pants.

"Fuck you," said Rick, just before his right fist caught Josh squarely on his left jaw, slamming him backward against the rear fender.

Josh crumpled into a heap, barely conscious, moaning as blood gushed out of his torn lip, pants twisted around both ankles. His head lolled backward as blood dripped down his face and onto his once-crisp white dress shirt.

Rick glared at Kim through the open door. She was sitting up, trying to fasten the torn straps of her dress around her neck. Her feet were bare; a pair of black panties had been tossed on the floor next to a single gold high heel. Kim's eyes were glazed as she looked up and saw him standing there.

"You fucking bitch." Rick picked up his sport coat, turned, and walked away.

"Fuck you, Rick!" Kim was out of the car, barefoot, screaming at the back of his head. "Where are you going? To see your girlfriend?"

Rick didn't even turn around.

19

When she saw Josh, he was leaning against the driver's-side door, bracing himself with both hands, staring down at the pavement. The seat of his pants was smudged with dirt.

"What are you doing out here?" Stacy asked, putting her hand on his shoulder.

He turned around, not answering. He stared at her while trying to steady himself.

"Oh, my God! You're bleeding!"

She pulled a tissue from her purse and started to dab at the blood on his face. He yanked the tissue from her, pushing her hand away from his swollen face.

"Stop it, you stupid bitch! That hurts!" he yelled. "Just get in the car."

He fumbled for his car key while Stacy walked around the Cadillac, got into the front seat, and slammed the door. Josh slid into the driver's seat and took a few deep breaths before starting the car. Stacy stared at her husband as he slowly pulled out of the Lakeview Country Club parking lot.

"You have to tell me what happened, Josh. You look terrible!" she exclaimed.

She hadn't missed the bloodstains on his shirt, and although she couldn't see the left side of his face, she knew it must be painful because he was careful when he pressed the tissue to his mouth. The cut bled quickly through the tissue, and Stacy dug in her purse for another one and handed it to Josh. He tossed the soaked tissue on the floor and grabbed the fresh one, applying it to his face.

"Do you need to go to the emergency room?" She was concerned when she saw how much he was bleeding.

"No. That's the last place I need to go." His words were slurred.

"When are you going to tell me what happened to you?"

"I fucking fell in the parking lot. Stop bugging me."

She could tell he was lying. He had a habit of clearing his throat right before he created a story that he expected her to believe.

"So you went out into the parking lot and fell? What were you doing out there? And why didn't you tell me where you were going?" She was pissed that he'd left her alone. But that wasn't unusual for Josh. "I've been looking everywhere for you."

"You must have been in the ladies' room. I was hot and went outside," he said. "I needed to clear my head a little."

"You're drunk." She was disgusted.

"Don't accuse me of anything." His voice was threatening.

"I'm not accusing you, Josh." She hesitated. "Sweetheart, why don't you let me drive?" she said softly, trying to cajole him into stopping the car.

She could tell he was trying to keep the car from veering into oncoming traffic. At times the car would cross the center line, and Stacy braced herself, trying not to scream.

"I've got this," he said. "Just shut the fuck up."

Stacy pressed her lips together and held tight to the armrest. She looked over at Josh again. He'd thrown the blood-saturated tissue out of the open window, and he was clutching the steering wheel with both hands, trying to keep the car from going off the road. It wasn't the first time he'd driven them home after he'd had too much to drink. It also wasn't the first time he'd disappeared when they were at a social gathering.

When she'd come back from the ladies' room at the country club, she couldn't find Josh anywhere. She'd asked a few people if they'd seen him. Someone said they thought he'd gone outside. That's when she found him slumped against their car. She knew that something had happened in the parking lot and that he'd never tell her the truth. But she had her ways of finding out.

20

Rick walked back into the country club, rubbing his throbbing hand and trying to control his anger. But he wanted to see Alexa one last time. Then he'd leave.

Sometimes you just need a wake-up call, he thought.

This was it between him and Kim. No way would he drag Alexa into his fucked-up life, but he couldn't go until he at least said goodbye. He seemed to keep making mistakes, and he didn't want to make another one.

The lights had been lowered, and the room was dark except for the candlelight and the twinkling lights over the dance floor. Rick saw Alexa standing next to a table near the back of the room talking to Katie, one of her friends. Rick walked over and said, "Excuse me." He grabbed Alexa's arm and pulled her to the side. "I need to talk to you."

Alexa, surprised to see him, glanced quickly around the room, then shook her head. "I don't think it's a good idea, Rick."

"Just give me a few minutes."

"Where's Kim?"

"I don't care." His jaw tightened.

Alexa turned and looked at Katie. "I'll be right back."

Rick stepped aside as Alexa led the way out of the noisy room. They walked side by side down the hallway, neither saying a word.

When they got to end of the empty corridor, Alexa turned and faced him. "What is it, Rick?"

He stared into her blue eyes. They were searching his, trying to understand what was going on.

"I wanted you to hear it from me. I'm leaving Kim, and it has nothing to do with you. But I had to tell you, in case I still mattered to you. Either way, Kim and I are finished."

Alexa reached for his hand, but he flinched and pulled it away in obvious pain.

"Oh, Rick," said Alexa, looking at his red, swollen knuckles. "What happened?"

"It doesn't matter." He shook his head.

"It does matter. How'd you get hurt?"

He ignored her question. "Alexa, I know I've made a lot of mistakes. Losing you was a big one." He stopped and took a deep breath. "I better get going."

He started to walk away.

"Wait, Rick."

He turned and looked at her.

"You matter to me. You always have," she whispered.

He stared at her in disbelief.

"I wanted to call you a thousand times. But I couldn't. At least until today." He stopped. "But you didn't answer."

He reached out to her. She placed her hand in his, and he pulled her against him.

"Alexa, I love you. I've always loved you," he said.

"I love you, Rick; you know that." She started crying.

He embraced her, and she put her arms around his shoulders. Nothing had changed between them. Tears filled his eyes. He pulled away from her and shook his head. The moment seemed surreal.

"Right now, I don't know what to say. I have to get through whatever's going on with Kim. Everything's all fucked up."

"Tell me what to do. I'll do anything you say. I just don't want to add to your problems with Kim," she said.

"You couldn't make things worse. But I don't want you involved in any of this. I don't know how to stop whatever's happening with her. I have to protect my daughter," he said. "And you."

"Don't worry about me. Just tell me how to help you. I'll do whatever you need me to do." Her eyes were swimming with tears.

"I don't know right now." He shook his head. Rick kept flashing on the image of Kim and Josh in the back seat of the car. "Come on, Alexa. I'll walk you back to the party."

His manner was brusque as he tried to stay in control of his emotions. He just wanted to get the hell out of there.

They stopped in front of the Oak Room. "I have to go," he said, looking into her eyes.

Just then, the pounding dance beat that had filled the hallway was replaced by the mellow strains of a popular love song.

"Rick, will you dance with me before you leave? One last dance?"

He didn't answer but followed Alexa into the banquet room. The lights were lowered, and couples began to make their way onto the dance floor as Savage Garden's "Truly, Madly, Deeply" began to play. She held his hand and led him through the darkened room and onto the dance floor, ignoring the stares of everyone around them. He took her in his arms, and Alexa reached up and wrapped her arms around his shoulders, her face buried against his neck. At that moment, the whole world disappeared as they held each other, moving slowly to the music and whispering words that only they could hear.

Suddenly a woman's voice could be heard above the music. She was out of control, screaming. "You fucking bitch!"

21

Everyone stared as Kim forced her way onto the dance floor and confronted Rick and Alexa, yelling at the top of her lungs. The couple let go of each other and stood motionless in disbelief. Rick was appalled at Kim's appearance. Her hair was damp and tangled, her makeup smeared, and her dress was torn, a strap hanging off one shoulder. But Kim seemed oblivious to everyone and everything as she continued her barrage of obscenities.

"You're dancing with that bitch?" she asked. "You asshole! I hate you!"

"Come on, Kim," said Rick. "Let's go."

Alexa stood, frozen, as Rick grabbed Kim by the arm and tried to get her to leave with him. She kept jerking her arm away while continuing her outburst. Finally, several of the women grabbed Kim and pulled her off the dance floor, but Kim kept looking back in the direction of Alexa and Rick, screaming and swearing. They dragged Kim out of the Oak Room and down the hall, managing to get her into the ladies' lounge.

Alexa and Rick stood there, astonished at the scene that had played out in front of them. Everyone had stopped dancing; some were stunned into silence, and some were laughing, the twinkling lights making grotesque patterns on their faces. The deejay quickly changed the song to an upbeat dance tune in an attempt to get everyone back into a party mood. A few couples started dancing again while others went to the bar, disturbed by what they'd just witnessed. Rick took Alexa's hand and led her back to her table.

"I'm so sorry," he said, releasing her hand.

"It's my fault," said Alexa. "I shouldn't have asked you to dance with me." She shook her head.

He looked toward the door. "I have to find Kim."

"Yes, you better go."

Rick went to the ladies' lounge and stood outside the door. He could hear several of the women talking to Kim, trying to get her to calm down, but they weren't having any luck. Rick knocked on the door, and Lindsay, one of Kim's friends, opened it slightly.

"She won't come out, Rick. She's pretty drunk, and she's locked herself in one of the stalls."

"I'm coming in to get her." Rick tried to shove past Lindsay.

"No, just wait. Seeing you now might make matters worse," she said. "I'm going to get her some coffee."

Rick stood there, helpless. He couldn't just leave Kim in there, but he had no choice. Maybe the coffee would sober her up. He was so fucking pissed. How could she behave this way? She'd made a fool of him in front of everyone they knew, but he really didn't give a shit. It wouldn't take long for the whole town to find out about Kim and Josh. Rick wondered if this was the first time Kim had been with Josh. Or who else she'd fucked. *It didn't matter now,* he thought. Kim's friends would take care of her. He'd had enough of her shit. She'd sealed her fate when he caught her fucking Josh. She'd walked away from him by betraying him. Rick knew this was the final straw. How could he continue to allow her to care for their daughter when she couldn't take care of herself? He knew the answer. He couldn't.

22

Alexa walked around the crowded room looking for Katie, but she couldn't find her anywhere. She checked her cell phone, and Katie hadn't responded to any of her texts. She'd just have to leave without saying goodbye. She knew she couldn't stay and face anyone after the scene Kim had made. She should have listened to her little voice, the one that had told her not to come to the reunion. But then again, she wouldn't have seen Rick.

Alexa's heart broke for him. He must have been so embarrassed by Kim's behavior. Alexa didn't know what had happened that caused Rick to decide to end his marriage to Kim, but after seeing Kim drunk and out of control, Alexa felt certain it wasn't Rick's fault. She wondered if the injury to his hand was somehow related to their breakup. How could he have stayed with Kim this long? But she knew the reason. He'd stayed because of his little girl. Rick would never walk away from his responsibility, and he'd proven that by marrying Kim.

She thought about Rick and how he'd gotten involved with Kim. Alexa didn't think they knew each other in high school. Kim hung out with a pretty fast crowd that had a reputation of partying a lot, and that meant drinking. After high school, she hadn't known what had happened to Kim. But she and Rick must have met, started dating, and even fallen in some kind of love. Alexa could understand Rick's attraction to Kim; she was striking and had a sexuality that would attract any man's attention. Kim's interest in Rick was understandable too. But whatever had brought them together didn't really matter now. All she knew was that Kim was hurting Rick.

Alexa had told herself that she wanted to attend the reunion to see Rick, to get him out of her system so that she could move on with her life. Then Katie had dropped the bombshell that Rick wasn't happily married. That might be an understatement, considering the events of the evening. But no matter how unhappy Rick was, Alexa had to remember that he was married. Even if he was planning to leave Kim, that hadn't happened yet. She made it a rule to steer clear of married men. Period. The uncertainty of this situation with Rick scared her. Losing both of her parents had taught her that the bottom could drop out at any moment. Losing Rick had been a life lesson too. She liked living on her own. That meant being in control of her own life and depending only on herself. She knew she should walk away and never look back.

The reality was that she hadn't seen Rick in ten years. But now that she had, those old feelings were still there and seemed very real. But were her feelings for him based on sentimentality and a longing for the past? Maybe she was in love with the memory of how they once were. But she didn't think so. The answer was simple. She loved him. She believed that loving someone doesn't need a reason or an explanation. That people don't choose who they love. It just happens. Rick was the good man she remembered, and he was facing a tough situation. And she believed in him. She would do whatever he needed. Even if it meant staying out of his life forever. That might be the best thing for everyone.

Alexa hated leaving without saying goodbye to Katie, but she couldn't stay any longer. She'd call Katie tomorrow and try to explain what happened. Alexa walked out of the country club, found the Mustang, and drove back to the Gold Palm. She let herself into her room, threw her purse down on the desk, fell across the soft duvet, and began to cry.

23

Saturday

She took off the gold hoops and bracelets, careful not to let them jangle, placed them on her dresser, and slipped off the too-tight high-heeled sandals. *What a relief!* she thought. Her feet had been killing her all evening. Katie walked into the large closet, unzipped her jumpsuit, and stepped out of it. Tim's voice startled her, coming from the darkness of their bedroom.

"Katie, how was the party?" He sounded sleepy.

"I'm sorry. I didn't mean to wake you up," she answered.

She picked up the jumpsuit, hung it on her side of the closet, and slipped on her cotton robe, tying the sash around her waist.

"That's OK. I was half-awake," he said. "Did you have a good time?"

Tim turned on the lamp next to the bed and propped himself up on the pillow. His slender shoulders and bare chest looked pale in the shadowed room, his brown hair swept across his forehead. He yawned, stretching his mouth wide as he grabbed his glasses off the night table. He slipped them on and patted the bed, inviting her to join him.

"Just a minute." She disappeared into the bathroom.

Tim was reading when she came to bed. She took off her robe, still wearing her black strapless bra and panties, and slid into bed next to him.

"How are the kids?"

"They're fine. We ordered a pizza and watched a DVD, one of the Disney movies," he said. "I guess you had a good time." He looked at his watch. It was after 2:00 a.m.

"I'm tired, Tim. Can we talk in the morning?" She fell back against the pillow and closed her eyes.

"It's pretty late," he said. "Where have you been?"

She didn't like him questioning her.

"If you must know, I've been with Alexa. There was kind of a scene at the reunion, and she got upset. She asked me if I'd go back to her hotel and stay with her for a little while, so I did."

"What kind of scene?"

"I'll tell you in the morning." She was half-asleep.

Tim gave up. "By the way, did I mention that you look very hot tonight?"

He put his book on the night table and took off his glasses. He leaned toward her and began touching the rounded tops of her breasts, his fingertips exploring the deep crevice between them. Katie rolled onto her side, facing away from him, and Tim pulled her close, kissing the back of her neck. His hands were all over her, fondling her breasts and hips, sliding up and down her thighs. He pressed his body against her, wanting her, the smell of wine and perfume intoxicating him.

"Come on, Katie, I missed you tonight." His voice was tender as his hand slid down the front her silk panties.

"Please, Tim. I'm tired." She pushed him away.

"I get it." Katie felt the bed shake when he rolled away and turned his back to her.

Tim was pissed, but she didn't care. She was tired, and she didn't want to deal with him right now. The evening hadn't gone quite the way she'd expected. It had turned out far better than she could have ever imagined.

24

The phone rang three times before Dan Hastings woke up. He looked at the clock as he placed the handset to his ear. It couldn't be good news at 3:00 a.m. And it wasn't.

"Are you sure?" Now wide awake, he leaned on his elbow as he spoke into the phone, fighting to keep his voice from breaking. He concentrated on what the caller was telling him before he answered. "I'll be there ASAP."

He ended the call and threw his legs over the side of the bed. He placed his hands on his thighs, trying to steady himself from the shock.

"What is it, Danny?" asked Lynn, who was only half-awake, her head still on the pillow. She reached over and touched his back, rubbing through the white T-shirt. "Let me make you some coffee."

"Go back to sleep," he answered brusquely.

"What's wrong, Dan?" She was sitting up now, and he could hear the worry in her voice.

"I'll call you when I know what's going on."

He somehow managed to stand. The motion helped him gain a semblance of control, but he wasn't ready to deal with Lynn or her questions. Not until he had the facts. And not before he had a tight grip on his emotions. And he wasn't there yet.

Dan Hastings had been chief of police in Cypress Lake for eight years, on the force for seven before that. He knew almost everyone who lived in the close-knit lakeside community, and it had been over five years since there'd been a murder. And it had been a robbery gone bad at a strip mall liquor store. Not someone he knew.

And maybe it wasn't murder. Maybe she'd just passed out from too much booze, had a heart attack or some undiagnosed health problem. He'd find out soon enough. But whatever had happened, it was bad.

He dressed quickly, strapped his holster around his waist, donned a light jacket, and drove to the familiar address. Sergeant Bert Lowe met him at the end of the driveway.

"Hey, Chief," said Bert.

"Is it Kim?" asked Dan.

"Yes, sir. The EMTs said it's probably alcohol overdose, but they thought it might be something else."

"Like what?" Dan wondered what Bert meant.

The sergeant shrugged his shoulders. "I'm not sure, but they thought you should have a look."

Dan Hastings hated this type of case. A close friend found dead, possibly murdered. But she wasn't just a friend. He'd been sleeping with Kim off and on for several years. He was married, and so was she. And he suspected that he wasn't the only one. But it hadn't stopped him. He'd fallen in love with her against his better judgment. But she was still a friend, and she'd been in trouble. He'd tried to convince her to stop drinking, but nothing he said would sink in. A hard head.

Damn! He took off his CLPD cap, ran a hand through his thinning blond hair, then put the cap back on. He took a deep breath.

Whatever had happened to her, it could blow up in his face in more ways than he could begin to imagine. *Shit!*

Dan looked toward the garage, the double door raised, yellow tape barricading the entrance.

"Is Rick here?" asked the chief.

"Yes. He and his mother-in-law are in the house."

"Did you talk to them?" He turned to look toward the house, illuminated by the swirling strobe lights of the police and ambulance vehicles.

"Yes. Patrice Langston, Kim's mother, is kind of out of it. She's upset and crying, and she seems pretty confused."

"What about Rick?" He turned his gaze back to Bert.

"Rick found Kim in the car when he got home from some party at the Lakeview Country Club. About two o'clock," said Bert. "But that's all I could get from him."

Dan stood silent for a moment as he processed the information.

"You took photos?" he asked the officer.

Bert held up his cell phone. "Yep."

"Guess I better take a look."

Dan recognized the two EMTs who were standing outside the garage. They stopped talking as he approached.

"What do you think happened, Mark?" Dan had known the older of the two medical techs a long time.

"Not sure. Probably an OD but thought you should make the call."

Dan nodded and looked into the garage at the silver Acura. He felt lightheaded as he approached the open driver's-side door and bent forward to look into the car. The first thing he saw was her crumpled red dress, a curve of pale shoulders, and the back of her tangled mass of hair. It looked like she'd leaned over the console to look for something on the passenger-side floor. But she hadn't. He walked around the back of the car and approached from the passenger side. Kim's head was at a ninety-degree angle, one side of her face resting against the leather seat. Her mouth was gaping open, tongue extended, lipstick smeared, hair disheveled and covering half of her face. Both arms were trapped under her body in an unnatural pose. A red strap with a frayed end was hanging over one shoulder. The smell of vomit and death was overpowering. It was all he could do not to cry out. Dan backed away quickly and made it halfway down the driveway before stopping to take deep breaths of fresh air.

"You OK, Chief?" Bert was now standing next to him, staring at him.

"Yeah, I'm fine." He looked at the sergeant. "Call Doc Jacobs."

"Yes, sir." Bert pulled out his cell phone.

"Get Jimmy to canvass the neighborhood. I want to know if anyone saw or heard anything unusual. And get one of the evidence kits and check out the car."

"You're acting like this is a murder, Chief," said Bert.

"I don't know what it is," said Dan. "Not yet. Just do what I told you to do."

"OK, Chief."

Dan looked toward the house but didn't move. He had to talk to Rick, and he knew this wasn't going to be easy. *Goddammit. How could this have happened?* His gut wrenched as he fought back tears. He had to keep his head together and find out what happened to Kim. She'd probably had too much to drink, went over the edge. But she'd had too much to drink before. Maybe she'd taken pills. But why now? Why would she die like this? None of it made sense. Unless something else had happened to her. If she had been murdered, he'd find her killer if it took his last breath. She never deserved this. He should have married her a long time ago. But she wouldn't. Why had she been seeing him if Rick had been treating her right? *Fuck!* If only he'd been able to help her. Now it was too late.

25

The house was bright with lights as Dan stepped into a foyer with a vaulted ceiling, a crystal chandelier, and an oriental rug on the light oak floor. Kim had always liked nice things, and Rick could afford to give them to her.

"Hey, Rick," said Dan, extending his hand.

"Dan." Rick looked dazed.

"I'm very sorry for your loss."

Rick didn't respond. Dan followed Rick into the formal living room, where a thin, middle-aged woman with short blonde hair was sitting on one end of a tufted gray sofa, her arms cradling a baby wrapped in a yellow blanket. An empty baby bottle sat upright on the end table next to them.

"Patrice, this is Dan Hastings, the chief of police," said Rick, his hands in the pockets of his jeans and the sleeves of his light-blue dress shirt rolled up.

Dan stood in the middle of the room next to Rick. "Mrs. Langston, I'm so sorry to bother you at this time, but I need to ask you some questions," he said. "I know this is difficult."

Patrice began sobbing, pressing her face into the pale-yellow blanket that she was clutching to her chest. Dan stared at the woman and the sleeping baby in her arms. Then he came back to the moment and motioned for Rick to move toward the other side of the living room, away from Patrice.

Rick lowered his voice. "I'm the one who found Kim. I came home; the garage door was open, and she was in the car. That's it." Tears welled in his eyes.

"What time did you get home?"

"It was around two this morning. I left the country club after Kim did. She was upset about something, got pissed, and took off; it was my fault," he said, regret strong in his voice. "If only I'd stopped her." His voice broke.

"Lakeview Country Club?" asked the police chief.

"Yes. Kim's high school reunion."

"Tell me what happened." Dan waited.

"Kim had a lot to drink. We'd fought about that before, and to-night wasn't any different."

"So that's what you fought about? Her drinking?"

"Yes," said Rick.

"That's when she got mad and left?" asked Dan.

Rick nodded, staring down at the carpet.

Dan was getting the picture—Rick looked like a man who felt guilty as hell about something, including letting his wife drive home drunk. "And you called the police right after you found Kim in the garage?"

"Yes. I thought she'd just passed out. When I opened the car door, I realized…" He stopped, disbelief hanging in the air.

"How long has your mother-in-law been here?"

"She's been here all evening babysitting."

The police chief looked over at Patrice. "Mrs. Langston, did you hear anything unusual before Rick got home?"

Patrice was looking down at the baby in her arms and didn't answer.

He spoke to her again in a louder voice. "Mrs. Langston, you didn't hear the garage door go up or talk to Kim after she arrived at home?"

"No, I didn't hear anything," she whispered, not looking at him. "Earlier I went out to have a cigarette on the patio." Her voice began to break. "I thought I heard a noise..." She stopped, tried to gain control. "But there was nothing there." She started rambling, her voice quivering. "I just can't believe my beautiful girl is gone. I told her to not to drink. Oh, my God! Why didn't she listen?" Patrice gasped. "Oh, my God! Oh, Kimmie!" She put a hand over her face and began sobbing uncontrollably.

Rick walked over to Patrice, sat down next to her, and put his arm around her. He spoke soothingly before offering to take Bethany, but she held the baby closer against her chest, tears streaking her face. Rick got up and walked over to Dan.

Dan glanced at Patrice and then lowered his voice. "Did your wife have any health problems?"

"She was fine, except she drank too much," he said.

"What about pills?"

Rick shook his head.

"Did you fight a lot?" Dan stared at Rick; his tone was cold.

"What do you mean?" Rick didn't seem to understand the question.

It was too soon. "I think I've asked you enough questions for now." He started walking toward the foyer. "Please call me if you remember anything that might be important."

Dan handed Rick his card and then walked out of the house and across the grass to the garage. The neighbors were out in their yards watching the activity, the police cars and ambulance lights having disturbed the usually quiet street. Bert met him before he got to the open garage door.

"The inside of the car reeks of alcohol and perfume," said the officer.

"That's not a surprise. What'd you find in the car?" asked Dan.

"A bottle under the driver's seat. Her cell phone was on the passenger-side floor," he answered. "It must have fallen out of her purse."

"Did you find the purse?"

"Yes, sir. There was money and a credit card in the purse. I put everything in two evidence bags."

"Doesn't sound like a robbery," Dan said to the officer. "When you go back to the station, put the bags in my office."

"Not in the evidence room?" Bert looked puzzled.

"I'll log it in." Dan ignored the questioning look Bert gave him.

"Sure thing, Chief."

Both men turned to look at the tan car that had just pulled in behind Dan's patrol car. It was the assistant medical examiner, Dr. Bob Jacobs. Dan met the doctor on the sidewalk, and the two men talked as they made their way to the open garage doors with the yellow police tape.

26

Dan was waiting outside the garage when the doctor came out, ripping off the latex examination gloves. The doctor told the EMTs they could remove the body, then he turned to Dan.

"What do you think, Doc?" asked Dan. He and Bob Jacobs had been friends for a long time. He was not only the assistant medical examiner in the district but also one of the most respected physicians in Cypress Lake.

"She was too young," he answered, shaking his head.

"Yes, she was." He tried to control the tremor in his voice.

"We'll know more after the medical examiner does the autopsy. It looks like alcohol poisoning, but other things indicate asphyxiation, maybe from the alcohol. Maybe drugs." The doctor hesitated. "Or maybe not an accident."

Dan looked into Bob's eyes. They looked tired, and the older man's gray hair was uncombed, his plaid shirt and khaki slacks wrinkled.

"Why do you think it might not have been accidental?" he asked.

"I don't know for certain. I scraped under her fingernails. Offhand, it looks like blood, but we'll have to wait for the forensics report, Dan." He paused. "Her body position is unusual for an overdose. If she'd passed out, she wouldn't have fallen sideways, on her arms. But it is possible."

"So it could have been an accident."

"Yes, possibly. But her dress was torn, like she might have struggled with an assailant."

"Yeah, I saw the dress." He was quiet for a moment. "How long has she been…" Dan's voice trailed off.

"Time of death? Not long—about twelve thirty a.m.," said the doctor.

"Can you get me a preliminary report by tomorrow?" asked Dan.

"I can try."

"Thanks, Doc." The older man nodded and started walking back to his car.

Dan watched as the EMTs put Kim's limp body into a black body bag and placed it on the stretcher. Rick had come out of the house and walked next to the stretcher as they lifted her into the ambulance. He just stood there, staring until the flashing lights disappeared from view. Dan tried to read what was going through Rick's mind, but he didn't have a clue. Maybe Rick was broken up by Kim's death, but he hadn't fallen apart. But what did Dan expect from a guy who didn't know where the hell his wife was half the time. *Shit!* He must be one coldhearted bastard.

Rick was still standing motionless when Dan walked through the damp grass and stood next to him. "I'd like you to come to my office later today. How about eleven?"

"Why?" Rick looked at Dan, a puzzled expression on his face.

"I need to ask you some questions." The words hung there.

"I've told you everything I know. I came home and found her."

"Well, first of all, your wife is dead. And it's possible that the cause is from an alcohol overdose, but we don't know for sure," answered Dan.

"What are you saying? It was an accident, goddammit! You know she drank too much." Rick glared at Dan.

"But if it was an accident, why is her dress torn? And why the hell didn't you drive her home?" He leaned close, put his arm around Rick's shoulder, and whispered in his ear. "You let your wife drive home drunk."

Rick stared at him in disbelief. "Fuck you, Dan."

The police chief headed toward his patrol car, lights still flashing. He called over his shoulder. "I'll see you at eleven." Under his breath, Dan muttered, "You bastard."

Kim was dead. And Dan was going to find out every detail of what had happened before Kim Young got behind the wheel of her car at the Lakeview Country Club and drove home alone, only minutes before her young life ended.

27

"What happened?" asked Lynn. She had been waiting for Dan at the front door.

"Kim Young. She's dead." He walked past her, heading for the kitchen. "I need some coffee, then I have to get down to the station."

"Oh, my God," gasped Lynn, putting her hand over her mouth. Still in her bathrobe, she followed Dan and watched him pour the freshly brewed coffee into the clean mug she'd set out for him. "What happened?"

"We don't know yet. She probably died of alcohol poisoning." He took a long swallow.

"I can't believe it," said Lynn, shaking her head. "How did it happen?"

"Rick found her in the car in the garage. They'd been to a party," he answered. "We don't know anything yet, so keep this to yourself. Got it?" His tone was sharp.

"Don't worry. I won't tell anyone." She looked at him. "You can trust me." She slung the words over her shoulder as she walked out of the kitchen and down the hallway into their bedroom.

Dan followed her. "What do you mean by that?" He set the half-filled mug on top of his bureau and looked at her, his large hands resting on his hips.

"I didn't mean anything, Dan. I'm sorry to hear about Kim."

She started making the king-size bed, pulling the lightweight blanket up over the top sheet. She straightened and plumped the pillows, not looking at him. Dan didn't respond. He took off his holster, hung it over the chair in the corner of the room, and unbuttoned his shirt as he walked into the bathroom.

When Lynn heard the shower running, she went into the kitchen. She looked out of the kitchen window. It was early, not quite dawn; she had plenty of time to get ready for work. She picked up her coffee cup, still full, and placed it in the microwave to reheat it. While waiting, she felt for the slip of paper in her bathrobe pocket. It was still there. She'd checked his cell phone's call history, but he'd been careful to delete any suspicious texts or phone calls. But he'd slipped up. She thought about the night a few weeks ago when she'd found what she was looking for.

She had waited until the pattern of his breathing transitioned to its usual low snore. She knew at that level of deep sleep, he wouldn't be easily disturbed when she'd made her move. She'd looked over at him one more time, flat on his back, mouth slightly open, a single sheet pulled up to cover his broad chest. Then she'd rolled quietly out of bed.

His slacks were thrown across the upholstered chair, the holster in its usual place, draped over the back. The chair functioned as his extended closet, and she'd learned never to complain about it. He always put his wallet in the top drawer of the tall bureau that sat along the wall closest to the bathroom. She'd looked for it earlier, but he must have been tired when he got home; he'd forgotten to put it away.

Lynn had walked in slow steps to the chair. She'd stopped, unmoving, when she heard the gasp, the loud snort; the mattress groaned as he flipped onto his right side, facing the wall. The room became still again. No breathing sounds. She'd waited and listened. It took only a minute or so for the rhythmic noise of his deep breathing to resume.

She hadn't wanted to pick up the pants for fear the belt buckle would jangle. She'd found the right-side pocket dangling off the chair, weighted down by the thick bulge of his wallet. Grabbing it, she'd slipped silently into the bathroom and closed the door without locking it, not chancing a possible metallic click. The night-light was enough for her to find what she was looking for. The yellow, torn remnant of a Post-it note was wedged between his driver's license and auto club card. She'd taken the sliver of paper and slipped it into her bathrobe pocket.

Returning the wallet to his pants pocket, she'd reversed her steps and climbed back into bed. She'd felt a mix of distress and deep anger at his betrayal, but she hadn't said anything. She'd known he was seeing someone, but she didn't know who. It isn't true what they say, that the wife is the last to know. The wife always knows. She doesn't necessarily know who her husband is cheating with, but she knows.

She'd memorized the phone number, but she'd held on to the slip of paper, in case. She wasn't certain whose number it, but she'd found out when she'd dialed it from work and had gotten voice mail.

How could he have been so stupid? She loved Dan, but he'd been hurting her for too long. Now it was his turn to hurt.

The microwave beeped, causing her to jump. She carried the cup of coffee to the kitchen table and sat down. She heard the shower stop running just as she started to cry, tears spilling onto her bathrobe.

28

Alexa woke up, not certain where she was. A muffled ringing sound that seemed to be coming through a thick fog had startled her out of a deep sleep. Then she realized it was her cell phone. She'd fallen asleep with her clothes on, and everything that had happened the night before came rushing back. The lamp on the night table was still turned on; she grabbed her phone but didn't recognize the number.

"Alexa, it's me, Rick," he said.

"Rick," said Alexa, surprised to hear his voice. "Are you all right?"

"No."

She could hear in his voice that something was terribly wrong, and she became frightened.

"Tell me." She waited.

"It's Kim. She's dead."

Alexa couldn't believe it. Had he just said Kim was dead? "You're joking, right?"

"No, this is no joke. When I got home early this morning, I found Kim." She heard him take a deep breath before continuing. "She was in her car. The police are still here, so I can't really talk."

"Oh, my God, Rick. I can't believe it."

"Everything is so screwed up. I don't know when I can talk to you again," he said. "She was drunk last night, and she drove herself home. She must have had too much to drink, overdosed or something. But the police are acting like something else could have happened to her."

"What do you mean?" asked Alexa.

"They're acting like I'm responsible. Fuck! I don't know," he said. "I guess I am. I let her drive home drunk. Jesus!" His voice broke.

"Oh, Rick, I'm so sorry," said Alexa.

"I have to go." Suddenly he was distant. "I just wanted to tell you what happened."

"What can I do to help you?"

"There's nothing you can do," he said. "Just remember I love you."

"I love you, too, Rick." He'd already hung up.

Alexa put the phone down and looked at the clock. It was 4:30 a.m. She knew she wouldn't be able to get back to sleep. She took her dress off, climbed back into bed, and stared at the ceiling. Seeing Rick again had been wonderful. But when Katie had told her that Rick was married to Kim, and on top of that, that they had a baby, it was a shock. Finding out that he wasn't happily married had been an even bigger shock. She had no idea how badly things had turned out for him. His life with Kim was not what it had seemed. The way she'd behaved at the reunion had been appalling, including the scene in the ladies' room when she had verbally attacked Alexa. Now Kim was dead.

Alexa felt a cold chill run through her. Why would the police be involved if Kim had died from an accidental overdose? What was Rick so afraid of? Alexa knew that something bad had happened at the reunion, and Rick wouldn't tell her what it was. Alexa believed he loved her and didn't want her involved, that he was trying to protect her. But from what? This trip was turning into a nightmare. How could all this be happening? Rick was wonderful, the only man she'd ever loved. But the questions kept coming. What had happened last night between Rick and Kim? And why was Kim dead?

29

The phone was ringing when Dan walked into the station house. He stopped at the desk and waited to see if the call was for him. He looked at his watch; it was 5:45 a.m.

Betsy looked up from the phone. "Bert wants to talk to you."

"You're here early," he said to the older woman.

"So are you." She shrugged her shoulders.

Dan stared down at her and tapped his fingers on the desk. Betsy's dyed-brown hair was cut short and styled in soft curls. She had on a red cardigan that she wore most days over a different colored blouse, and her reading glasses were propped on the end of her nose. She'd been here long before Dan had joined the CLPD, and he was almost certain she'd be here after he left. He relied on her and was especially glad to see her today.

"I'll take it in my office." He walked through the door, sat down behind the worn metal desk, and picked up the black handset.

"Yeah, Bert. What have you got?" he asked.

"Larry from county forensics went over the car. He checked for fingerprints. He'll send a report later."

"How's Rick doing?" asked Dan.

"He's cooperating, but he's very quiet," answered Bert. "The mother's taking it hard. She's looking after the baby when she's not in her room."

"What about the neighbors? Anybody see anything?"

"Nope. Nobody saw a thing."

"Ask Jimmy to stay there. I need to talk to the coroner."

"Right, Chief," he answered.

Dan hung up the phone. He looked through his contacts for the number and hit dial. The call was picked up after one ring.

"Dr. Jacobs speaking."

30

"Hey, Doc," said Dan.

"Dan, I was going to give you a call," he answered.

"What do you have?"

"Just remember, these are preliminary findings. Samples have been sent to the county forensics lab, but I can give you some information that will be helpful."

"I'm listening," said Dan as he pulled a legal pad out of the desk drawer and a ballpoint pen from the ceramic cup stuffed full on his desk.

"I found bruises on both of the victim's wrists. They could have been made by someone grabbing her. These types of bruises are common during a domestic dispute. She also had intercourse within the last eight hours. There were traces of semen and lacerations on her tissue, so it could have been forced or rough sex. It's hard to tell. A strap on her dress was torn."

Jesus, thought Dan. "What about her blood alcohol level?"

"High. I'll send the final toxicology report to you when I get it."

"So she could have died from alcohol overdose."

"Yes, it's possible. But there's something else." The doctor hesitated. "At first I thought she might have hit her face on the steering

111

wheel. Bruising and swelling of her face and mouth indicate some kind of blunt force. But Kim's face was tinged blue, especially around her mouth. Her lips were swollen, and she had bruising of her gums and tongue."

Dan waited.

"These are all indications of asphyxiation," said the doctor. "I also found a trace of fibers in her nasal passages."

Dan was having trouble writing down the words. "So you think she may have been suffocated? Is that what you're saying?"

"I'm just telling you what I found on the initial exam, Dan. Don't jump to conclusions." He stopped. "But it's possible. With the alcohol level so high, it would have been easy. Three minutes and she'd have been finished."

Dan dropped the pen, leaned his weight back into the desk chair, and rubbed his eyes with his free hand, still holding the phone to his ear.

"Are you there?"

"I'm here."

"I'm sorry, Dan. You knew the victim?" asked Jacobs.

"Yeah. I knew her."

"I'm very sorry. I'll get back to you when the final report is completed."

Dan hung up, stared at the notepad in disbelief, and threw the pen across the room. He looked at his watch. He wasn't going to wait until 11:00 a.m. to talk to Rick. There were too many unanswered questions that needed to be answered. Now.

31

D an stood on the brick front porch and rang the doorbell. He leaned
back against the scrolled wrought-iron railing and looked at his
watch. It was 7:00 a.m. Jimmy was still there, placing yellow police
tape along the length of the driveway. Rick's pickup truck was in the
driveway, parked next to an older model tan Camry. The front lawn
was manicured and perfectly landscaped, with two large oak trees
on each side of the brick sidewalk leading to the front door, shrubs
and flowers accenting the beautiful lakeside home. *Funny how you can
have everything and nothing, all at the same time,* thought Dan. He'd had
only fleeting moments with Kim, but they'd been everything. His
thoughts began to drift to the last time he'd seen her. It was about a
week ago, the memory vivid.

The silver Acura was going about seventy-five miles per hour when
he'd pulled up behind it and flashed the lights, no siren. It was late
at night, and it wasn't the first time Dan had pulled this car over.
Dammit! He was sure she was doing it on purpose. He didn't like

being put in this position. He liked making the moves. *Goddammit,* he'd thought. She had him under her thumb, and she knew it.

He'd put on his baseball cap, opened the glove compartment, pulled out the half pack of stale cigarettes, a book of matches tucked inside the cellophane wrapper, and stuck them in his pocket. He'd been trying to quit, but he kept them handy in case he needed one. He needed one now. He'd gotten out of the car but took a deep breath before he walked up to the passenger side of the Acura. He looked up and down the dark two-lane road before he opened the car door and slid into the passenger seat.

"Hey, sweetheart," he'd said.

"I've missed you, Danny." She shook her hair over her shoulder and looked at him.

He'd glanced at her bare legs and then stared out of the front windshield. She'd shifted in the seat, positioning herself to face him. He'd pulled the pack of smokes and matches out of his uniform shirt. He shook a cigarette into his mouth, then he'd offered the pack to Kim. She'd taken it with a graceful movement, her red fingernails flashing, and smiled at him. Dan struck a match, held it first for her, then for him. He'd sat back in his seat and exhaled at the same time he rolled down the car window. He'd taken his cap off, thrown it onto the back seat, and unfastened his belt and pants.

"I've missed you, too, baby." His voice was rough, and he started to feel out of control.

He'd flicked the barely smoked cigarette out of the window, turned toward Kim, and slid his hand under her short skirt, her legs widening for his touch. He'd leaned over the console, lifted her long hair, and placed his mouth on the nape of her neck, just below her earlobe. His mouth lingered, tasting her skin, while his fingers found the mound of silk between her thighs. Kim had placed her hand behind Dan's neck, cigarette still between her fingers, and they'd kissed, her mouth open to his. Without a word, she threw the cigarette away and reached for his open zipper. Dan leaned back into the seat, both feet braced on the floorboards, his hands on the back of Kim's head. He had gasped and shuddered, breathing out the words, "I love you, baby." Later, he'd kissed her before he got out of the car and told her to slow down, that she knew how much she meant to him, and that he didn't want anything to happen to her.

"Nothing's going to happen to me." Kim smiled, waving good-bye to Dan, who was standing on the side of the road next to her car.

She'd hit the accelerator, a cloud of dust swirling around him as the car's taillights disappeared into the darkness.

He swallowed hard, holding back tears, wishing he could go back to that night, change the course of their lives, and make all this go away, when the front door opened.

"Come in," said Rick.

He was wearing the same clothes he'd had on when Dan talked to him earlier. The house was quiet, with no sign of Kim's mother or the baby.

"Where's your mother-in-law?" asked Dan, trying to shift his thoughts back to the present.

"She's asleep," he answered in a monotone. "Can I get you some coffee?" Rick looked exhausted and pale, his eyes bloodshot.

"No, thanks." Dan took his time. "Look, Rick. I know this is hard, but I have to ask you some questions."

"OK," said Rick. "Why don't we talk in my office? I don't want to disturb Patrice or wake the baby."

"Sure."

Dan followed Rick past the kitchen to the back of the house and into Rick's office. Rick took his place behind the large polished oak desk.

"Have a seat," said Rick, pointing to the upholstered chair sitting next to his desk.

Dan stood, staring out of the large window facing the lake. It was early, but the sun was already glinting bright off the water. He imagined Kim sunbathing in the backyard, sitting on the patio or walking out on the dock to get into the boat. He turned to face Rick.

"This won't take long." He paused. "Why did Kim drive herself to the country club last night?"

"She didn't want to wait for me. So she left."

"Did she have a friend with her?"

"Not that I'm aware of."

"Was she mad at you for some reason?" he asked.

"No more than usual," said Rick.

Dan didn't like Rick's evasive answers. "Look, Rick. I'm just trying to figure out what happened."

"I don't see how it will help. Kim's dead now. The fucking details don't really matter." He took a deep breath before answering. "But if you really want to know, she came home late yesterday afternoon, and I was pissed. I asked her where she'd been. She wouldn't answer me. She got dressed and left the house before her mother got here."

"So you two had a fight." Dan was starting to get the picture.

"Kim had her own mind about things," said Rick, looking Dan square in the eyes.

"What happened at the country club?" Dan took a notebook out of his pocket and began writing.

"After Patrice got here, I drove to the country club. I got there after nine. I saw Kim's car, but I couldn't find her. So I looked around, saw a few people I knew, and talked with them."

"How long did you look for Kim?"

"I don't know," said Rick. "Maybe an hour or so."

"Who'd you talk to?" Dan looked up from the notebook.

"I talked to a lot of people." Rick was getting angry.

"Did you ever find your wife?" Dan put the notebook back in his pocket.

"Yes." Rick put his elbows on the desk, wincing with pain as he folded his hands under his chin. He stared straight ahead, his face blank, not looking at Dan.

"Maybe you should start by telling me what happened to your hand."

"Maybe you know better than I do what happened," said Rick, looking up at Dan. He leaned back in his chair, folding his arms across his chest.

"Stop being a smartass, and just tell me what the fuck happened to your hand," Dan demanded, leaning down and putting his hands on the desk, his face close to Rick's.

"I found Kim." Rick was eyeball to eyeball with the police chief.

"What does that have to do with your hand?" Dan was becoming impatient.

"The details aren't important," he answered calmly. "Let's just say she wasn't alone."

"So you found her with another guy?" Dan stepped back from the desk, the answer catching him by surprise. "Under what circumstances?"

"I'll bet you can guess what the circumstances were."

"Did you have a fight with someone last night? Someone who was with your wife at the time?"

"Yes, you could say someone was with my wife. Absolutely." Rick's voice was filled with sarcasm.

"Stop playing games, and tell me who the fuck she was with."

"Josh Logan."

"You found your wife with another man. Where were they?"

"They were fucking in the back seat of his car." Rick's face flushed red with anger.

Dan felt his jaw clench. "You hit him. Then what happened?"

"I hit him, and he went down. I guess I yelled at Kim. Then I left, went back into the party." Rick's voice drifted off, and he leaned farther back in the chair, staring into space, his jaw clenched.

"And then what?"

"Kim got pissed off that I hit her boyfriend, and she was pretty drunk. She and some of her friends were in the bathroom, and Kim wouldn't come out. So I left." He directed his gaze back at Dan.

Dan just nodded. His eyes narrowed as he looked down Rick.

"So where'd you go after you left Kim in the bathroom?" It was an accusation.

"I drove around for a while, and then I came home." His face was a mask. "And I found Kim."

"Did you see Josh again?"

"No."

"You were alone when you were driving around?" asked Dan.

"Yes."

"Were you with anyone else before you left the party?"

"No. I told you I talked to a few people, but that's all," he answered. "Why are you asking me all these questions?"

"It's my fucking job. Answer me."

"Kim drank a lot," said Rick, looking away. "At times she was irrational."

"So you were pretty sick of it, and then you found her with another man, and you lost it," said Dan, standing closer to the desk, staring down at Rick.

"Yeah, I lost it," said Rick, glaring up at Dan. "How would you feel?"

"Did you ever hit Kim?" Dan felt as though he was going to explode.

"Are you fucking out of your mind?" He looked at Dan in disbelief.

"Maybe Kim drove home and you followed her. She was drunk, still in the car, and you decided you'd had enough."

Rick stood up and walked around his desk, his face inches from Dan's. "What the fuck are you saying? That I killed my wife?"

"I'm not saying anything. I'm just asking." Dan stood with both hands on his hips, not moving.

"Like I said earlier, fuck you, Dan." He spit the words into Dan's face.

Dan stood for a moment, not moving a muscle; then he walked to the door of Rick's office and turned around. "I'll call you when I get the report from the medical examiner. Don't go anywhere."

Dan left Rick's office, headed to the front door, and slammed it as he left. He walked to the patrol car, started it, and rolled down the windows. While the car cooled off, he thought about everything Rick had told him. What had Rick and Kim fought about before the reunion? The fight he had in the parking lot. There were too many unanswered questions. What really happened to Kim? Where had Rick gone after he left the country club? Dan pulled his sunglasses off the visor and put the police car in drive. He was going to find out.

32

It was about nine thirty on Saturday morning when Dan pulled into the parking lot of the Logan Cadillac dealership. He found an empty space marked Customer Parking near the showroom doors and nosed the cruiser into it. The lights inside had been turned on, the floor cans aimed at the shiny new cars on display, but he couldn't tell if the dealership was open. Dan got out of the car and tried the front doors. They were locked. He shaded his eyes and looked through the glass; he thought he saw movement in the back of the large room. He knocked on the doors and waited, but there was no response.

He walked down the sidewalk in front of the building, following signs to the service department. The doors of the service bay were open, with one car inside; the owner was standing at the counter talking to a uniformed clerk who was typing information into a computer. Dan waited until one of the service techs drove the car out of the bay, and the owner walked through the door marked Customer Lounge. The clerk—Lonnie, as identified by his name tag—turned his attention to Dan.

"Can I help you?" Lonnie saw the uniform and put his pen behind his ear.

"I need to speak to Josh Logan. Is he in?" asked Dan.

Lonnie looked nervous and glanced out toward the lot. "Yes, I think I saw his car when I came in. Let me page him."

He stepped to a wall phone, punched a button, and spoke into the receiver. The page was loud, asking Josh Logan to come to the service desk. Dan stepped back from the desk and waited. Lonnie seemed relieved when another customer pulled a late-model Cadillac into the service bay. Dan told Lonnie that he'd be in the customer waiting area. The clerk nodded at Dan as he walked past.

The customer lounge was decked out with comfortable leather couches; a coffee table with an array of car, golf, and travel magazines; a coffee machine; a big-screen television; and Wi-Fi—everything the discerning luxury car buyer could possibly want. Dan poured some coffee into one of the white mugs with gold trim. He was adding fresh cream when he saw a tall figure come through the door. He'd never met Josh Logan, but he'd seen him around town and knew his family owned the dealership.

"Can I help you, Officer?" asked Josh.

"Hope so," answered Dan. "I'm Dan Hastings, Chief of Police."

Josh shook the extended hand and introduced himself. "What can I do for you, Chief?" He turned toward the coffee machine.

Dan had to strain to understand what Josh was saying. Josh's face was swollen and purple; he had an open cut on his lower lip, and when he spoke, his lips barely moved. His hand shook when he held the coffeepot, causing him to partially miss the mug and splash some coffee onto the tile floor.

"Is there someplace private where we can talk?" Dan asked.

"We can go to my office."

Josh led the way out of the lounge and down a long corridor. There were numerous glass-walled offices on either side of the hallway, and Josh's office was at the very end. The sign on the door read, JOSH LOGAN, General Manager. Dan followed him into the plush surroundings, and Josh motioned for Dan to have a seat across from the stainless-steel desk. Josh sat down behind the desk and placed his cup on a square metal coaster.

Dan shifted his position, uncomfortable in the straight-backed leather chair with the wide metal frame. The office decor was all cold steel, with slate-gray carpet and a large silver-framed black-and-white photograph of a classic 1968 Cadillac El Dorado on the wall behind the desk. The desk was bare except for Josh's coffee cup. A tall chrome lamp stood in the corner.

"Looks like you had a bad night," said Dan, taking a sip of the hot coffee and crossing an ankle over his knee.

"I guess you could say that." Josh stopped midlaugh, flinching from the sudden pain.

"Do you want to tell me about it?" asked Dan, his face expressionless.

"I was at the country club last night. I guess had a few too many, and I fell in the parking lot."

"Have you seen the news?"

Dan's pivot caught Josh off guard. "What do you mean?"

"Kimberly Young is dead."

"What the fuck are you talking about?" Josh's eyes narrowed with doubt.

"She was found dead in her car last night. At home." Dan stared at Josh, deadpan.

Josh stood up fast in shocked reaction. He held on to the desk, and his arms began to shake in an effort to support his unsteady weight.

"I think you'd better sit down." Dan got halfway out of his chair, thinking Josh was on the verge of collapse.

Josh lowered himself back into his chair. "I can't believe it." He looked as if he'd gotten punched in the gut. "Not Kim," he whispered.

"Let me get you some water," said Dan, now standing.

"No, I'm OK." Josh was trying to regain his composure, but he was visibly shaken.

"Did you have a fight with her husband last night?" Dan settled back into the leather chair.

"I don't know." Josh seemed to be confused, and he shook his head, attempting to gather his thoughts. "No. I was drunk. I fell."

"That's not what Rick said."

"Wait a minute." His brows furrowed, trying to grasp what Dan had told him. "What happened to Kim?"

"We don't know. She'd been drinking. That's all I can tell you."

"We were all drinking pretty heavily. I don't remember much about last night." His voice trailed off.

Josh picked up his coffee cup and took a drink. His arm was unsteady, and some of the coffee spilled onto his shirt, but he didn't appear to notice.

"Maybe I can help you out a little bit. Do you remember being with Kim in the back seat of your Cadillac in the parking lot at the country club? Rick Young, her husband, found you with his wife? And he got pissed off and hit you?" He waited. "Does any of that ring a bell?" Dan raised his shoulders.

"Is that what Rick told you?" He was indignant.

"He said he caught you banging his wife." He stared at Josh.

"He's lying!" He snorted. "Maybe you should ask him what he was doing last night with one of his old girlfriends."

"Her name?"

"Alexa Smith."

"You saw Rick with this person, Alexa Smith?"

"Oh, yeah. They were together, all right." Josh smirked before bracing his jaw in his left hand from the jolt of pain.

"You know her?"

"I knew her in high school," he said, mumbling the words. "She doesn't live here now."

"How can I reach her?" asked Dan.

"How should I know?"

Dan ignored the sarcasm. "I need to ask you a few more questions."

"Ask away," said Josh.

"How long had you been seeing Kim Young?"

"I hadn't been seeing Kim. I saw her at the country club last night. That's all." Josh shrugged his shoulders in denial.

"I guess I can always check your phone," said Dan, looking squarely into Josh's eyes without blinking.

Josh put his hand on his shirt pocket, felt the phone, and shook his head. "There's nothing to check," said Josh, breaking eye contact. "You're talking to the wrong guy. I have nothing to hide."

Dan stood up and put his coffee cup on the corner of Josh's desk. "Good. I'm glad to hear it." He started to walk out of the office, but he stopped and turned around. "Did you go to the party with your wife last night?"

"Yeah, I went with Stacy." His face was blank.

"Good. She might be able to remember more about the evening than you do."

Dan left Josh sitting at his desk, walked out to the cruiser, and started the engine. He pulled the notebook from his pocket and jotted down the name Alexa Smith, then grabbed his cell phone.

"Cypress Lake Police Department," answered Betsy.

"I need to find out where someone named Alexa Smith is staying. She's probably at a local hotel, one of the chains, or maybe higher end."

"Right, Chief. I'll call you back."

"Thanks."

He sat in the police car and waited. It didn't take long until the phone rang. "Yeah, Betsy."

"Gold Palm Resort. Do you want the phone number?"

"Give it to me." Dan wrote the number down in his notebook. "Thanks, Betsy."

"Ten-four."

Dan looked at his watch as he placed the call. It was 10:30 a.m. It took four rings before Alexa Smith answered.

33

Alexa wrapped a towel around her wet hair and grabbed the white terry cloth robe that was hanging on the back of the bathroom door. She put a Columbian blend K-cup in the coffee maker, hit the start button, and grabbed her cell phone off the night table. There was a text message from Katie with two words: "Call me." Alexa sat on the bed, her back propped against two pillows resting against the headboard, and tucked her bare feet under her. She hit dial and muted the television while waiting for Katie to pick up.

Katie didn't even say hello. "Have you seen the news?"

"Yes," said Alexa. "I can't believe it."

"Oh, my God, it's unreal."

"I'm in shock. We just saw her last night."

"I guess I'm not surprised. If anyone was going to get into trouble in this town, it would be Kim," said Katie. "She's always lived on the edge."

"Katie, the news is pretty vague about what happened," said Alexa. "When we saw her, she was drunk, and it sounds like it was an accident. Maybe even an overdose."

"Knowing Kim, she'd gotten herself into some kind of trouble." Katie snorted a half laugh. "I wouldn't be surprised by anything that girl did."

"Whatever happened, remember that there's a little girl who's lost her mom, and Rick must be devastated."

"How do you know about Rick? Did you talk to him?"

"Look, Katie. I don't know anything." Alexa's alarm bells started going off. Why was Katie questioning her?

"You don't have to tell me. I know you're protecting Rick."

"I don't have any reason to protect Rick. He hasn't done anything wrong," said Alexa. She was starting to feel defensive, and she didn't like Katie's implications.

"Sorry, Alexa, I didn't mean anything by what I said." Katie's tone softened. "I need to talk to you about something. Do you want to meet me somewhere for lunch?"

Alexa was exhausted and really didn't want to do anything. If she was truthful with herself, she wanted to be available if Rick called her. But she knew it wouldn't happen. And she shouldn't see him. Not until the timing was right, and she didn't know when that would be.

"Sure," she answered reluctantly. "Do you want to come to the hotel?"

"I'd love to," she responded. "I've never been inside the resort. I hear it's fabulous."

"Yes, it's beautiful. Can you meet me in the lobby? We can have lunch at the Terrace."

"Is around eleven thirty OK? I'll give the girls an early lunch," she said.

"See you then." Alexa ended the call.

She looked forward to seeing Katie. It might help to talk with her. Maybe she'd learn more about what had been going on with Rick and Kim. And she wondered what Katie wanted to talk to her about.

Maybe she wanted to tell Alexa where she had disappeared to last night.

Alexa grabbed the remote and turned up the sound on the flat screen. A local television reporter was standing in front of an up-scale home that was cordoned off by yellow crime-scene tape, and she was talking to a uniformed police officer. The reporter had beads of sweat on her upper lip, and she was squinting into the sunlight as she spoke into the microphone. She thanked the officer as he walked away.

"We've just spoken with Cypress Lake Police Sergeant Bert Lowe about Kimberly Young, who was found dead in her car early this morning. The car where her body was found was parked in the garage of the family residence, 1502 Lakeside Drive, and was discovered by her husband, Richard Young. You can see behind me the house where the deceased Ms. Young resided with her husband, who is a businessman and local contractor, and their infant daughter.

"I'll try to sum up what Officer Lowe told us. Ms. Young's death is being investigated to rule out foul play. He would not give any further information, but we've learned that Mr. and Mrs. Young attended a party last night at Lakeview Country Club, and Mr. Young has been questioned by Chief of Police Dan Hastings. We will update you when we get any more information about the tragic death of this young mother, Ms. Kimberly Young."

Alexa couldn't believe what she was hearing. She was so upset for Rick. He must be heartbroken, and the reporter sounded so callous and detached. Why would there be an investigation? She only hoped that Rick wasn't involved. How could she even think that? He'd sounded so broken up when he'd called her early this morning. And all he wanted was to forewarn her about what had happened and to tell her that he loved her. She couldn't imagine how he'd felt when he'd found Kim dead.

An icy coldness swept through her, and Alexa pulled the thick robe tighter, trying to offset the chill. But the feeling wouldn't go away. Then she recognized what it was. It was fear. Then she heard it. That little voice, the one inside her head that wouldn't shut up. The one that kept telling her something was very wrong. Only this time it was louder and more ominous.

34

Tim was sitting on an antique white barstool at the island, chomping on a toasted bagel, eyes glued to the flat-screen television mounted underneath the kitchen cabinets. Katie wished she could have slept in, but she didn't want Tim to bring up her late night again. She'd brushed her hair and thrown on a pair of black leggings and an oversize T-shirt. She'd taken two aspirin for her headache, but they hadn't started working. She poured fruit-flavored cereal into two bowls and called to the girls to come downstairs for breakfast.

"Can you believe the news about Kim Young?" asked Tim, talking with his mouth full. He turned off the television set.

"No, I can't," said Katie, getting the orange juice pitcher out of the refrigerator. "But she always did drink too much."

"The local news said she'd been at the reunion. Did you see her?"

"I saw her, but I didn't talk to her," said Katie as she carried the pitcher to the girls' table and began pouring juice into their cups.

"I don't think you should see Alexa anymore." It was a statement.

"Why not?" Katie's arm jerked, spilling the orange juice onto the floor, missing the intended plastic Little Mermaid cup. "Dammit!" She walked to the kitchen counter, grabbed a handful of paper towels, got on her hands and knees, and began wiping up the sticky mess.

"With everything that's going on with Rick, you need to steer clear of anything to do with him, and that includes Alexa," he said. "You always said she was trouble."

"She's been my best friend since we were in elementary school," said Katie, throwing the soiled paper towels into the trash compactor. "She was in our wedding, for Christ's sake. How can you say that?" She turned around and gave him an exasperated look.

"I didn't say it. You did, remember? How she dropped out of college, and you two used to smoke cigarettes and drink beer on your birthdays. Besides that, she had quite a few boyfriends in high school. God knows what she's doing now. Maybe she's been involved with Rick."

"We used to have fun, but we were pretty tame compared to a lot of the girls," said Katie defensively.

"Look, this thing with Rick is serious, and you're a teacher, remember?" Tim was warning her. "Don't get involved with her. And by the way, you never told me what happened last night at the reunion. You said there was some kind of scene?" Tim looked at Katie.

Why is he so curious? His questions were beginning to annoy her, and she wasn't in the mood to talk about last night.

She was carrying the bowls of cereal to the children's table when their two little girls came running down the stairs and into the kitchen, talking and laughing. "I got here first," said Sophia, touching the miniature chairback with her outstretched hand.

Her younger sister was only a step behind. "No, I did," said Ava, swatting her chair with her chubby hand. The girls sat down at their special table and started eating the crunchy, fun-shaped cereal.

"Shh," Katie whispered to Tim, her index finger vertical against her lips. "I'll tell you later. It's no big deal."

Katie took a carton of half-and-half out of the refrigerator and sat down on the barstool next to Tim. She poured coffee into her cup and added a little of the cream. She put her elbow on the counter and placed three fingers on her forehead. The headache was still there.

Tim turned to look at her. This time, his stern warning sounded more like a friendly suggestion. "Please stay away from Alexa."

"Don't worry, Tim." She tried to reassure him. "I'll just have lunch with her, and that'll be it. I don't think I can get out of it now." She took a sip of coffee, picked up the remote, and turned on the television set. A reporter was standing in front of Rick's house, giving updates about Kim's death.

"When are they going to stop talking about Kim?" Katie exclaimed, punching in the Disney channel on the remote. The girls squealed and turned their chairs toward the set to watch the cartoon.

"Promise me," Tim said, reaching over and touching her thigh. "You owe me after last night."

"I promise," she said, not looking at him.

She had to see Alexa one more time. Then she'd keep her promise. Maybe.

35

A soft, feminine voice answered, "Hello?"

"My name is Dan Hastings, police chief here in Cypress Lake," he said. "Is this Alexa Smith?"

"Yes, I'm Alexa," she answered.

"Ms. Smith, I'm investigating the death of Kimberly Young," he said. "I'm sorry to bother you, but I wonder if I might ask you a few questions. "

"Yes, of course." She hesitated. "But how did you get my number?"

"I understand you're a friend of Mr. Young's." He ignored her question.

"We went to high school together, and yes, we were friends."

"Were you at the reunion last evening?"

She paused for a moment before answering. "Yes, I was at the reunion."

"Did you talk to Mr. Young last night?"

"I'm sorry," said Alexa. "I don't really know you, and I think I better go." She sounded afraid of something.

He waited a minute. "Would it be all right if I meet you somewhere, just to ask you a few questions?"

There was another pause, this one longer, and Dan thought she'd hung up. But then she responded. "I guess so."

"May I have your cell number, please?" He wrote the number down in his notebook. "Thank you, Ms. Smith. I'll be in touch." He ended the call.

Dan stuck the phone in his pocket, pulled out of the dealership parking lot, and headed back to the station. As he drove, he thought about the phone call. This Alexa Smith sounded very frightened. That could mean one of two things: either she was covering something up and scared shitless, or she had no idea what the hell was going on and was scared shitless. He was going to find out which one it was.

36

Alexa realized she was trembling. Why was Chief Hastings calling her? How did he know where she was staying? It was all beginning to seem unreal. Everything was catching her off guard. She had to calm down and think things through. She looked at her watch; she'd better hurry if she didn't want to keep Katie waiting. She blew her hair dry before slipping on slim white capris, a black jersey with three-quarter-length sleeves, and black flats. After taking one final look in the mirror, she found a red-and-white silk scarf in her carry-on and tied it around her neck. *Good enough,* she thought.

After tossing her cell phone in her purse, she double-checked that she had her room key and headed down the hallway toward the elevator. But she kept thinking about the phone call from the police chief. She'd have to tell him everything she knew, but she didn't want to say anything that could get Rick into trouble. But she wouldn't lie. If nothing else, maybe she'd learn more details about Kim's death from this police officer. But if Kim had died accidentally, why would he want to talk to her? Someone must have told this police chief about her relationship with Rick. But who?

As she rode down in the gold-paneled elevator, Alexa thought about the things Katie had said about Kim. Why would Katie not be surprised that Kim was dead? It was shocking under any circumstance. Alexa felt a chill come over her. She needed to learn a lot more about what had happened last night, especially where Katie was when Kim was making a horrible scene. She needed to learn more about Katie, period. They'd been lifelong friends, and Katie had always been there for her. Whatever was going on, Alexa would do everything she could to be there for Katie.

When she stepped off the elevator and saw Katie standing next to the fountain, Alexa felt a surprising wave of relief. Last night seemed like a bad dream, and Katie might be able to help her get a grip on everything that was happening. All her doubts suddenly felt far away.

"Hey, Alexa," said Katie, flashing a bright smile. Katie looked attractive in her summery blue A-line dress with colorful blue, pink, and green fish appliques at the knee-length hem. Large neon-pink oval earrings were a bold contrast to Katie's dark hair.

"Katie!" Alexa gave her a warm, clinging hug. "I'm so glad you're here." Her voice must have given her away.

"Alexa, what's wrong?"

"I'm not sure," said Alexa. "I guess I'm a little shaky after everything that's happened."

"Yes, it's horrible about Kim. It's all over the news."

"Let's go to the restaurant and get a table. Then we'll talk," said Alexa.

They strolled to the Terrace, the beautiful outdoor restaurant that was adjacent to the lobby. The hostess seated them at a wrought-iron table in a corner, framed by miniature palm trees and blooming white hibiscus. The hotel air-conditioning spilled out through the open doorway, offering cool comfort in the warm May temperatures.

A waiter in black pants and a white shirt appeared with ice water and menus and asked if they cared for something from the bar. Alexa needed coffee after her almost-sleepless night, and Katie ordered a white wine spritzer with extra lime. The waiter promised a quick return to take their orders. Alexa looked at the luncheon menu, but she realized she'd lost her appetite. Katie was looking at the menu, chattering away about something.

Katie became aware that Alexa wasn't listening and put down her menu. "What is it, Alexa?" She grabbed her friend's hand.

"I'm sorry. I'm not very good company today," said Alexa, shaking her head.

"You need something to eat. You're tired and hungry, and let's face it, last night didn't turn out too well," she said, taking a gulp of water.

"No, it didn't." Alexa's eyes began to fill with tears, and Katie leaned over and gave her a hug.

"It's going to be all right. Don't worry." Katie smiled at her.

Wanting to believe her, Alexa smiled back and picked up the menu. She was glad they'd met early. The restaurant was nearly empty, so they could enjoy a leisurely lunch with plenty of time to talk. She needed to tell someone about the disturbing call from the police chief. Alexa remembered that Katie had said she needed to talk to her as well. Alexa wondered what that was all about. Whatever was going on, Alexa had to find out. She just hoped that she could help Rick. His wife was dead. And he blamed himself for it. But Kim had been drunk. That wasn't his fault. But what if something else had happened to her? Why were the police questioning him? And why would the police chief want to talk to her? She loved Rick. But she couldn't stop asking herself what really happened to Kim. That was the big question.

"I'd like the crab salad," Katie said, handing her menu to the waiter.

"That sounds good. I'll have the same, please," said Alexa.

"The food here is supposed to be wonderful," said Katie. "I'm glad we could meet."

"Is Tim watching the girls?"

"Yes, they're playing in their kiddie pool in the backyard. Then they'll take a long nap."

"You're very lucky, Katie," said Alexa. And she meant it. Katie seemed to have it all.

Before Katie could respond, the waiter brought their drinks, along with a basket of warm rolls and butter. Katie rimmed the wine-glass with the lime, tossed it into the bubbly drink, and took a sip. "I hope this helps my headache."

"Why don't you have one of the rolls? They smell delicious."

"Yes, that might help too." Katie placed a roll and a pat of butter onto her plate.

"Did you know that when I left you to go to the ladies' lounge last night that Kim followed me?"

"You're kidding!" said Katie, her eyes wide with surprise.

"I wish I was. She said some pretty awful things about me and Rick."

"Like what?"

"That I couldn't have Rick. It was pretty vile stuff. I went back to the Oak Room and looked for you. I was really upset," said Alexa.

"I must have been at the buffet." She took a bite of the roll, not looking at her friend.

"She'd had a lot to drink, but it was still upsetting. I went outside, and by chance, ran into Rick. He had just arrived and was looking for Kim."

"They obviously didn't come together," said Katie, stating a fact.

"What happened to Kim was horrible, but I'll never forget the way she screamed at me. The things she said were untrue, but a lot of people overheard her."

"Alexa, everyone knew about her drinking. Sadly, she hadn't changed much since high school."

"I wouldn't know. I just know that things could get really bad for Rick."

"What do you mean?"

"I got a call this morning from the Cypress Lake police chief."

Katie put her glass down and looked at Alexa. "What did he want?"

"He wants to meet and ask me some questions."

"Oh, my God," exclaimed Katie. "It sounds like they suspect that Kim's death wasn't an accident."

"I don't know. I just know that Kim confronted me last night and said some pretty vicious things. Rick and I danced together, and Kim left the party drunk. Plenty of people saw us, and it looks bad. But nothing happened." She wanted Katie to believe her.

"You and I know that, but everyone saw you and Rick together last night, right?" Katie had a look on her face that Alexa didn't understand.

"What are you saying?"

"I'm saying Cypress Lake is a small town, and people talk. Everyone will think the worst." She paused. "I don't, but other people might."

"That's what worries me."

Alexa didn't know what to say now. Every word that came out of Katie's mouth sounded almost accusatory. She decided it was time to change the subject. "Katie, you'd said you needed to talk with me, and I've been doing all the talking." Alexa waited.

"It's nothing, really. But I need a small favor," Katie answered.

"I'll help if I can. What is it?"

"I know my timing is bad because of everything that's going on."

"Just ask me." Alexa was getting impatient.

"It's a little complicated, but I got home a little late last night. I had too much to drink, and I didn't want Tim to know. So instead of taking a chance on getting a DUI, I sat in the car at the country club until my head cleared."

"You did the right thing," said Alexa. "But what can I do to help you? It doesn't sound like a problem."

"Well, I told Tim that I'd come here when I left the country club to spend some time with you. That you wanted to talk." Katie took another drink of her spritzer, avoiding Alexa's gaze.

Alexa didn't know what to say. Why was Katie asking her to back her up in a lie that she told her husband? Alexa didn't know Tim that well. And the Cypress Lake police chief wanted to ask her questions. How could she say that Katie had been with her at the hotel if she wasn't? It could backfire in so many ways that Alexa couldn't even imagine. And what was Katie trying to hide? The questions just kept coming, and nothing was making sense. Alexa's little voice was speaking to her loud and clear.

"Katie, don't you think you'd better tell me what really happened last night?"

"I told you what happened! Are you going to help me out or not?" Katie words were stinging.

At that moment, the waiter brought their lunch—plates of delicious-looking crab salad on beds of mixed greens surrounded by an arrangement of sliced melon, oranges, and grapes. The interruption gave Alexa time to think about what Katie had asked her.

"It sounds like something's wrong, Katie." Alexa stared at Katie.

"Nothing's wrong. If Tim happens to ask you, just say we spent some time together, that's all. I'm sorry if I put you on the spot."

"It's not that. The police are going to ask me questions. This isn't a game; this is serious, and lying could make the situation worse. For both of us."

"Well, maybe it could be in your best interest to say I was in your hotel room."

Alexa was dumbfounded. "What are you saying?"

"I'm just saying that the police might learn about your fight with Kim, and they might just think something happened that didn't," said Katie, an innocent expression on her face.

"I'm sorry, Katie, but you're not making sense. Are you saying I need an alibi?" Alexa had a sick feeling in her stomach.

"No, I'm just saying help me out here. It can't hurt for the police to think we were together. Right?" Katie's tone took on a desperate quality.

"It could hurt both of us if the police or Tim found out that we lied," stated Alexa. "I wish I knew what's really wrong. We're friends, and I want us to stay that way."

Katie didn't say anything; she just stared at her food before looking at Alexa. "I'm sorry. Please forgive me. Let's just pretend this conversation didn't happen."

"It's really for the best, Katie. I may not even see Tim, and if I do, hopefully he won't ask me anything. I hope you'll trust me enough to tell me what's really going on. And the most important thing to remember is that Rick is alone with a baby girl. Don't ask me to do anything that will hurt anyone, OK?"

Alexa took a bite of her salad, thinking about what Katie had asked her to do. Katie didn't really seem sorry, and Alexa was more certain than ever that something was really wrong in Katie's world. She hoped her friend would eventually tell her. But Alexa wasn't going to start telling lies. Too much was at stake.

37

Dan drove back to the station. He'd call this Alexa Smith again later and arrange to meet with her, but first he needed to check out the evidence that Bert had collected from Kim's car. He walked into his office and locked the door. Two plastic evidence bags were sitting on the credenza behind his desk. Dan opened the lower right desk drawer, pulled out a pair of latex examination gloves, and snapped them on. Standing over the credenza, he opened each bag, removed the items, and placed them one by one on the wooden surface. One bag held an empty pint-size vodka bottle that had been dusted for prints. The other bag contained a cell phone in a blue butterfly case and a red velvet evening purse. The purse contained a tube of lipstick, a mirror, a debit card, and a twenty-dollar bill, as well as a half pack of cigarettes and a BIC lighter. A wave of sadness hit him as he touched the things that Kim had held in her hands only hours ago.

Dan shook off the feeling, picked up the cell phone, and sat down at his desk. The battery had about 65 percent of its charge left. He wrote down all the numbers in the call history, then carefully deleted the three calls she'd made to his cell phone. He brought up the contact list and copied the names and numbers. Some entries were just initials. "*J*" was one. He scrolled through the list looking for his name. It wasn't there. He brought up her email account, but nothing out of the ordinary jumped out at him.

Then Dan remembered something. He put the cell phone down and dug his wallet out of his back pocket. *Where is it?* he thought. He pulled his driver's license and credit cards out, opened each of the leather folds, and riffled through the cards again. Nothing. It was gone. Maybe it slipped out when he'd gotten his last fill-up. Maybe. He thought for a few moments. *Shit!* He put the cards back in the wallet and stuck it in his hip pocket.

He put everything back in the evidence bags, tore off the gloves, and tossed them in the trash can under his desk. After unlocking his office door, he walked downstairs to the evidence room in the basement. He unlocked it, placed the bags on one of the shelves, and secured the room. He'd log the items in later. Fatigue and stress were catching up with him. He stopped at Bert's office, told him that he was going home to get some sleep, and suggested that Bert do the same. He told Betsy where he was going and left the station house. Everything that could be done was done. Now it was wait time.

38

Josh went into the bathroom and checked himself out in the mirror. *Jesus Christ*, he thought. His lower lip had a nasty split, and the left side of his face was purple, his eye nearly swollen shut. He left the bathroom and found Seth, the assistant sales manager, in his office. Josh told Seth that he was leaving and would be back later in the day. Seth stared at Josh's face and said, "Sure."

Every step Josh took across the hot pavement jarred his head, sending jolts of pain through his skull. He couldn't separate the pain of Rick's punch from the aftereffects of last night's booze. Either way, he had to get out of the office. He got into his SUV and drove out of the dealership parking lot. He needed to get home and put ice on his face to reduce the swelling. Maybe he should have gone to the ER last night as Stacy had suggested. His lip was cut pretty badly, probably needed some stitches, and he was beginning to wonder if his jaw was broken. But he didn't want to be interrogated by some emergency room doctor. He wondered if Stacy and the kids would be at home. Hopefully not, but he'd take his chances. He didn't need any more questions from her either.

The news about Kim had hit him hard. Worse than the impact of Rick's fist against his jaw. What the hell had happened to Kim?

Goddammit! She'd been the best thing that had happened to him lately. The only good thing, really. Except for his kids, he had nothing else. Kim was intoxicating, like a drug, and fulfilled a need in him that only she could satisfy. She gave him everything and asked for nothing. That was the only problem too. She never asked him for anything. He would have done anything for her. She came when he called her and did exactly what he wanted, when he wanted it. And she never lied to him.

His vision was blurred, so he slowed down. The pain was so intense he thought his head would split. He was getting close to the turnoff, one that he went to as often as possible. But not as often as he wanted. He kept driving until he saw the motel. He turned into the gravel lot and parked in the vacant space in front of the same unit where they'd spent their last afternoon together. Josh put his head down on the steering wheel. His shoulders shook—but not for long. He slammed his palm against the steering wheel. *Damn!* He should have asked more questions. How did this happen? Why was the police chief questioning him? It could only mean one thing. The police thought Kim had been murdered, and maybe they suspected him. The anger was making his head hurt.

Josh started the SUV and began to focus on what he should do. First things first. He'd better check his cell phone. He pulled the smartphone out of his pocket and checked the call history; it was blank. He hit Delete again to make sure, then stuck the phone back in his shirt pocket. But if the police had Kim's cell phone, his calls would show up in the history, unless she'd deleted them. *Christ!*

Looking around, he backed out of the parking space and pulled onto the highway, gravel spinning under the big tires. He turned on the radio, wondering if there was any news about Kim's death. He drove fast, ignoring his headache. He had to calm down, get himself under control. But if someone had hurt Kim on purpose, he'd make that person pay. Who would do something like that? Josh didn't have to think for very long. It could only be one person.

39

Stacy was the last person he wanted to deal with, but he had to talk to her. Before that cop got to her. Josh had to make certain that the story she told Hastings matched his—that he was drunk and fell in the parking lot. And he hoped she hadn't talked to any of her girl-friends. But that was unlikely. By now, everyone in town had heard some sordid version of his encounter with Rick. With Kim dead, the story would be embellished. He'd lie, of course. But Stacy would have doubts, and she'd make his life hell. She already did, but he'd learned ways to control the bitch.

He drove to his street in the gated community, pulled the Escalade into the wide driveway, and opened the double garage door. Stacy's white Caddy CTS was in the garage. He went into the house, through the combination laundry and pantry room, and entered their sleek custom-designed kitchen. *She must be at home,* he thought, *unless she's taken the kids to the neighbors.* It was Saturday, and she wouldn't ex-pect him home until at least 6:00 p.m. when the dealership closed. He looked in the family room, and she wasn't there. He didn't hear the kids playing anywhere in the house. He looked through the French doors off the kitchen and saw them in the swimming pool with Lisa, the teenage babysitter who lived next door. Stacy was on a lounge chair under an umbrella, sipping from a can of Coke and reading a magazine.

He opened one of the doors. "Stacy, can you come into the kitchen?"

"Josh! I didn't hear you come home." She walked to the open door in a flattering one-piece black swimsuit, a black, flowing gauze cover-up open in the front. "What are you doing home so early?" Her hair was in a loosely wrapped bun, tendrils falling around her suntanned face.

"I'm in a lot of pain. Can you make a drink for me?" he asked, leaning on the island.

"Just a minute, Josh." She called to the babysitter. "Lisa, watch the kids, OK?"

"Sure, Mrs. Logan."

"That looks pretty bad. Why don't you let me call the doctor?" She frowned with concern.

"I told you I don't want to see a doctor. Just fix me a goddamn drink." He grabbed her wrist.

She didn't resist his tight grip. "I can't get your drink if you don't let go of me," she said sarcastically.

"Go," he snapped, releasing her with a jerk. "I'll be in the family room. And get me an ice pack."

He went into the family room, closed the shades, and fell onto the leather sofa. He rested his hand on his forehead, the pain relentless. A few minutes later, Stacy came in with an ice pack and a scotch on the rocks with a twist.

"Let me put this on your face," she said, sitting down next to him. She placed the chilled bag gently on the side of his cheek. She stuck a straw in the tumbler and held it near his mouth. Josh bent forward, took a long sip, then fell back onto the sofa pillow.

"Thanks, baby," he said, eyes closed, patting her bare leg.

"What happened last night?" she asked. "I don't know why you won't go to the doctor."

With great effort, he lifted his head halfway off the pillow, his voice loud and emphatic. "I told you what happened. I drank too much, and I fell. And if anyone asks you, that's what you tell them. Do you understand?"

"I will. Don't worry, Josh. But I guess you've heard the news."

"About Kim Young? Yes, I heard some of the guys at work talking about it," he answered, lowering his head back down and closing his eyes. "Too bad."

"I didn't know her that well," said Stacy. "But it's very sad."

"I wonder what happened?"

"I don't know," said Stacy. "But some of the girls were talking about her. She and Rick must have had a fight last night, and Kim had a meltdown about him being with Alexa Smith. You remember her, right?"

"Yeah, I remember her."

Josh knew that Stacy was being vague on purpose. She knew that he'd dated Alexa in high school. She didn't know that Alexa had broken it off.

"Kim had too much to drink last night, but she was always wild," said Stacy, glaring at him. "You know that too. Right, Josh?"

"I don't know anything about Kim. And I'm not in the mood for your fucking accusations."

"I'm not accusing you of anything, but you knew her, didn't you?"

He sat up suddenly, grabbed her shoulder, and squeezed it so hard that she let out a yelp of pain. "Drop it! Do you hear me? Don't mention her name to me again."

"Yes, Josh. I hear you. Stop, please. Let go of me. You're hurting me. Please!"

He released his grip on her shoulder and took another sip through the straw. Stacy was whimpering, rubbing her shoulder as she walked out of the room. "Come back here, Stacy," he demanded.

She stood in the doorway, crying.

"Please come here," he coaxed her. "Please."

She walked over and stood next to the sofa, pulling the gauze cover-up tight around her. He grabbed her hand and pulled her down next to him.

"I'm sorry I lost my temper," he said. "Please stop crying. I don't want the kids to see you upset. You know I'm in pain."

"It's all right, Josh," said Stacy, sniffling.

"You know I love you, Stacy. Now go wash your face, and bring me another drink."

She got up, and he patted her ass as she walked away.

Goddammit, he thought. He didn't need this headache. He just wanted all this to go away. And he hoped Stacy kept her fucking mouth shut. She'd better, if she knew what was good for her.

40

Stacy tiptoed into the family room; Josh was in a deep sleep, his arm hanging over the edge of the sofa, the ice pack still resting across his swollen face. She felt a momentary twinge of pity for him, even though he'd brought all this on himself. Despite his injuries, he still looked handsome, just lying there asleep, so much like the loving man she thought she'd married. She remembered their wedding day. Her handsome groom waiting at the altar, the flowers, the lovely bridesmaids in lilac gowns, the elegant, choreographed reception—everything picture-perfect, with a Caribbean honeymoon as the finale. Then things changed.

After their fairy-tale honeymoon, Josh began criticizing her for everything, from the way she wore her hair to her wardrobe and her housekeeping. And of course she had to quit her job. No wife of Josh Logan's was going to work. He was the provider, and her job was to take care of him. He compared her to his friends' wives. She just didn't quite measure up in her appearance and behavior for someone of his high social standing. She'd tried hard, doing things the way he liked, but he let her know when he was displeased. And the way he expressed his displeasure was often very painful.

She knew about his affairs, but she'd learned to ignore them. If she confronted him, it was very bad. For her. She remembered the first time he'd hit her. She'd waited until he was in the shower, gone to his office, and found his cell phone in his desk drawer. She opened a text message and saw a photo of a half-dressed woman. She didn't hear Josh until it was too late. The blow to her stomach caused her to double over, knocking the wind out of her. She'd learned to be much more careful.

It hadn't taken Stacy long to find out the truth about what Josh was doing in the parking lot last night. Her girlfriend Julie had texted her with all the details, including the fight between Rick and Josh. Apparently everyone at the reunion had heard about Kim and Josh. Now everyone was talking about what had happened to Kim. As far as Stacy was concerned, Kim had gotten exactly what she deserved.

She crept out of the room, making certain that Josh was asleep, and dialed the number she'd written in the leather address book she kept hidden in her night table. It was Saturday, but she hoped she could reach Avery Miller. The firm of Miller, Davies, and Michaelson was well known but came with a price. But if she got the settlement she expected, she'd have enough money to pay the legal fees with plenty left over. Josh had inherited a lot of money from his dad, including the business, and she planned on getting half of it, maybe more. Especially when she showed the attorney the photos she'd taken of the bruises that Josh had inflicted on her over the course of their six-year marriage. Once Josh knew she had documentation of what he'd done to her, he'd have one of two choices: pay up or face charges of spousal abuse. Josh would hate the bad publicity.

She just didn't want Josh to know what she was planning until she'd talked to the attorney and was assured that she'd get half of the money and custody of the children. Stacy hoped she could keep up the pretense of the loving wife for just a little longer. If he found out that she was planning to leave him, she was afraid to think of what he might do to her. He would never know the pain she'd already caused him. And it was just the beginning.

41

Sunday

Alexa put the top down on the Mustang and followed the resort's palm tree–lined driveway to the highway, enjoying the cool, early Sunday morning. She wanted to drive around Cypress Lake, see her hometown again, and just get out of the hotel for some fresh air. She was looking forward to a jog along the lakefront. After her stressful lunch with Katie, she'd spent all Saturday afternoon and evening in her room watching the news, trying to learn as much as possible about what had happened to Kim. Nothing new had been discovered, according to the media reports, with Kim's death still being called accidental. If it was something other than an accident, they weren't saying.

The newspeople were camped in front of Rick's house, watching and waiting for any sign of the family so that they could shout questions at them, hoping for a dramatic sound bite they could play over and over again for ratings. Around eleven o'clock last evening, the family had released a statement asking for privacy at their difficult time of loss. Alexa wished the media would leave Rick and his family alone. It was a tragedy beyond her comprehension that would affect him and his daughter forever.

If it hadn't been for Rick, Alexa would have flown back to Chicago. Her weeklong visit had ceased to be a vacation, but she decided she was going to stick around, just in case. Of what, she wasn't sure. If Alexa was truly honest with herself, the reason she wanted to stay was Rick. He didn't want to see her. He'd made that clear. But it was because he wanted to protect her. He didn't realize she didn't need to be protected. Alexa had learned self-reliance a long time ago, even before her father had died. She was confident she could take care of herself, and maybe, if given the chance, she could even help Rick. Maybe in some way she could be there for him, if only as moral support.

Alexa drove through the town's main business district, happy to see that little had changed since she'd been away. Cypress Lake was still the comfortable small town she remembered, and pristine, in spite of the tourists that flocked to Florida each year. The lake drew tourists, but they were the kind that loved fishing, not the dazzle of the theme parks or beaches. The diner, deli, and hardware store were still there, with specialty stores scattered in between. The pretty, wide streetscape, with flowers and palm trees planted in the median, was just as she remembered. The older storefronts bore the names of families who had lived in the tightly knit community for generations. She drove slowly until she reached the end of Main Street, made a left turn at the light, and drove past the community center and over the railroad tracks. It was only a few blocks farther when she caught her first glimpse of the shimmering blue water of Cypress Lake.

42

The sun had just cleared the horizon, and a cool breeze was coming off the lake. Alexa parked the convertible in one of the angled parking spaces facing the lake, a short distance from the yacht club and boat ramps. She got out of the car and stood on the wide concrete sidewalk that ran the full length of Lakefront Drive. She gazed at the water and watched a small aluminum boat, its two passengers heading out for early fishing, the low sound of the motor humming in the distance.

Alexa leaned on the iron-and-wood park bench and did some stretching, trying to relieve the stiffness from her restless night. She touched her toes and extended her arms upward, inhaling the fresh air mixed with the scent of water hyacinth and the musky lake. Checking her sports watch, she began a slow jog, her stride easy as she followed the sidewalk, lined with palm and oak trees, along the floodwall, covering the first mile in about ten minutes. Only a few cars were parked sporadically along the waterfront, the locals enjoying the early dawn, with some sipping coffee on benches, reading newspapers, or walking their dogs in the cool Florida early morning.

After another half mile, Alexa stopped at the park for a drink from the stone water fountain. The playground was empty except for two pigeons sitting on a trash can rim, searching for breakfast. She was getting warm, even with the cool breeze, and she could feel trickles of sweat running down her back. She turned around and headed back to her car, now a blurred orange object about a mile and a half from where she was. She'd just picked up her pace when another vehicle pulled into the space next to hers, blocking her view of the Mustang. As she got closer, she realized it wasn't a car; it was a blue pickup truck. She kept running, her eyes on the blue pickup, when suddenly she saw a dark-haired figure climb out of the truck. He was leaning against the door, arms crossed, appearing to look in her direction. Was this a dream? She found it hard to breathe when she realized it was Rick. *Oh, my God,* she thought. *What is he doing here?*

She ran faster until her heart felt like it was going to jump out of her chest. He was staring directly at her, and she was so close, she could almost look into his eyes, until suddenly he got back into the truck and reversed out of the parking space. The blue truck moved slowly at first and then picked up speed, turning onto one of the lakefront access roads. Alexa sprinted back to her car, trying to catch a glimpse of the truck, but it was too late. The blue pickup had disappeared.

43

Dan sat at the kitchen table, took the last bite of a fried egg, and washed it down with the remaining coffee in his cup. He looked over at Lynn, sitting across from him, not eating and already dressed in slacks and a blouse. His gaze tracked from the thin slip of paper she was holding to her eyes. They were flashing with anger.

"I found this phone number in your wallet." She slid the piece of paper across the table until it was positioned next to his coffee cup.

He kept his eyes fixed on Lynn's. "So what? I keep lots of phone numbers in my wallet."

He didn't want to look at the number because he knew whose it was. He suspected she knew too. *Fuck!* Kim was dead, and now he had to deal with Lynn. Maybe she had a right to be pissed off, but he couldn't do this. Not now.

He took the fresh pack of cigarettes off the table, tore it open, and pulled one out. Sticking it in his mouth, he dug into his left shirt pocket for matches, but they weren't there. He got up, turned on a burner on the stove, and tipped his head sideways to get a light from the blue flame. Inhaling deeply, he walked back to the table and picked up the piece of paper. He looked at the number, wadded the paper into a ball, and tossed it in the ashtray. He stood there, waiting for the accusation.

"I know whose number it is, Dan," she said.

"So what?" he said. "I called her a few times, that's all."

"Really? That's all?" Her voice dripped with sarcasm.

"Don't make a big deal about it." He tried to sound casual, inhaled a deep drag, and crushed the barely smoked cigarette into the ashtray.

"Why wouldn't I? My husband calling another woman, keeping her phone number hidden in his wallet. I'm overreacting—is that what you mean?"

"I know how it looks." He shook his head in denial. "I'm sorry, Lynn, but it's not what you think."

"Maybe I wouldn't overreact if you hadn't come home so late last Friday night. And so many other nights." She pursed her lips and crossed her arms over her chest.

"I have to work late sometimes," he said. "It goes with the job."

"I didn't realize that screwing other women was part of the job too."

She jumped up from the table, and in a quick motion, picked up his dirty plate and threw it against the wall. The china dinner plate shattered as it hit the white wallpaper with miniature green leaves, sending slivers of porcelain spraying into the air, larger pieces crashing onto the tile floor.

"What the hell are you doing?" He stepped backward, trying to get out of the way of the flying shards. "Jesus, Lynn!"

"What the hell were you doing, Dan? Did she mean that much to you?" She was shouting, her face red, her whole body shaking.

"I don't know what you're talking about," he said. "You're out of your fucking mind."

He grabbed his cap, keys, and holster and stormed out of the kitchen, broken porcelain crunching under his heavy boots as he slammed the door. He couldn't believe she'd gone through his wallet. *Goddammit!* What the hell did Lynn want from him? He had to get out of the house, get away, and try to reason out some way to deal with her. He couldn't now. He had to focus on finding Kim's killer. Then maybe, somehow, he could try to fix his marriage, but he wasn't so sure that Lynn would ever forgive him. Maybe he didn't deserve to be forgiven. *How did things get so fucked up?* He got in the patrol car, started the engine, and roared out of the driveway, not looking back. If he had, he would have seen Lynn standing in the doorway, watching as he drove away.

44

Dan didn't want to go to the station, so he drove around, asking himself who might know something that could fill in the missing pieces that could lead him to Kim's killer. The one missing piece was obvious. It was about 10:00 a.m. when Dan pulled the cruiser under the portico and turned off the engine. He'd been inside the Gold Palm Resort a few times for minor complaints, but it had been a while. The lobby was nearly empty. The few people he saw looked like businessmen on their way to golf games or families going to the pool. Dan turned when he heard someone call his name.

He smiled, walked over to the long reception desk, and shook hands with the older man behind the desk. Mike was short, balding, and dressed in a navy-blue sport coat and red-and-blue tie with diagonal stripes. His beady eyes darted behind black-framed glasses, watching the guests as they came and went.

"Hey, Dan, long time, no see," he said, turning his gaze toward Dan.

"You're looking spiffy there, Mike," said Dan, glad to see an old friend. "I didn't know you still worked here."

"Yeah, I'm still here. I need the extra bucks. I have one left in college." He shrugged. "You know how it goes."

Dan turned and looked at the elegant lobby. "Nice place to work, though."

"It's the ritziest hotel I've ever worked at." The older guy lowered his voice. "You can imagine the tips I get."

"Yeah, I'll bet you rake it in," said Dan, looking back at the clerk.

"You look like you're here on business. What can I do you for?"

"You have a guest here, Alexa Smith?"

"Yes, she checked in on Friday, I think." He turned toward the computer screen on the desk, hit a few keys, then waited. A minute or so later, he looked up. "I was right. It was Friday. I carried her bags up to her room. She's a pretty, young flight attendant, and she drives an orange Mustang." His smile widened. "She gave me a nice tip."

"You notice anything else about her?"

"As a matter of fact, when I took her bags to her room, some guy was there with her. He looked like trouble."

"What do you mean?" asked Dan, leaning both elbows on the desk. "Do you know who it was?"

"Nope, but I could tell she didn't like him. She seemed uncomfortable, kind of nervous. I looked around the room, and he hadn't gotten her into bed yet, but he wanted to. I can spot an asshole a mile away."

"What'd the guy look like?" asked Dan, more than curious about the man in Alexa Smith's room.

"He was tall, hair combed straight back, a player. I waited down the hall to see if there might be a problem, but he left soon after I did, and he looked pissed. I ran down the stairs and watched him get off the elevator. I followed him and saw him drive off in a big white Escalade with dealer plates."

"You read this guy right. He's bad news," said Dan, amazed at Mike's detailed account. "You notice anything else about Ms. Smith?"

"Yes, but it might not mean anything."

"It might," said Dan, trusting Mike's instincts.

"This Ms. Smith left early this morning. I'd just gotten here, so it was about 6:00 a.m. She looked like she was heading out for a jog."

"That sounds pretty innocent," said Dan.

"Yeah, maybe. The valet brought her Mustang to the front of the hotel, and she got in and drove off. I walked over to the entrance and watched her drive out of the lot. A blonde in a Mustang is eye candy." He smiled at Dan.

"I would agree with you on that," smiled Dan. "What did you notice after that?"

"I saw a blue Ford pickup truck pull into the lot just as she was pulling out. The pickup made a circle and appeared to follow the Mustang."

"That's interesting," said Dan. "Do you have video surveillance of the lot?"

"Sure. You want to see it?"

"Yeah, I would."

Mike motioned for Dan to step behind the desk, and it only took a few minutes for Mike to bring up the video footage from earlier that morning. Dan stared at the computer screen and saw a blue Ford pickup leaving the lot. He was fairly certain it was Rick's pickup truck. The license plate wasn't clear, but there was a sign on the side of the truck that looked like the one on the side of Rick's that read Rick Young Construction.

"Can you save this video footage for me?" said Dan.

"Sure," answered Mike, punching some keys to save the surveillance video from that morning.

"You've been a big help," Dan said, shaking Mike's hand. Dan thought for a few minutes. "Do you have a house phone?"

He was going to call this Alexa Smith and see if she'd talk to him now. Now that he knew that Rick had followed her out of the parking lot this morning, he had a lot of questions for her.

Mike pointed to an alcove to the right of the desk. Dan was connected to her room number, and she answered quickly. "Hello?"

"Ms. Smith, this is Dan Hastings. I'm sorry to bother you, but I wonder if you have a few minutes. I'd like to talk with you, and I happen to be here at the Gold Palm. Would now be a convenient time?" He waited through a long silence.

"Well, I have to finish getting dressed," she answered, hesitating.

"I'd be happy to wait," he said pleasantly.

"I can be down in the lobby in about a half hour."

Dan looked at his watch. It was now 11:00 a.m. "Thank you. I won't take up much of your time."

Good, thought Dan. He wanted to find out where Alexa and Rick went this morning when they left the resort.

Dan walked over and chatted with Mike for a while, keeping his eye on the elevator. It was about twenty minutes later when Mike looked over at the young blonde woman wearing slim jeans, a white tailored blouse, and black flats who'd just stepped out of one of the elevators.

"There she is now."

"Thanks, Mike," said Dan, turning to look in Alexa's direction. "You've been a big help."

"Anytime."

▲

When Alexa got off the elevator, she looked around for a man in a uniform. She saw a sturdy police officer in a baseball cap standing at the front desk talking to the clerk. The clerk looked in Alexa's direction, then the police chief shifted his gaze to her. He said something to the clerk before he stepped away from the desk.

"Good morning, Ms. Smith," said Chief Hastings, greeting her with a handshake. "Thanks for meeting with me."

"Hello," she answered as his hand engulfed hers. He was nice-looking, and he had kind eyes, making her feel a little more relaxed.

"Why don't we take a walk, maybe sit outside somewhere?" he asked.

She followed him to the wide entrance doors, which slid open automatically as they approached. The police chief put on his sunglasses and led her to a curved teakwood bench surrounded by flowers under a tall oak tree. It was warm, even in the shade, but a light breeze made it feel almost pleasant.

"Let's sit here, OK?" He smiled at her.

She sat down on the bench before he sat down, allowing about two feet of space between them.

"Nice place," he said, looking around.

"Yes, it is."

"You came into town for your class reunion, is that right?" he asked.

"Yes, that's right." She nodded.

"You grew up here?" He looked at her.

"Yes, we lived in Coral Estates. My dad passed away about seven years ago, and that's when I moved to Chicago."

"Your dad." Dan looked at her, thinking back. "Robert Smith?"

"Yes, that was my dad."

"I think I remember him. Your family has lived in Cypress Lake a long time."

"My dad's family is from here," she answered.

The police chief suddenly changed the subject. "You left the hotel early this morning. Where did you go?" He looked through his aviator sunglasses into the distance.

"I went to the lakefront downtown." She was caught off guard by the question. How did he know she left the hotel early?

"Did you meet Rick Young there?"

"Of course not."

"His blue truck was seen leaving the parking lot right after you left the resort."

"That's not true. I never saw him—" She didn't finish her sentence.

"The hotel has a video of the parking lot, and Rick's truck has been identified. He pulled out of the lot right after you did in the orange convertible." He turned and stared at her. "A coincidence, wouldn't you say?"

"I didn't know that he followed me." She wasn't going to be falsely accused of anything.

His tone changed. "What if I told you that Kimberly Young was murdered. A young mother, pretty, twenty-seven years old with a little baby girl. Her name is Bethany."

He placed an upside-down photograph on the wooden bench between them. Alexa stared down at the photograph, then at the police chief.

"Pick it up!"

She winced, shoulders jerking at the command. She slid the picture toward her, lifted the corner, and brought it up to eye level, focusing on the image. Her mouth opened in shock; she dropped it as though it had burned her fingers. The police chief picked it up and stuck it back in his pocket.

"What are you doing here, Ms. Smith? You're gonna pick up the pieces for your Rick? You love him, right? Are you part of his plan? Good money, ready-made family. Everything all set, including the dream house?"

"No! No! Never!"

"But you love him."

Alexa couldn't think. What was he saying?

"Stop it! You're wrong!" She shook her head, crying.

"I don't think so, Ms. Smith. Where was your Rick after the reunion? Did he go straight home? When did you last see him before you came back to Cypress Lake? How do you know what he's capable of doing?"

She jumped up from the bench and ran into the hotel, away from the oppressive heat, the gruesome photo, the fear, and the lies. She ran up the stairs to her room and struggled to get the magnetic key to signal the latch to open the door. To escape.

Dan watched as Alexa ran into the hotel. He sat there for a minute thinking about what she'd said. He wondered if he'd pushed too hard. She didn't react as if she was guilty of anything except coming back to town and maybe getting caught up in a series of events that probably would have happened anyway and were now out of control. He'd loved Kim, but she had been self-destructive. He couldn't change that now.

He walked to the patrol car and slid into the front seat. He'd parked it under the portico in the shade, but it hadn't helped. The car felt like an oven inside. His damp shirt stuck to the vinyl seatback. He felt hot and drained; the fight with Lynn had been unexpected. He wondered if he could have handled it differently, if he should have stayed and tried to talk to her. But she wasn't ready to talk.

Dan spent the rest of the day driving around town, doing what he considered was part of his job: patrolling. The truth was that he didn't want to go home. It was an "on the surface" normal Sunday afternoon in Cypress Lake, with no signs of anger, distress, or murder, just some tourists and locals strolling along the sidewalks downtown. A few threw up their hands in greeting as he drove past. He headed toward the lakefront. He hadn't been fishing in a while. He wanted to do that again and lose himself in aimless thoughts. But he didn't know if he ever could again. He compulsively touched his shirt pocket, the one with the photo of Kim. He wanted to get rid of it, out of his sight, out of his thoughts, but he couldn't. He felt the burn of hot tears forming. He couldn't stop them. He couldn't stop anything.

It was after five when he got back to the police station. He went into his office and closed the door. He reached into his pocket, pulled out the photograph, and stuck it in the file folder on his desk without looking at it. He swiveled around in his chair and let the tears run down his face.

45

Her hand was shaking as she held the phone. Finally, Rick picked up.

"What do you think you're doing?" she demanded.

"Alexa, what are you talking about?" he asked, perplexed.

"The chief of police was here, questioning me. He's accusing you and me of plotting to be together, saying we somehow planned for this terrible thing to happen to Kim." Her voice broke. "It was horrible."

"Stop it, Alexa. Dan Hastings has a complicated problem. I'm not going to get into it, but he wants to blame me, and he's doing his best to hold me responsible. And he's right. I am..." He paused. "He's trying to make me react by coming after you."

"But he's implying it was murder. And he knows you followed me out of the parking lot this morning. Why did you do that? Are you insane?"

"I'm not going to act guilty when I'm not. I just needed to see you again." He sounded desperate. "The newspeople were gone, and I had to get out of here. I drove to the resort, and when I saw you leaving, I followed you to the lake. Then I realized it was a mistake, and I got out of there as fast as I could." He stopped. "I'm sorry you've been dragged into this mess."

"It's not your fault," she responded. "But why is this police chief after you? How can he blame you for her drinking? She's responsible for that."

"I know that," said Rick. "But Hastings keeps suggesting that something else may have happened to Kim. I don't know what he's talking about, but he wants to blame me."

"I shouldn't have come back here." Alexa was talking to herself as well as to Rick.

"Maybe you shouldn't have."

They were both quiet.

Alexa broke the silence. "But I'm here now, Rick, and I love you. And I meant what I said. I'll help you in any way that I can. I know you blame yourself, but you shouldn't. You tried to stop her."

"Honestly, I don't know. I told her so many times to stop drinking, but I'd given up."

"You can't change people if they don't want to change."

"I know that. But Hastings shouldn't have questioned you. You're not involved in this, and, bottom line, it's my fault that you are."

"I don't think it matters now. And if Kim drank too much, you can't be charged with anything."

"It's still bad, Alexa. Her mother is staying here. She barely talks. She just sits and holds the baby all the time."

"I can't imagine how you both must be feeling," she said softly.

"Bethany keeps me going, Alexa. And you do too." He hesitated. "When this is over, can I see you?"

"Let's not talk about that right now," she answered.

"I've never stopped loving you."

"I have to go, Rick."

"I shouldn't have said that. I'm sorry."

She didn't answer.

"I'm going to talk to Dan Hastings and tell him to back off. He had no right to question you."

"If you do, it might make things worse."

"Worse than what? Kim's dead. Everything is different now, and the police should leave you the fuck out of it." She could hear the anger in his voice.

"Be careful, Rick," she warned him. "We've done nothing wrong, so it doesn't matter. You just take care of yourself and Bethany."

"I'll call you when I can. Remember how much I love you. Nothing's changed."

"For me either."

He hung up without saying goodbye. She hoped he wouldn't cause more trouble for himself by talking to the police chief. At least she understood why he'd followed her to the lake. But she didn't know if the police chief would accept Rick's explanation. There must be something more that he hadn't told Rick. She wanted to know what it was. But there was nothing more she could do now but wait.

46

Monday

Dan was stiff from sleeping on the vinyl sofa in the break room. He'd showered in the locker room facilities, put on a fresh change of clothes that he kept in his locker, and grabbed a cup of coffee. He'd just gotten back to his office when there was a light tap on the door. It was Betsy.

"Dr. Jacobs is on the phone." She closed the door behind her.

Dan picked up. "Hey, Doc."

"I got the report from the medical examiner."

"And?"

"It confirms that Kimberly Young had a blood alcohol level over 0.300 and that she died of asphyxiation." He repeated it. "She was suffocated, Dan."

Dan was silent, letting the news sink in. He didn't want to know, but he had to ask. "How?"

"The killer must have held an object, possibly a pillow or a soft glove, over her face until she stopped breathing. She was likely unconscious when it happened."

"This is a game changer," said Dan.

"I'm afraid it is," he said. "But one other thing."

"What?"

"The blood under her nails? It was type O-positive. Kim was A-positive," said Dr. Jacobs.

"Could she have tried to fight off her killer?" asked Dan.

"Let's just say it's possible but not probable."

He felt his gut wrench, thinking about Kim's last moments, gasping for air.

"She'd also had intercourse earlier that day. It's possible that she'd scratched whoever she was with."

"Yeah, I guess that's possible too."

"I'll email the report to your office." The doctor hung up.

Dan sat there, stunned. Now it was definite. Kimberly Young had been murdered. Dan didn't wait to read the report. He grabbed his baseball cap, put on his holster, and walked to the outer office.

"I'm going out for a while," he called over his shoulder to Betsy. He turned around. "Look for an email from Doc Jacobs. Print the report and fax it to Judge Harris's office. I'm going over there now. Call him and tell him I'm on my way."

"Sure, Dan," said Betsy, looking up over her glasses.

"One more thing. Tell no one what's in the report, and stick it in the file folder on my desk. Then lock my office."

"Will do."

He walked out, slamming the door.

47

Dan walked into Judge Harris's office, and the assistant told him to have a seat. He was too wound up to sit, so he walked around the well-appointed waiting room and looked at the collection of family photos that filled the wall space. Even the family dog had a special framed photo, alone, then one with the children, the whole family, and finally the judge and his wife. He thought of the bare walls in his office; they'd been that way since he'd become chief of police.

Dan had just sat down in one of the framed leather chairs when the assistant said, "Judge Harris will see you now."

Dan walked determinedly into the judge's office. "Jerry, how are you?"

They exchanged a warm handshake over the desk, and the judge motioned for Dan to have a seat. "Good, Dan. How're you?" asked Jerry.

"Well as can be expected. How's the family?"

"Everyone's fine. The kids are getting big." He smiled.

"I saw the photos. Very nice. Especially loved your dog's photo. German shepherd?" asked Dan.

"Mostly. Holly's part of the family, but she's getting up there."

"That happens," said Dan. "Enjoy her while you can."

"You're married, right? I'm sorry, I can't remember your wife's name," said the judge, shaking his head.

"Yes, Lynn and I've been married about six years."

"You'll have to bring her around sometime. I'll throw steaks on the barbecue."

"Lynn would like that." Dan nodded.

The judge picked up several pieces of paper from his desk and frowned. "I got your fax. And of course I've been watching the news. A very sad case, to say the least." He looked up at Dan.

"Yes, that's why I'm here. I need a search warrant. The residence and garage of the decedent."

"You have probable cause?"

"I suspect Rick Young of murdering his wife, Kimberly Young. She was found dead in her car at home after a party last Friday night. She had a high blood alcohol level, became unconscious, and was suffocated." He paused. "You've read the ME's report?"

"I read it." He put down the report he was holding. "Why do you suspect Rick?" asked Jerry, putting his elbows on the desk and resting his chin on his folded hands.

"He and Kim had had an argument earlier in the evening. After the argument, she left the house without him to go to a party, a class reunion. While at the event, he caught his wife having sex with another man, and Rick hit the guy she was with. Another aspect of the case involves an ex-girlfriend of Rick's who shows up at this reunion. Witnesses say they were seen together." He paused. "I've talked to her too."

"You talked to her?" asked the judge, raising his eyebrows.

"I've been doing some investigating. I have every reason to believe Rick Young is responsible for his wife's death. She drove home drunk and left him at the party. He was with the ex-girlfriend, and they were pretty cozy. He goes home much later after who knows what, and he finds his wife drunk and unconscious in her car in the garage. It would have been pretty easy to hold his hand over her mouth or to use something else to cover her mouth, and he kills her. Simple as that."

"I guess you have this all figured out, Dan."

"It doesn't take a genius to figure this one out, Jerry. He had motive and opportunity. Plus an ex-girlfriend on the scene. It seems pretty clear-cut."

The judge got up and walked around the cluttered desk. He sat on the edge of it and stared down at his friend.

"Dan, you're a good police officer, and this case is an extremely tough one because of the circumstances. I'll give you the search warrant, but I warn you to take it slow. Hunches can be wrong. A lot of people show up at reunions and drink too much. A lot of people cheat on their spouses. It doesn't mean conspiracy to murder."

"I know that, Jerry. But Kim wasn't happy with Rick. He had plenty of reasons to want her dead."

"How do you know?"

"I just know."

"You knew Kim Young?" he asked.

"I knew her, yes. She's a hometown girl. I know she drank. I've stopped her for speeding in the past." He shifted in his chair, discomfited by the question.

The judge walked back around his desk and sat down. He took his glasses off and rubbed the bridge of his nose, then put his glasses back on. "I know Rick Young and his dad. They're nice people. Rick has no criminal record and a pretty good war record, from what I understand. He's lived in Cypress Lake all his life, and I knew him as a kid." The judge took a deep breath. "I'll give you the search warrant. But I'm warning you, Dan. Go slow on this one. It sounds like you've made up your mind. What if you're so convinced of Rick's guilt that you're overlooking the real killer?"

"I'll learn more if I can get into the house," Dan answered. "Rick's been evasive when I've talked to him. I just have a feeling."

The judge picked up his phone and asked his assistant to get the paperwork started for the warrant. He hung up and spoke to Dan.

"Will you call me as you proceed?"

"I'll do that." He stood up.

"Is there anything else you want to talk to me about, Dan?" asked his friend, raising his eyebrows.

"No. Why would you ask me that?" asked Dan, bristling at the question.

"I'm sorry. Just call me when you want to talk." He paused. "My assistant will send the warrant by courier when it's complete."

"Thanks, Jerry."

Dan left the judge's office, walked out into the heat, and down the courthouse steps. For the first time, an uneasy feeling that he might be missing something came over him. It was the slightest shiver, almost physical, as he began to question his own judgment. What if his reasoning was all wrong? He'd held the belief that Rick was responsible ever since he found out that Kim was dead. For Christ's sake, Rick let her drive home drunk. Dan hated Rick and blamed him for a lot of things, but did he murder his wife? Now Dan wasn't quite so certain.

48

Dan walked back to the station. The sun was hot, and sweat was running down his temples. He was relieved to step back into the cool building. He took his sunglasses off and stuck them in his shirt pocket.

"Betsy, did you put the report from Dr. Jacobs on my desk?" he asked, stopping at her desk.

"Yes, I faxed it to the judge and put it in the folder. Just like you asked."

"Thanks."

Dan unlocked his office door, threw his damp hat on the chair in the corner, and sat down at the desk. He stared at the folder but didn't open it. He pulled his cell phone from his pocket and dialed the number. He had to try.

"Good morning, Mayfair Village Shops," a pleasant female voice answered.

"Women's department, please," asked Dan.

He was placed on hold and listened to the song "Raindrops Keep Falling on My Head" until a voice he recognized answered.

"Women's wear, may I help you?"

"Hey, Tina. This is Dan. Is Lynn around?"

"Hold on, Dan. I'll see if she's available."

He waited several minutes, but this time he had to listen to an upbeat pop song that he didn't like, and he had no clue who was singing it. He was about to hang up when Tina came back on the line.

"Dan, she's with a buyer right now. May I give her a message?"

"Just tell her that I called."

"Sure will. Oh, Dan, it's too bad about Kim Young."

"Yes, it is," said Dan. "Thanks, Tina."

He ended the call and let out a deep breath. He needed a cigarette, but he wasn't going to have one. He opened the manila folder that was sitting in the middle of his desk, put on his glasses, and began reading.

49

The house felt too quiet, unsettled and disturbed by an invisible and powerful force. Rick felt it, along with the almost-crushing imbalance of his life and world. None of it felt real. He looked at Bethany in her crib. She didn't seem aware of any change in her world. But she would, and he felt a great sadness for his beautiful daughter, the innocent victim of everything that had happened.

Dads were supposed to fix things. Rick was a fixer. But he couldn't fix this. It was a nightmare, even after he woke up. It wouldn't go away. He wished he could go back and do something to save Kim. But she hadn't wanted to be saved. Not by him. At least, it had appeared that way.

Why the hell had she married him? Money? Probably. He wasn't stupid, but he'd acted impulsively. He couldn't escape blame when it stared him in the face. This mistake would never go away. He let the most important person in his life down. He touched his daughter's cheek, and she smiled reflexively. He fought back the tears. Fatigue was wearing him down.

The doorbell rang. He knew Patrice was sleeping in her room. She must have taken something. He walked down the stairs, hoping it wasn't another reporter. When he opened the door, he saw Chief Hastings, with two police officers standing behind him.

"I have a search warrant, Rick." He held a piece of paper in his hand.

Rick moved out of the way, letting Dan and the other officers into the house. "What's going on, Dan?"

"We just want to look around," said Dan. "And I need your cell phone."

"Sorry, it's my business phone," said Rick.

"You'll get it back as soon as I look it over."

Rick pulled his phone out of his hip pocket and handed it to Dan. "My daughter's asleep upstairs in her crib, and Kim's mom is asleep in her room."

"We'll be as quiet as possible."

Rick was seething with anger. "I don't know what the hell you think you're doing. You don't have the right to come into my house and go through my private property."

"Sure I do," said Dan as Sergeant Lowe walked back toward Rick's office. "Your wife was murdered." He handed Rick the warrant.

Rick stood there in complete shock. "What do you mean she was murdered?"

"Someone suffocated Kim after she passed out in the car. In your garage, Rick."

"Jesus Christ," Rick whispered, shaking his head. "I can't believe it."

"I got the report from the medical examiner. She was probably unconscious when she was suffocated," said Dan. "Made it pretty easy for the killer." He kept looking at Rick.

"Are you sure?"

"Yes, I'm sure." He stared at Rick's face. "I need to see your arms, Rick. Roll up your sleeves."

"What the fuck for?"

"Are you gonna roll up your sleeves, or am I going to have to make you?"

Rick pushed the sleeves up and extended his forearms. Dan grabbed each arm forcefully and looked them both over. Satisfied, he let go.

"What was that all about?" Rick pulled his sleeves back down.

"She had blood under her fingernails, may have fought with her killer."

"You're a bastard, Dan. I could never have hurt Kim." Rick's face was red, his hands flexed into fists.

"Oh, and as I recall, you had on long sleeves that night. I'll need the shirt you were wearing," said Dan, a smirk on his face.

"You can have it, but it won't prove anything."

"We'll see," said Dan.

50

Donna Pratt placed her briefcase and newspaper, along with the white paper bag that contained her breakfast, on her desk before she opened the venetian blinds. The sunlight poured into the stuffy office, and she walked to the thermostat on the wall and turned the AC down to sixty-seven. It was only May, and it already felt like the middle of August. She moved the briefcase to the floor, sat down at her desk, and opened the newspaper while taking a sip of coffee from the disposable cup. The hot liquid scalded her mouth, and she coughed, splattering brown specks on her white silk blouse.

"Shit!" She found a napkin stuffed in the sack that held her sausage biscuit and started dabbing at the spots that had already stained the front of her blouse.

Suddenly her eyes moved from the coffee stains to the headline of the Monday morning paper: LOCAL WOMAN FOUND DEAD IN GARAGE. She stopped dabbing, put on her reading glasses, and picked up the newspaper. After a few minutes, she threw the paper down on her desk and called to her assistant in the outer office.

"Gloria, get my dad on the phone," said Donna.

Donna took a large bite of the biscuit and a sip of coffee while she scanned the article again. *Christ!* This was going to turn the town upside down. She was washing the biscuit down with more coffee when the phone rang.

"Hey, Dad," said Donna. "I was away all weekend and just saw the news about Kimberly Young."

"Yes, it's an unbelievable tragedy."

"What do you think?"

"Off the record, she died of asphyxiation. It's what I suspected from my initial exam, but the ME's report confirms it," Dr. Jacobs answered. "Don't tell anyone what I just told you."

"Of course I won't. Rick must be devastated," she said.

"I'm sure he is. The police chief seems to suspect him, though."

"That's absurd. Rick's a good guy. What happened?" Donna asked, taking notes on the legal pad in front of her.

"She was intoxicated, passed out in her car, and someone suffocated her. A cloth of some type, maybe a pillow."

"You're sure it wasn't an accident?"

"Not possible."

"I better call Rick," she said.

"Wait a minute, sweetheart," he said. "How was your weekend?"

"Nice, Dad," she said, rolling her eyes.

"You were with that guy in Saint Pete?"

"Yes, Dad. I was with that guy. His name is David." She didn't want to get into it with him. "I've got to go." She hung up before he had a chance to ask any more questions.

She threw the rest of her breakfast in the trash can; grabbed her purse, briefcase, and coffee; and walked to the outer office. "Call me on my cell if you need me."

"OK, Donna," said Gloria, her eyes never leaving the computer screen. "Don't forget your meeting at two p.m."

Donna had already slammed the door.

The phone rang. Gloria ran out into the hall and stopped her boss, who was halfway down the flight of stairs.

"Donna, you have a call. I think you'll want to take it."

51

Bert came out of Rick's office and looked for Dan. He passed the kitchen, walked down the hall, and stood at the bottom of the staircase in the foyer.

"Chief Hastings?" he called up the stairs.

Dan appeared at the top of the steps. "What is it?"

"I need the combination to the safe in Rick's office."

Rick walked down the stairs and led Bert back to his office. Grabbing a Post-it note off the desk, Rick wrote down two sets of numbers with dashes between them. He handed the yellow note to Bert.

"The large safe in the basement has several firearms, including long guns. The second combination opens that one. The safe in the bedroom has the same combination as the one here in my office," he said. "And don't fuck with anything on my desk."

The doorbell rang. Rick left his office and walked to the front door. When he opened it, he let out a sigh of relief, grateful to see Donna Pratt standing there.

"Donna, thank you for coming," he said, wrapping her hand in both of his and ushering her into the house.

"I'm so sorry about Kim, Rick. I just found out," she said gently.

"I fucking can't believe it," he said. "I can't even think straight, and the police think I did this." He shook his head in disbelief.

"First things first. I need to see the search warrant." She shifted into lawyer mode.

"Here it is." He pulled the warrant out of his jeans pocket and handed it to her.

Donna unfolded it and took her time reading it. "It looks OK." Her eyes narrowed as she pressed her lips together. "I know the judge who issued this. There must be probable cause, Rick."

"What do you mean?"

"They have to have a strong reason to search your house. They're looking for evidence that can implicate you or others as possible suspects in her death."

"I haven't done anything wrong," he said defensively.

"Where can we talk?" she asked. "I need to know every detail of what's been going on with you and Kim."

"Let's go in here," he said, motioning in the direction of the living room.

Donna sat in one of the burgundy leather club chairs placed in the alcove formed by the large wraparound front windows. Rick stood with his arms crossed over his chest and stared out of the windows at the chaotic scene playing out in front of his house. One patrol car was in the driveway, and another one was parked in front of the driveway entrance. Two news vans were parked along the curb, and a group of curious onlookers was gathered in front of the house. Two young men with cameras were positioned at the end of the sidewalk.

"Start at the beginning," she said, taking a legal pad and pen from her briefcase.

52

"What'd you find?" asked Dan, standing in the kitchen and talking to Sergeant Lowe.

"Rick has a lot of handguns and some rifles in a large safe in his workshop. Hunting rifles and ammo. I found a .45 Kimber in his desk. He's licensed to carry," said Bert, looking down at his notes.

"What else?"

"I found a stack of letters hidden in the back of the safe." He handed Dan a thick manila envelope.

Dan looked at the envelope. "Who are they from?"

"All from the same person. Someone named Alexa. They were old, postmarked 2005. Some 2006."

"That's fine, Bert. Good job."

"His office has lots of paperwork, all from his business. I couldn't really check it all out, but I guess I don't know exactly what I'm looking for," said the officer.

"I know what you mean," said Dan, not mentioning the two bottles of vodka that he'd found hidden in the master bedroom closet. They proved nothing beyond the obvious. Kimberly Young had a drinking problem.

"So what now, Chief?"

"We'll check out the cars. I'll take Rick's truck; you look in Mrs. Langston's car." He handed a key to Bert.

"What's in there?" asked Bert, pointing to a large paper evidence bag that Dan was holding.

"Rick's jacket, a pair of gloves, and the clothes he was wearing the night she was killed. We have several bags of pillows already in the cruiser."

Bert nodded.

"You go ahead and check out the car. I'll tell Rick we'll be finished soon," he said.

"OK, Chief," he said, walking toward the front door.

Dan unclasped the manila envelope and pulled out one of the pink envelopes. It was addressed to Rick Young at a college mailing address. He pulled out the two-page letter, written on pink scallop-edged paper. The purple-inked words were written in the swirling script of a teenage girl who was obviously very much in love. He folded the pages, returned them to the envelope, and placed the letter back in the manila envelope. Only a man with deep secrets would keep love letters from an old girlfriend hidden in his safe, out of sight of his wife.

53

"What happened, Rick?" Donna asked him again.

He turned away from the window, looking as if he was coming out of a fog. "I don't know what happened to Kim," he answered, a blank expression on his face.

"When did you see her last?" Donna was jotting notes on the legal pad.

"We were at a party at Lakeview Country Club." He answered slowly, as though he was trying to remember the details. "She'd had too much to drink."

"OK. But what happened? Did you and Kim have a fight that night?" She prodded him.

"Yes, we did." He was quiet for a moment. "I got to the dance after she did. And I started looking for her. When I found her, she was with Josh Logan in the back seat of his SUV."

"Josh Logan? The same Logan who owns the Cadillac dealership?"

"Yes, he's the sales manager." Rick nodded.

She stopped taking notes and looked at Rick. "They were having sex. Is that what you mean?"

"Yes." He answered in a monotone.

"Then what?"

"I don't know for sure, except I grabbed Josh. I hit him, and he went down. Kim screamed at me, and I left."

"Did you leave the country club?"

"No, I went back inside. I wanted to say goodbye to someone," he answered.

"Who was this person?"

"She was a friend I knew from school." He turned and stared out of the window again.

"So did you say goodbye?" She looked up at him, studying his face.

"Yes, I said goodbye." He went on, his thoughts drifting. "She asked me to dance before I left, so I danced with her."

"What's her name?"

"Alexa Smith."

"Then what happened?"

He turned back to Donna. "Kim saw us and got really mad. She said some pretty nasty things. Then she went into the ladies' room with some of her friends. I tried to get her to come out, but she wouldn't."

"Did you see Kim after that?"

"Not until I came home," he answered. "Then it was too late." He sat down in the matching chair near the window. He put his elbows on his thighs, clasped his hands, and shook his head.

"I'm sorry, Rick. I know this is hard, but I have to ask." She paused. "Did you kill your wife?"

"No, I didn't." He looked at Donna. "But I may as well have. I let her drive home alone."

"That's not what this is about, Rick. This is about murder."

"No, I didn't kill her, Donna. I wouldn't do that." He was adamant.

"Had she cheated on you in the past?" she asked.

"I don't know for sure, but I think so."

"Do you know who with?"

"I would guess Josh, maybe others. I don't know." He shook his head.

"Are you having an affair?" asked Donna.

"No. I'm not." He looked directly at her.

"Who would want to kill Kim?"

"Honest to God, I don't know." He shook his head.

"Someone obviously did." She stood up and tucked the legal pad in her briefcase. "Let me talk to Chief Hastings. I'll find out what I can."

Donna picked up her purse, and before leaving the room, she turned to Rick. "Where were you between the time you left the party and when you found Kim in the garage?"

"I was driving around."

"Did anyone see you?"

"Not that I'm aware of."

"That's fine, Rick. Don't answer any more questions that the police ask you, and don't talk to the news media. I'll find out what I can."

Her high heels clicked on the hardwood floor as she walked toward the back of the house. She saw the police chief in the kitchen, placing a stack of letters inside a manila envelope.

"Chief Hastings, may I have a word with you?"

He looked up.

"Sure," he said. "How are you, Ms. Pratt?"

"I'm fine, Chief." She gave him her best smile, tipping her head slightly sideways. "Please call me Donna."

"You can call me Dan." He smiled back. "I know your dad."

"I guess you talked to him," she stated.

"I did."

She stared at him, and he stared back. "You know Rick didn't kill his wife."

"I don't know that," he answered.

"You don't have anyone else. You're just assuming the husband did it. I've watched those crime shows too. And I know the statistics. But you're wrong about this."

"Rick had motive and opportunity," said the police chief, raising one of his shoulders.

"What motive?"

"Witnesses saw them fighting, and he caught her having sex with some other guy. He's hot-tempered and lost control." He paused. "And he has a girlfriend."

"But you have no evidence." She smiled and shook her head. "No case, Dan."

"Not yet. But I will."

"You will call me if you find anything?" she asked.

"Are you representing him?"

"I represent his family's interests."

"Then I'll call you. Out of courtesy, but I don't have to."

"I'd appreciate it very much," she said. "And I'd like to see the ME's report."

"I'll send a copy to your office," he said.

She handed him her business card, smiled at him, and walked back to the living room where Rick was waiting. "I'll be in touch, Rick," she said. "Remember. Don't answer any more questions."

Donna walked down the sidewalk, past the photographers. One took her photo as she got into her car. She started to pull away but then stopped. The police chief had stepped outside the house, and the reporters rushed him. One she recognized from a local station shoved a microphone in his face while another started filming the impromptu interview. *Shit!* she thought. He would probably give up the fact that Kimberly Young had been murdered. That would send the media into a feeding frenzy of speculation, none of it good for Rick. She put the car in gear and drove away, knowing she'd find out what he'd said on the evening news. But she also wondered what Chief Hastings knew that she didn't.

54

Rick sat alone in the dark kitchen. He'd felt somewhat reassured after talking with Donna. But she could help him only with the legalities of the investigation into Kim's death. The one thing he couldn't accept was that someone had actually murdered his wife. He hadn't told Patrice. Not yet. She'd been in a daze ever since she found out about Kim. He dreaded telling her that someone had actually harmed her daughter. It was bad enough that Kim was dead. Now they were faced with knowing that someone had intentionally hurt her. It was unfathomable to him. How could he explain it to Patrice when he couldn't understand it himself?

What kind of madness would cause someone to kill Kim? Someone had invaded his property and killed her. Who would have suffocated her in the garage? Who would have even known she was there? She had a few friends, but when he thought about it, he didn't really know about her life. She came and went without telling him where she was going. He'd gotten used to her disappearances. She always had an excuse when he'd question her. After seeing her with Josh, he had to accept she had another life, a secret life. He'd always suspected it, but maybe there were many others besides Josh.

In the beginning, when Kim came on to him, he'd been caught off guard. He hadn't wanted to get involved. But he had. She was an enticing, sexy woman. But it was not the kind of relationship he thought would last. And he didn't want it to. She needed excitement and attention, and she liked living on the edge without thinking of the consequences. After the baby, she must have wanted more excitement. The drinking added to her dangerous life. But who would have wanted to murder her? Rick had wanted to hurt Josh when he saw him with Kim. But had he wanted to kill him? He wasn't sure. He'd killed before. But that was in combat. Part of his duty in the military, but he wasn't a cold-blooded murderer, and he would never in a million years have hurt Kim, no matter how angry she'd made him—and she had pushed his buttons many times.

Rick now knew Dan suspected him of killing his wife. He'd hated her at times, the way she'd neglected Bethany. He'd thought of leaving her, but he never would have hurt her. Ever. Who would have thought of doing that? It wasn't a robbery; nothing was stolen. It was murder. The word kept repeating over and over in his mind. And it didn't appear to be a random murder. Kim had been the target. Someone had wanted her dead.

Rick went into his office, grabbed the .45 out of the desk drawer, and released the magazine; it was fully loaded. He shoved it back in, checked for a round in the chamber, and flipped on the safety; he stuck the pistol in the back of his jeans. He checked that all the doors were locked and set the security alarm, disarming the interior motion detectors.

He heard Patrice coming down the stairs. He'd have to warn her about the alarm. And also tell her that her daughter had been murdered. He went back into the kitchen, grabbed a cold beer from the refrigerator, and twisted off the metal cap. He took several long gulps of the dark liquid, the froth burning his throat. He drank another long swallow. He had to tell her now. Before someone else did.

55

Patrice looked exhausted. Her eyes were red, but she wasn't crying anymore. She sat down at the kitchen table across from Rick.

"The baby's asleep," she said.

"I'm glad she's too little to understand." The words caught in his throat.

"I don't believe it, Rick. It can't be real, can it?" She looked at him, wanting reassurance he couldn't give to her.

He reached across the table for her hand. He held it and looked at her. She seemed fragile, her fingers brittle and cold.

"Patrice, when did you last have something to eat?" he asked.

"I was going to get something, but…" Her voice trailed off.

Rick got up and placed a kettle of water on the stove. "I'll make you some tea."

He opened the refrigerator and pulled out a casserole that a neighbor had dropped off. He lifted the lid and spooned some chicken and vegetables onto a plate. He covered it, placed it in the microwave, and set the timer.

"I don't want anything." She shook her head. "I don't think I can eat."

"You need to eat something. Do it for the baby," he coaxed. "She needs you."

He set a fork and knife in front of her. He put a tea bag in a cup, poured the water from the kettle, and set the tea in front of her. She looked down at the cup of tea but didn't respond.

Rick sat down across from her. The microwave beeped three times, but he ignored it. "Patrice, I need to tell you something."

"What is it?" She was looking away from him, bleary-eyed.

"The police chief was here. He got the report back from the medical examiner. It's bad news. About Kim."

He was trying to find the right words, but nothing was coming to him. There were no right words.

"What? What could be worse than my darling girl being gone?"

"Someone suffocated her," he answered.

"Oh, Rick," she said. "Maybe that's a mistake. She drank too much. I knew it would happen. It was the drinking that took her away from us."

Patrice put her face in her hands and began to cry, deep, out-of-control sobs. Rick got up and stood behind her, placing his hands on her trembling shoulders.

"I know," he said, trying to console her.

Rick stood there for a long time while she cried. There was nothing he could do to erase this moment in time.

56

Alexa sat on the sofa in her suite, sipping a glass of red wine and watching the late news. The local station was showing a clip of the Cypress Lake police chief answering questions the reporters were shouting at him; he looked uncomfortable but measured, limiting what he told them. He said they were proceeding to investigate what they now knew was the murder of Kimberly Young. No one had been charged, and he wouldn't give any details. But he was standing in front of Rick's house. It was obvious that the police were questioning Rick. *He must be devastated,* thought Alexa. *Oh, God. Who could have killed Kim?*

It was frightening to think that someone had committed a murder in Rick's house. She was afraid for him. And Bethany. Alexa had only until the weekend—that was when she was supposed to fly back to Chicago. She wanted to leave now, but it might look even worse for her and for Rick. She couldn't abandon Rick. Not now.

But that police chief had scared her. He was trying to imply something about her and Rick. That they were involved and had planned something terrible. But they hadn't. She hadn't seen or talked to Rick in years. The truth was simple. She'd done nothing wrong, and she felt certain that Rick hadn't done anything wrong. Even though he blamed himself for Kim's drinking.

Maybe the wine was clouding her judgment, but she felt desperate to see him, talk to him. Let him know she loved him. If there was some way to help him, she would. Even though he'd told her to stay away, she couldn't. She could feel his pull, the hold he had on her. He was the love of her life. If fate was giving her a second chance, she was going to take it.

57

Tuesday

Katie couldn't tell Alexa what she'd done. Alexa would think she was a terrible person. Maybe she was. But it wasn't her fault. If anyone was to blame, it was Tim. He'd caused everything to fall apart. Somehow she was managing to hold it together. No one at school thought Katie was anything more than the cheerful teacher with the holiday earrings and happy emoji stickers who brought special treats for her students on their birthdays. Her class had voted her Teacher of the Year last year. Even the other teachers loved her. No one knew she was living a lie.

When she'd married Tim, she thought life was going to be wonderful. But seeing Alexa again had reminded her of what could have been. When Katie had been happy and full of hopes and dreams. When she and Alexa had sleepovers, they'd lie in bed and talk about the future. They had their lives all planned out. Alexa was going to marry Rick, and Katie was going to marry Mr. Right, who was out there somewhere, waiting just for her. But it hadn't quite turned out that way for Katie.

Alexa had escaped Cypress Lake and had a career as a flight attendant, flying to exciting destinations and meeting exciting men. Katie almost hated her for it. Maybe she did. Alexa was beautiful and had her pick of any man she wanted. It was all so easy for her. So maybe Rick had cheated on her. It had been only the one time. But Miss Perfect wouldn't forgive him. How stupid of Alexa to give up a great guy like Rick. Alexa didn't know that Katie had had a secret crush on Rick. But of course he'd chosen Alexa, the pretty cheerleader with lots of friends. And that needy act she was able to pull off. Everyone pitied her when she lost her dad, but Katie saw through it. She was the only one who did. What did Alexa have that she didn't have? Katie was even smarter than Alexa. Alexa had good grades, but Katie was the one who made it into graduate school. Alexa couldn't even finish college. The excuse about her dad dying was just that—an excuse so that she could be with any man she wanted. She'd probably slept with every guy who asked her. Her holier-than-thou act hadn't fooled Katie.

Josh Logan had told everyone at school about Alexa—that she'd had sex with him and who knows who else. As far as Katie was concerned, Rick was better off without Alexa. She couldn't comprehend what he'd seen in her. Or Kim. But men weren't very discriminating. She'd learned that the hard way with Tim. He was like all men. None of them could be trusted. She wished she'd found that out before she married him. She'd even fallen in love with him. She'd been so impressed that he was a bank manager. Guess that's how he'd been able to hook up with so many women. That's how she met him. How fucking stupid was she? She wondered how many times he'd cheated, but it didn't matter now. It had been one too many.

Katie wished she hadn't had so much wine at the reunion. What a mistake! Then Alexa had let her down. Why couldn't she do one small favor for her and just tell one little lie? That's all she'd asked. But no. Miss Perfect had refused to help her BFF.

Katie was alone in the teachers' lounge when she pulled the cell phone out of her purse. When the dispatcher answered, Katie deepened her voice and whispered, "Why don't you check out Alexa Smith at the Gold Palm Resort? She was with Rick the night Kim Young was killed."

She ended the call and put the phone back in her purse. She grabbed her purse and briefcase and left the teachers' lounge before anyone came in. She walked down the empty hallway, through the double door, and outside onto the covered walkway. The trash can was nearly full, but she shoved her hand deep inside the metal opening and dropped the burner, burying it among the candy wrappers, chewing gum, aluminum cans, and paper cups. It only took about a minute. The final bell rang as she walked into her classroom, slightly out of breath, her mouth turned up into a half smile.

58

Dan had instructed Bert to deliver all the evidence they'd collected from Rick's house to the county forensics lab. Maybe something would show up on the pillows or on Rick's clothing. It was a long shot, but there was nothing else to go on. Dr. Jacobs said the blood under Kim's fingernails could have been from someone she'd scratched earlier. Maybe Josh. She'd been with him, according to Rick. And Josh looked bad, beaten up. *Fuck!* thought Dan. If blood showed up on Rick's shirt, it could be Josh's blood. He'd have to talk to Josh again. More than that. He wanted to look Josh over and see if he had any scratches. If Rick's blood was under her nails, it could mean that she'd struggled with him. But he had no visible cuts. He'd have to call Dr. Jacobs about getting DNA testing on the blood. It could identify for certain whose blood it was. But it still wasn't proof of who killed Kim.

He held Rick's phone and looked at the call history. The only long-distance calls that Rick had made were recent. One was made on Friday morning at 11:00 a.m. Rick had called the same number on Saturday at 4:30 a.m., right after Dan had left Rick's house. He recognized the number—it belonged to Alexa Smith. It also appeared that

Ms. Alexa Smith had placed a call to Rick after Dan had visited her at the Gold Palm Resort on Sunday morning.

So the lovebirds have been talking to each other, thought Dan. Rick had called Alexa's number on Friday morning before the reunion. Then he'd called her again in the early morning after Kim's murder. And Ms. Alexa Smith must have warned Rick that Dan had questioned her about Kim and that he'd been seen following her to the lakefront. So maybe Kim knew that Rick was having an affair with Alexa Smith. Or that they were planning to see each other. Rick was an asshole, but maybe he and Alexa Smith were just old high school friends who wanted to reconnect. Shit like that happens. But usually no one ends up dead.

Dan shook his head. He didn't really know anything yet. Except one thing. Everything kept pointing to one person. Rick. But did he want it to be Rick? Was he so convinced of Rick's guilt that he was overlooking vital information that could lead him to the real killer? What was he missing?

He didn't hear her at first. He looked up when Betsy walked into his office, holding a notepad. "Hey, Chief. I just got a strange call. Someone disguising their voice," she said.

"No identification?" he asked.

"No. The voice sounded female." She held up the notepad, looked through her bifocals, and started reading. "*Why don't you check out Alexa Smith at the Gold Palm Resort? She was with Rick the night Kim Young was killed.*"

"That's all they said?"

She tore off the note and handed it to the chief. "That's it. The phone carrier is tracing the call."

Who the hell would want him to think that Rick was with Alexa Smith on Friday night? The implication said it all. The caller is the killer. Or someone wants to throw Rick, or Alexa, under the bus. Or maybe the judge was right. He was barking up the wrong tree. Or maybe someone knew about Alexa and Rick, and they wanted to do their civic duty.

Dan grabbed his CLPD cap and his cell phone and strapped on his holster. "Call me. I'll be out for a while," he said as walked out the door.

"Wait, Chief. You have a phone call. Someone named Mike."

He turned in the doorway and stared at her. *What now?* he thought. "I'll take it in my office."

59

One Year Ago

Kim turned her compact car into the rutted sandy driveway next to the white-frame house and parked a few feet behind her mother's Camry. Kim pushed the driver's seat forward against the steering wheel and reached into the back seat to get the basket stuffed with a week's worth of dirty laundry. Her apartment complex had coin-operated machines in the basement, but she couldn't afford to spend the money. It was hard enough making ends meet on her modest salary as a salesclerk at the discount department store. If she worked overtime or on the weekends or holidays, it helped. But not enough.

"Hey, Mama," she called out. "Where are you?"

"Hey, Kimmie," Patrice answered from the kitchen.

Kim carried the basket to the kitchen and dropped it onto the chipped linoleum. Her mom was leaning over the sink, running a soapy dishcloth over a dinner plate. She turned around when she heard the basket hit the floor, saw the stack of laundry, then rinsed the plate and placed it in the drainer. She dried her hands on the dish towel and turned to face her daughter, who was sitting at the kitchen table, lighting a cigarette.

"I'm not going to do your laundry again, Kimberly," her mother said.

"I didn't ask you to," Kim said, throwing the match in the thin metal ashtray in the center of the table.

Patrice was wearing baggy knit pants, stretched out at the knees, and a faded blue-and-white striped jersey and slippers, and she looked very tired.

"I just had dinner, but I can warm up some leftovers if you want," she offered.

Kim opened the refrigerator and took out a dark-brown bottle and twisted off the top.

"I'll get something to eat while I'm doing my laundry."

She took a drink of the beer, set her cigarette in the ashtray, and carried the overloaded basket to the enclosed porch located just behind the kitchen. She put a load in the washer and added detergent, and the machine began to fill. When she got back to the kitchen, her mom was sitting at the table. Waiting. Smoke trailed into the air from the burning cigarette.

"How are you, sweetheart? I don't see you much, except when you want to do laundry."

Kim hated the guilt trip her mom always tried to lay on her. "I'm busy, Mom." She carried the beer to the refrigerator, opened the door, and stared inside. She grabbed a container of leftover potato salad, opened a drawer, and picked out a fork. She sat in the chair across from Patrice and began eating.

"So what have you been doing with yourself?" asked Patrice.

Kim knew it was a loaded question. Her mother always wanted to know what she was doing. She always seemed to be accusing her of something, even when she was in high school.

"I've been busy working at the store," answered Kim, washing down a large bite of the salad with several swallows of beer. She took another bite.

"Are you dating anyone?" asked her mother.

Kim knew where this was going. Her mother had heard the rumors, and she wanted to know the juicy details. *Too bad,* she thought.

"I date a lot of different guys, Mom."

Kim slammed the beer bottle down on the table and carried the empty plastic container to the sink. She filled it with warm water and dishwashing liquid, letting the foamy water do the work.

"Sorry, Kimmie, I just like to know about your life. I'm your mom, and I love you." She walked over to the sink and put her arm around her daughter's shoulder. Kim shrugged her off.

"I know, Mom. There's nothing to tell."

"I've heard otherwise."

"What have you heard?" Kim got another bottle of beer from the refrigerator, not looking at her mother.

"I've heard that you're seeing a married man." She shook her head. "You know it will go nowhere, don't you?"

"It doesn't matter. I'm dating someone else now, so you don't have to worry about me anymore."

"You're my daughter, and I do worry about you, honey," she answered. "I don't want to see you throw your life away." She was nearly in tears.

"You mean the way you threw yours away." Kim's voice was filled with hatred.

"This isn't about my life. It's about yours. You're beautiful, and you can have any man you want. It's about making the right choices, Kimmie."

"Stay out of my life!"

"I want you to know you can talk to me if you need to. Don't you understand?" pleaded Patrice.

Kim didn't answer. She walked into the drab living room at the front of the house, sat on the threadbare sofa with the coffee stains, and turned on the television set really loud so that she couldn't hear her mother's voice. Canned laughter from a sitcom rerun filled the small room, but Kim didn't hear it. All she could think about was how to break the news of her pregnancy to her mother. And she had made the right choice. It might take a little time; she had some details to work out, but she was not going to throw her life away. She wasn't going to spend her life waiting for a lowlife who had deserted her to come home. Her mother had been a fool. Kim was going to get exactly what she wanted.

60

Tuesday

Josh felt groggy, not sure how many days he'd been in bed. Stacy had been attentive, bringing him ice, milkshakes, pain pills. But he couldn't tell her that it wasn't just the physical pain that had left him wasted and unable to function. He was fucked up over Kim's death. He was devastated to think of her gone from his life. She hadn't been part of his game plan and never would have been. *But damn.* She'd deserved more, even more than him. A lot more.

He thought of the day she'd wanted to marry him; it had come from out of the blue. He'd laughed it off, and she'd dropped it. Maybe if things had been different. He realized how alike they were, even though deep down, he knew it would have been disastrous. Freedom had its advantages, and Kim liked her freedom too. Then she'd married Rick, probably because of the baby. With Kim gone, Josh realized how truly alone he was. He closed his eyes tighter, as tears rolled from the corner of his eyes down the sides of his face. He wiped the tears away. *The pain must be getting to me,* he thought.

When he reached for the pill bottle, he knocked the glass of water off the nightstand. "Shit!" He raised his head off the pillow and squinted to read the time; it was 9:15 a.m. The house was still, not normal for this hour of the day. He placed his head flat on the pillow and took a slow assessment of his pain. The steady ache probably meant it wasn't worse, but he'd learn more when he looked in the mirror. But first, he'd have to get vertical.

Josh couldn't open his left eye as he struggled to sit up. A wave of nausea swept over him when he finally made it to his feet. It took a few moments before he was steady enough to make it to the bathroom. The reflection told him he was hurt pretty badly, especially his eye. It was a deep purple, and it looked like the lids were glued together. His cheek was so swollen that it was pressing upward, adding to the pain in his eye. Maybe he should go to the doctor as Stacy had suggested. *Where is she?* he wondered.

Wearing his boxers and a T-shirt, he went down the steps, one at a time, each one like a hammer against his skull. He gripped the bannister so that he wouldn't stumble, and when he reached the bottom, he had to stop and take a deep breath. He went into the kitchen—nothing. Not even coffee. No dishes in the sink. Where the hell were they?

He'd look upstairs again. Maybe the kids were asleep. Bracing his head, he walked up the staircase slowly, stopped on the landing, and saw that the doors to the kids' rooms were closed. He opened Joshua's door first. The *Star Wars* blanket was neatly in place, as though the bed hadn't been slept in. He scanned the room. Something seemed wrong. Toys were missing that usually sat on the children's furniture, and the red-and-white storage bins that held books and games looked oddly half-empty.

It took Josh eight strides to get to Anna's room. The white canopy bed was draped as usual with the princess comforter, but bare spots were noticeable on the storage shelves. Lucy, her favorite doll, the one she took everywhere, was absent from its normal resting place. Her pink princess pillow was gone.

Fuck! Where the hell were the kids? And where was Stacy? He walked as fast as he could to the bedroom. He threw open the closet doors and looked for the blue soft-sided zip-up, the one she had always taken on their trips ever since their honeymoon. It was gone. And so was she.

"Damn!"

He slammed his fist into the closet door, breaking through the slender white slats, and slivers of wood became embedded in his forearm. *That fucking bitch,* he thought. *If she thinks she's going to get away from me, she's out of her fucking mind.*

How the hell did all this happen? His life was spiraling out of control, and it was not his fault. None of this would have happened if he hadn't lost Kim. There was only one person responsible for this fucking mess. And he was going to get what he deserved. He'd destroyed Kim, and he'd destroyed Josh's marriage. He would make Rick pay if it was the last thing he ever did.

Josh found the pill bottle on the floor next to the bed. He threw two into the back of his throat and washed them down with a shot of whiskey. Then he got into the shower and turned on the cold water, letting it run through his hair and onto his face. His eye was still swollen, but it had opened slightly, allowing him to see more clearly. He stayed in the shower for twenty minutes, until the pain had begun to recede as the pills started working their magic.

After drying himself off, he put on the wrinkled khakis he found on the back of a chair and a clean white golf shirt that was hanging in the closet. Some blood from the wound on his arm smeared on the sleeve, but he didn't notice. His phone started ringing as he put on his loafers.

He picked up the phone, his voice demanding as he answered. "Stacy, where the hell are you?"

"Sorry, Mr. Logan. It's Christina. I just wondered if you're coming in. A customer says he has an appointment with you. A Mr. Elliot?"

"Tell him that I'm out today. Maybe I can see him tomorrow. Have him call back." He stopped. "No, wait a minute. Is Bev there?"

"Yes, she's here," answered Christina.

"Tell her to handle it."

"Yes, sir," she said. "Will you be in tomorrow?"

"I don't know yet." He hung up. He didn't like that bimbo questioning him. What the fuck was happening? Josh knew what he had to do. Stacy had a lot of fucking nerve to leave like this. And to take his children with her. If she thought for one second he would take her back, she was shit out of luck. This was the last time this bitch or any bitch would ever hurt him. Even when Kim had told him about the baby—their baby—he didn't care. He didn't need the complication, and she had a plan in place that would work out to her benefit and to his. He was fine with it, and she'd still fuck him. But Stacy leaving him had pushed him too far. He was going to make sure that no one would ever push him again.

61

Thank God she'd come to her senses. The wine last night had momentarily affected her judgment, but Alexa had stopped herself just in time. She hadn't called Rick. That would have been not only stupid but also dangerous. Now that he might be accused of murdering his wife, it would have given that police chief more reason to suspect both her and Rick of plotting to get rid of Kim. It sounded reprehensible, like a true-crime mystery on a reality television show. How could this whole thing have happened? Rick was a wonderful man, and she knew he'd never hurt anyone, especially the mother of his beautiful little girl.

Alexa had to escape from the television. She'd spent all morning listening to the local news and their continual broadcast about Kim's murder. But everyone must be glued to the news. A murderer was at large in the small town. It was frightening, and Alexa felt so vulnerable with many of the local residents aware of her history with Rick. It might be easy to draw the wrong conclusion. Even she could reason that out. She thought of her lonely but stable life before coming back to Cypress Lake. How simple it was, perfect in many ways. Now fate had brought her back. Maybe she was meant to come back and be here for Rick. Maybe it was their time at last. She'd have to stand by him, especially now when he needed her the most.

She slipped on her aqua two-piece swimsuit, white fishnet cover-up, and white wedge sandals. Room key in hand, she walked to the elevator and pressed the down button. A whirring sound signaled the car's approach before the soft ding. When the doors slid open, Alexa stumbled backward as he lunged at her. He grabbed the key card from her grasp, twisted her arm behind her back, and shoved her down the hallway. His hand was over her mouth, so no one could hear her desperate cries for help.

62

The hallway was empty as Josh maneuvered Alexa toward her room. She struggled against him, but when he pulled up hard on her twisted arm, she stopped fighting and moved along with him. The magnetic key worked the first time, and he pushed the door open, not letting go of her. Once in the room, she tried to bite his hand, but he slapped her face hard, and she collapsed in his arms.

"I let you go the first time, but I won't this time, Lexie." His voice low and raspy as he pushed her toward the bedroom. "No one is here to save you."

She tried to yell, but her screams were muffled as he pressed his hand tighter against her face. He was getting more and more excited as she tried to escape his strong hold on her.

"I'll stop hurting you if you promise not to scream," he whispered in her ear, his strong hand gripping her bent arm, the other pulling her body against his. She nodded, and he took his hand from her mouth.

He shoved her facedown on the bed, her arm still bent backward and her wrist pressed into her back. He planted his right knee between her legs and spread them. Unsteady, he fell on top of her, his heaviness pressing her body and face into the duvet, muffling her calls for help. He released her arm, his body weight keeping her from moving, and ripped the flimsy cover-up, exposing her back. With one hand holding her down, he unfastened her bikini top and leaned forward, licking and kissing her neck and shoulder while slipping his other hand under her body, cupping one breast.

"You want this, too, Lexie, as much as I do," he hissed, struggling to hold her down on the bed.

"Stop it, Josh!" she screamed, kicking her legs and fighting to get him off her.

"Shut up!" The words came out as a groan of animal desire.

He raised himself up and, in one quick motion, flipped Alexa onto her back, exposing her breasts. She tried to hit him, pushing to sit up, but he grabbed both of her wrists and held them above her head, her body pinned under him as he tried to kiss her. Alexa turned her face away from his, pressing her lips together. His one hand still locked around her wrists, he placed his legs between hers and spread them apart. He unzipped his pants and began fumbling with the fly of his shorts as her body writhed beneath his. Alexa's screams muffled the sound of the hotel door banging open.

"Get the fuck off her. *Now!*" Chief Hastings yelled.

Josh froze. Dan grabbed him, threw him facedown on the floor, and cuffed his wrists behind his back.

Alexa tried to sit up, covering herself with the torn swimsuit cover-up. Dan went into the bathroom, found a robe, and placed it over Alexa's shoulders. He helped her off the bed as another police officer stood over Josh, reading him his rights.

"Ms. Smith, are you all right?" he asked.

She didn't answer, collapsing into Dan's arms instead.

He held her close, wrapped in his arms, and walked her into the living room area of the suite. Dan glanced toward the open doorway and saw Mike standing there. Dan raised his chin and nodded.

"Good call."

63

The officer had Josh by the arm and pushed him toward the door. Josh yanked his arm free from the policeman's grip and turned toward Dan.

"You're making a big mistake! She invited me to her room!" he shouted, gesturing with his head toward Alexa.

"Get him out of here. I'll be down in a minute," said Dan, ignoring the veiled threat.

Dan could hear Josh swearing as he was led down the hallway to the elevator. His shouts were becoming fainter and fainter, finally disappearing after he was escorted into the elevator and the doors shut. Dan closed the door and looked at Alexa, who was sitting on the sofa, her arms folded around herself as though she was trying to hold herself together.

Dan got a bottle of water from the bar and sat down next to her. "Here, drink this."

She took a few sips from the bottle. "Thanks," she said, not looking at him.

"Can you tell me what happened?" His voice was calming.

"It was so fast." She hesitated.

"I know," he said. "Take your time."

"I was on my way to the pool." She paused. "Everything was getting to be too much." Tears began to run down her face.

"What happened?"

"When the elevator doors opened, he lunged at me, grabbed my arm, and forced me into the room." She was crying. "I tried to scream, but he had his hand over my mouth." She covered her face with her hands, her shoulders shaking as she sobbed.

Dan waited. "Do you know him?"

"We dated in high school but not for very long." She had stopped crying and looked at Dan. "He came here the day I checked in. He tried to kiss me, but I stopped him."

"I understand," he said. "Maybe we should take you to the hospital."

"I'm OK. He didn't touch me, not like that." She shook her head.

"Are you sure?" He didn't know if she was physically injured, but she'd been through a traumatic attack that would shake anyone up.

"I don't know. I think I'm OK."

Dan knew she was still upset with him. And afraid. He'd come down pretty hard on her. "Look, I'm sorry about showing you the photo when I was here before. Sometimes I have to push. You understand?"

She just nodded and looked at him, her eyes red and puffy.

"Do you think you could come down to the station and make a statement?" He waited for her to answer, but she was silent. "He's not going to come after you again. I promise. Do you understand, Alexa?"

"Yes." She nodded.

"Are you sure you're OK?" His concern was growing. He saw a young woman, very alone and vulnerable, in the middle of something bad.

"I'm all right, Chief Hastings." Her voice sounded stronger.

"Good. I'll wait for you to change," he said.

"I can drive myself."

"No, I'll send one of my officers back to drive you to the station. Just keep your door locked."

"Thank you." She smiled at him, grateful.

Dan was trying to remain objective in handling this case, but it was difficult. And he was beginning to feel compassion for this Alexa Smith. He had a gut feeling that she wasn't involved in Kim's death. And maybe Rick wasn't guilty. He'd admitted that he hadn't stopped Kim from driving home drunk. His remorse seemed real. Maybe too real for a murderer. But Rick's long-lost love was back in town. Quite a coincidence—and perhaps a well-planned one. But now Dan wasn't sure.

Dan didn't want to leave Alexa alone in her room, even for a short time, but she'd assured him that she was all right. He gave her his cell phone number and told her to call him if she needed anything. She seemed to be calm, in spite of what she'd been through. He had a different impression now. She appeared to be vulnerable but self-assured, like someone who'd learned to take care of herself. Maybe because she'd had to.

He left Alexa's room and walked to the elevator. He'd get Josh checked out at the hospital. The way Josh looked, Dan didn't want the case muddied with accusations of police brutality. And he'd get some blood tests, including blood type. He had plenty of questions for Josh Logan. And he planned to keep him locked up for a long time.

Dan made his way to the front desk, ignoring the stares of a few curious guests who had gathered in the lobby.

"Keep an eye on her, Mike. I'm sending one of my female officers to pick her up."

"Sure, Dan. I'm glad you caught that bastard."

"Thanks to you, he didn't hurt her."

"Glad I could help," he said. "I can spot assholes from a mile away."

"You sure did."

Dan walked into the glaring sunlight, put on his aviators, and got in on the passenger side of the police car. Through the metal screen, he saw Josh slumped down in the back seat. As soon as he saw Dan, he sat upright, leaned forward, and started yelling.

"You've got the wrong guy, Dan. You should arrest Rick Young and his girlfriend. Not me! You fucked up!"

"Shut your fucking mouth."

The police sergeant drove away, following Dan's instructions to take Josh to the emergency room. Dan didn't know what had caused Josh to go off the deep end and attack Alexa. It could be drugs, alcohol, or the murder of Kimberly Young. Or maybe it was all three.

64

Officer Marjorie Davis had met Alexa at the resort and had taken her to the police station. Chief Hastings had been gentle with her, asking a few routine questions for the police report. She was more than willing to sign the complaint against Josh. Alexa felt shaken and sore from the brutal attack, and Chief Hastings finally convinced her to go to the hospital, just as a precaution. The officer drove her to the hospital, where Alexa checked out just fine, only some minor bruises, but the doctor advised her to please call him if she began to feel worse or had any questions. He gave her a prescription for a mild sedative in case she had trouble sleeping.

When she got back to the resort, the officer walked her back to her room and opened the door.

"Are you sure you'll be all right?" asked Officer Davis. "I can stay with you as long as you'd like."

"You're very kind," she answered, her eyes welling with tears. "But I'll be OK."

"Promise you'll call me if you need anything." The woman handed her a card.

"Thanks so much," said Alexa, hugging the officer in gratitude.

She appreciated the concern of this policewoman and also of Chief Hastings. He seemed different now, and she was grateful for the way he took care of her. She'd never been so frightened in her life. Suddenly she felt afraid to be in the hotel room. Alexa looked around before putting her purse down. The staff had done a thorough job of cleaning the room, even putting fresh linens on the bed. But Alexa felt unsettled. She'd never gone through such a violent experience. She called the front desk, and Mike answered.

"Thank you so much for calling for help," she said, truly thankful.

"I'm glad I was here," he said.

"Not as glad as I am." She managed a laugh.

"How can I be of service?" he asked. "Can I get you anything at all?"

"I wonder if I could possibly move to another suite. I'm just not sure I can handle staying in this one," she said.

"Of course, Ms. Smith. I'll arrange it right away."

"Thank you, Mike. You've been so kind. I can never thank you enough." Her voice was filled with emotion.

"I have a daughter almost your age, miss. I'm glad to do it."

Alexa hung up and looked around the room. She was suddenly overwhelmed. She just wanted to see Rick and to have all this go away. His life had turned upside down, just as hers had. She couldn't believe it had been only days ago that she was excited to be back home, looking forward to seeing old friends, hoping to put some long-held feelings behind her. Now she knew her life would never be the same. Sad memories rushed back. So many good things were gone. She touched the curved metallic shape that fell just below the nape of her neck. It reminded her of the one man who owned her in every way. He just didn't know it. But how could he? She'd tried to run away from him, but she couldn't run from her feelings. Not anymore.

She knew what she had to do. She'd pack her belongings and move into the new suite. Then she'd call him. She needed to hear his voice and look into his eyes. And tell him how much she loved him—if he'd see her. She'd let him decide. But she knew she had to call Rick. Sometimes life changed in an instant. And she wasn't going to let another minute go by without telling the man she loved how she felt about him. She loved him so much. She knew nothing would ever change that. Not in a thousand lifetimes.

65

"Chief, I got something," Betsy said, sticking her head inside Dan's door.

"What is it?" asked Dan.

He leaned back in his swivel chair and stuck his hand out for the papers she was holding. She gave him the two sheets of printouts from the cell phone carrier.

"The anonymous call was made from a burner phone. The phone records show that the call was made from the Cypress Lake school property. They hit the GPS locator, and the phone may still be somewhere on the school grounds."

"I love you, Betsy." He blew her a kiss as she closed the door.

Dan sat there thinking. Who would have made a call from the school trying to implicate Rick Young and an ex-girlfriend in a murder? Former students and teachers would have been invited back to the class reunion. Could it have been a previous teacher with an ax to grind? Finding the cell phone on the school property would be like trying to find a needle in a haystack. And the phone could have been dumped there by anyone, not necessarily by someone connected to the school. He'd have to talk to Rick or Alexa. Maybe they'd have some ideas about who might have placed a call implicating them.

Everyone at the class reunion saw them together anyway. It wasn't new information, but he needed to know who made the call. Even though it may have been a false lead, it was possible that the killer made the call, or someone who was close to the killer. He was going to find out.

66

Alexa was relieved to be in a different suite, which was even more beautiful than the first. But she started to feel shaky, as the reality of what had happened began to sink in. She didn't even unpack but went straight to the shower to get all traces of Josh off her skin. The image of his swollen and disfigured face was hideous, and she couldn't get it out of her mind. His brutal attack was so evil, like a horror movie that kept playing over and over in her head.

She let the warm water flood over her, relaxing her sore, tense muscles, as she washed herself thoroughly. Thank God the police chief had gotten there in time to stop Josh. She hated to think of what might have happened if he hadn't. Josh looked as if he wanted to kill her. He'd said such terrifying things. She even wondered if Josh might have had something to do with what had happened to Kim. It was too frightening to think about.

After drying her hair, she put on the soft robe she found hanging in the bathroom and crawled into bed. She checked her cell phone on the night table and saw a text from Katie. She'd also missed a call from Dan Hastings. *It must be something important,* she thought. She hit the redial button, and he picked up.

"Ms. Smith, I'm sorry to bother you. I heard from Officer Davis that you checked out fine at the hospital," he said.

"Yes, I'm still a little jittery but all right, thank you," she answered.

"I'm glad to hear it. I need to ask you a question. Is now a good time?"

"Yes, I'll answer if I can."

"Someone phoned in an anonymous tip, saying you and Rick were together the night of Kimberly Young's murder."

"We were together. Everyone saw us at the reunion. It wasn't a secret," she answered, surprise in her voice.

"Whoever called used a cell phone that we traced to the Cypress Lake Middle School. Do you know anyone at the school who might have a grudge against you or Rick?"

Alexa was in shock. What was he saying to her?

"Are you still there, Alexa? Hello?"

"I'm here." She could barely answer him.

"Do you know someone at the school?"

"Yes, I do." Alexa sat up on the edge of the bed. A cold shiver ran through her body. "One of the teachers is a friend of mine. We were together at the reunion."

"Is there a reason this friend may have called us? Is she upset with you about something?" Dan asked.

"Yes, she's upset with me."

"I think you better tell me who she is and what's going on."

67

"Her name is Katie Cavanaugh, and she teaches at the middle school. I've known her almost all my life." Alexa was stunned by his questions.

"Why is she upset with you?" Dan asked.

"She wanted me to tell her husband that she was with me after the reunion. She didn't get home until late, and she was afraid he'd get mad at her."

"Did she tell you what she was doing when she stayed out late?"

"She said she had too much to drink, and she didn't want her husband to find out. She told him that she was here at the hotel with me." She paused. "She said that she was sitting in her car at the country club until she sobered up."

"So she wanted you to give her an alibi," he said.

"Yes, but I don't know Tim that well. I haven't talked to him since their wedding," she said. "But I know Katie was lying."

"How do you know that?"

"She wanted me to cover for her. That's not like her." She was afraid she'd said too much. "Look, Katie's my friend, and I think she's in trouble. I'd do anything to help her, but I told her I wouldn't lie, especially after I'd heard the news about Kim."

"What did she say when you told her no?"

Alexa stopped and thought carefully before she told him. "She got mad at me."

"Are you sure Katie was lying to you about where she was that night?"

Alexa thought for a minute. "I'm pretty sure she was lying."

"Did she know Kimberly Young?"

"Everyone knew Kim."

"Thanks, Alexa. I think I've asked you enough questions for now," he said.

"I don't know why she would have called you. Maybe it was someone else who called from the school."

"Yes, maybe it was," he responded. "I'll call you back later. OK?"

"Thank you," she said.

"You call me if you need anything."

"Thank you, Chief Hastings."

After Alexa hung up, she felt sick to her stomach. She knew deep down it was Katie who'd made the anonymous call. But she didn't know why. Why would a friend try to implicate her in a murder? It was beyond Alexa's comprehension. Something was terribly wrong, and Alexa was more frightened than ever. She knew she had to talk to Rick. She needed him now more than ever. She hoped he needed to talk to her too.

68

Bert came in with the forensics reports and handed them to Dan.

"Looks like they came up with nothing unusual on any of the items that we took from the house or the vehicles," he said to Dan. "Rick's shirt had blood on it, but it wasn't Kim's. It could be the blood that he got on his shirt when he fought with Josh."

Dan studied the report from the forensics lab. Nothing so far tied Rick to Kim's murder.

The sergeant continued. "The doctor's report from the hospital said that Josh had marks that looked like healing lacerations on his back." He handed another piece of paper to Dan. "His blood type matches the blood found under Kim's fingernails. He had a high alcohol level, but the toxicology report isn't back yet."

"Thanks, Bert."

Dan stared at the two reports. Everything was coming up a big fat zero. Josh had been with Kim the night she was killed. He wondered if they'd fought about something. Maybe Kim had become a problem for him. Kim's drinking had been a big problem for a lot of people, including Dan. Maybe Kim had wanted Josh to leave his wife. When Dan had asked Josh if he wanted to call his wife, his exact words were, "The bitch left me. I don't know where the hell she is."

Josh seemed to have been shaken by Kim's death, but maybe he was shaken because he'd killed her. Killing someone would be upsetting, unless you were a psychopath. He didn't think Josh was a psychopath, just a prick who liked cheating, and Kim had been convenient.

The facts were leading nowhere. Dan hated Josh and hoped he rotted in jail, and if he'd killed Kim, he would pay dearly. God, how could Kim have wasted her time with such a lowlife bastard? Dan's heart sank each time he thought of the baby, every time he thought of the last time he saw Kim. She was a lonely young woman in so many ways. He'd wanted to give her a life with someone who truly could have loved her the way she needed. But she hadn't wanted him. How could he blame her? He was married, older, not much to offer on a policeman's salary. But he'd loved her. He couldn't explain it to himself. Except that she'd seemed to need help. And he'd wanted to help her. But she hadn't wanted his help. And she didn't seem to care about Rick. He'd been convenient, a means to an end.

But Rick seemed very upset about Kim's death. Who the hell had killed Kimberly Young? Who'd wanted her out of the way, enough to commit murder? And why had Josh attacked Alexa Smith? He was drunk, probably on drugs or some kind of painkiller. Maybe he'd wanted Alexa for a long time. He was used to getting what he wanted. Or maybe he had a vendetta against Rick. Nothing was making sense. But he'd get to the bottom of it. His next step was to talk to Katie Cavanaugh. Maybe she had all the answers to his unanswered questions.

69

"Is Chief Hastings in his office?" asked Donna.

Donna could almost feel her hair frizzing, and she used the back of her hand to wipe the sweat off her forehead. The heat was making her edgier than usual.

"Just a minute. I think he's on his way out, but I'll check."

Donna stared down at Betsy until she hung up the phone. "He'll talk to you." She pointed toward the hallway.

Dan stood up when Donna strode into his office.

"What's happening with the investigation of Kimberly Young?" she demanded. "Did you get the reports back on the forensics?"

"Calm down," Dan said. "Have a seat, and let me get you some coffee."

"I'm calm, Dan." She smiled. "I need to know what you've got. My client has been under suspicion of murder, and I think he deserves some answers."

"OK."

Dan looked at the stack of papers on the corner of his desk, pulled three sheets off the top, and handed them to her. She sat down, pulled her glasses on, and started reading. A few minutes later, she looked up.

"So you've got nothing on Rick." She stared at him.

"Not yet," said Dan.

"The talk is that you've arrested Josh Logan. He's the one involved in the altercation with Rick the night of the murder. Correct?"

"You heard right," said Dan, leaning back and folding his arms over his chest.

"I guess you have more than one suspect. Can you talk to me about it, Dan?" she asked, her tone softening.

"There's nothing to tell," he answered, staring at her.

"Are you going to charge my client?"

"Not at this time."

"So you have no evidence against Rick." It was a statement.

"We covered that," he answered.

She picked up her purse and briefcase. "May I have copies of the forensics reports?"

"I'll send them to you as soon as I can."

"I'd appreciate it." She stood up, headed toward the door, and turned around. "You know he didn't do it."

"I don't know anything," said Dan.

She knew that Chief Dan Hastings knew plenty. He just wasn't telling her.

70

He walked through the school and followed the signs to the administration office. It was 3:30 p.m., and a few students passed him in the hallway, carrying books and backpacks, casting curious glances his way. Dan could hear music coming from one of the rooms, and a few of the teachers passed him as they left school for the day.

He found the office and opened the door. A woman was sitting behind a counter; only the top of her curly brown hair was visible. She stood when she saw him.

"May I help you?" She looked nervous behind her glasses.

"Yes. Is Katie Cavanaugh here? I understand she teaches here at the school," he said.

"She's one of our teachers. I think she's still here. If you can wait, I'll page her," the nervous woman answered.

"Thanks," said Dan.

He stepped away from the counter and turned to look at the bulletin board on the wall behind him. But he wasn't thinking about the notices posted there. He was thinking about the questions he was going to ask Katie Cavanaugh. If he asked the right ones in the right way, he wouldn't have to search the school dumpster for the burner phone. He turned around just as a stylishly dressed young woman walked into the office. She was attractive, with dark, shoulder-length hair, carrying a briefcase, her purse over her shoulder. She was wearing a full bright-yellow skirt, a frilly white blouse, and leopard-print flats. A strand of chunky yellow-and-white beads hung around her neck.

"Hi, Viv. Did you page me?" asked the young woman.

"Yes, Katie. This officer wants to speak to you."

She turned around. Her face seemed to lose its color when she saw him. Dan walked up to her.

"Mrs. Cavanaugh, are you all right?" She started to wobble, and Dan grabbed her arm.

The other woman ran to get some water. She brought back a paper cup and handed it to Katie, who was now sitting in one of the chairs in the row lined up against the wall. Katie drank the water, taking deep breaths.

"I'm all right now, thanks," she said. She looked up at Dan. "You want to talk to me? What about?"

He saw fear in her eyes.

"Can we talk somewhere private?"

"My room is just down the hall." She got up, leading the way, and Dan fell into step with her.

"You sure you're OK?" he asked, glancing over at her.

"I'm fine, thanks. I'm just tired. Not much lunch today," she answered, but he didn't believe her.

He followed her into the classroom, and Dan looked around as Katie put her things down on the desk. The room was cheerful, with kids' artwork scattered on the walls, flowering plants on the windowsill, an aquarium with yellow and blue tropical fish—the typical middle school classroom. She stood by her desk, waiting for him to start the conversation.

"You know why I'm here." He was standing in the center of the room, staring at her.

"No, I don't." She spoke too quickly.

"You called the station. You left an anonymous message. You said Alexa Smith and Rick Young were together the night of the murder."

She didn't say anything. She picked up the snow globe that was sitting on the corner of her desk. She shook it and held it at eye level, watching the silver glitter swirl around the three blue dolphins inside the clear glass ball.

"Alexa is my friend. I was afraid she was in trouble. So I called. That's not a crime, is it?"

"No, it's not a crime. But why didn't you give your name?" asked the chief. He had walked closer to her desk, standing about four feet from her.

"I didn't want to get myself into trouble," she answered, putting the globe down. She looked at him.

"Where'd you go after the reunion?"

"I sat in the parking lot. I'd had too much to drink. Is that a crime too?"

"No, ma'am, it's not. Ms. Smith said you wanted her to tell your husband, Tim, that you were with her after the reunion. Is that right?"

"Is that what she said?"

"Yes. I can take you down to the police station if you'd like. We can talk about it there." He walked to the door.

"I didn't do anything wrong." She started crying.

"But you made the call."

She was crying, nodding yes. "I didn't mean to get her in trouble. I just didn't want my husband to know where I was. You can't tell him." She was sobbing now, and Dan walked to the door and closed it. He turned back and looked at her.

"Look, Mrs. Cavanaugh. I just want to find Kim Young's killer. Do you know who killed Kimberly Young? Are you covering up for someone? Did you hate Kimberly Young?"

"Yes! I hated her! She had an affair with my husband!" She paused and then caught her breath. "But I didn't kill her! I swear."

"Where were you that night?" he asked, still standing in front of the door.

"I told you! I was in the parking lot, in my car. I drank too much." She was lying.

"I don't think so. Who were you with? Did you meet someone after the party? Someone you don't want your husband to know about?" He was getting to her.

"You can't tell my husband or anyone."

"I'm not your priest. I'm a cop. I'm trying to find a killer. Tell me."

"Yes, I was with someone." She was crying. "I left with him. He's a teacher here at the school. I don't want his wife to find out."

"Or your husband."

"Yes!" She covered her face with her hands.

"I don't care who you sleep with, Ms. Cavanaugh. I'm trying to solve a crime here. May I ask why in the hell you called my department, trying to implicate Ms. Smith and Mr. Young in a murder?"

"I don't know." She wouldn't look at him.

"You don't like Ms. Smith, do you?" he asked. "You were mad at her because she wouldn't lie for you? Is that it?"

"No, it's not like that," she said.

"I think it is," he said. "Or you killed Kimberly Young. You left the reunion, snuck into her garage, found her passed out, and killed her. Is that what you did?"

"No, I didn't."

"Give me the name of the teacher you were with, and I won't share your little secret unless I have to," he said. "I just need to corroborate your story."

She sat down in her chair and grabbed a tissue out of the bright-green holder on her desk. She sniffled into it. "Frank Howard."

"Thanks, Mrs. Cavanaugh."

He left her sitting at her desk, her head bent down, crying uncontrollably.

71

Alexa had ordered room service. She couldn't face getting dressed and going down to the restaurant. She'd checked the peephole when the food was delivered to make sure it was one of the hotel staff. The food had helped, and she'd turned on the news to see if there'd been any further updates on Kim's murder. She didn't think they'd found the killer, or the police chief or someone would have called her.

Alexa couldn't wait any longer. She needed to see Rick again. They were in limbo, waiting, and there was no reason for her not to call him. She'd done nothing wrong, and she didn't think seeing Rick could make matters worse. Maybe it would help him to know he wasn't alone.

She looked up his home number, and he answered. "Rick Young."

She drew in her breath, hearing the sound of his voice.

"Rick, it's me, Alexa."

"God, I needed to hear your voice."

"I needed to hear yours too."

"Can I see you?"

"Yes, but where?"

"Kim's mother is here at the house. Do you want to meet me somewhere?"

"Come to the hotel," she said. "I need to talk to you about something."

"I'll be there around four p.m.," he answered.

"I can't wait to see you." She whispered the words that she'd been longing to say to him for a long time.

72

She dressed quickly, in comfortable jeans and a white T-shirt and tennis shoes. But when she looked in the mirror, Alexa was alarmed to see the bright-red marks on her neck, raised like welts on her pale skin. Rick would be so upset if he knew what Josh had done to her, so she grabbed a scarf, tied it around her neck, and went down to the lobby to wait for him. She stared out through the wide glass front doors until she saw his blue truck pull up under the portico. She ran out and climbed into the pickup. He looked over at Alexa, reached for her hand and held it firmly in his before releasing it. He put the truck in gear and pulled away from the hotel. It was a moment of déjà vu, as if no time had passed, and nothing had changed between them.

Rick drove down the long driveway and turned right, through downtown Cypress Lake, and headed toward the outskirts of town. Within twenty minutes, they were outside the city limits and surrounded by farmland. As they drove, Alexa watched him—his facial muscles flexed, a few strands of gray at his temples. His forearms were muscled and tanned, his hand strong as he shifted through the gears. He was wearing old jeans, a faded blue polo shirt, and brown work boots. He drove south another ten miles and then turned onto

Foggy Creek Road, a rural two-lane road with orange groves on both sides. The trees went as far as the eye could see, full of Valencias ready to be picked.

"Where are we going?" she asked, breaking the silence.

He didn't answer. He just kept driving, focusing on the road. Traffic was sparse as they drove farther and farther into the groves. The blacktop two-lane road shimmered with radiating heat from the late afternoon sun. Rick slowed and made a right turn onto a narrow dirt road, almost invisible, that cut through a thick section of the groves. He maneuvered the truck slowly over the dry, uneven terrain until he pulled up to a wide steel gate. He got out, unlocked the chain, and swung the heavy gate open. He pulled the truck through the gate and drove about a half mile farther until he reached a white two-story farmhouse with green shutters, surrounded by grandfather oaks and tall pine trees. Rick followed the circular gravel driveway and parked in the shade in front of the house. He turned off the engine.

He looked over at Alexa. "My dad's been asking about you."

"I can't wait to see him again," she answered, smiling.

Rick got out of the truck, and she opened the door, stepping down onto the driveway as Rick came around to meet her. He held her hand and led her up the worn wooden steps onto the covered front porch. The old boards creaked under their feet, a comfortable sound, and Rick tapped lightly on the screen doorframe before stepping into the cool house, out of the late afternoon heat. Buddy, a golden retriever, ran up to him, whimpering and twirling in excitement, and Rick bent down, scratched his head, and rubbed the excited pet's ears. The older dog nuzzled against Alexa, just as Hank, the grove manager, met them in the living room.

"Hey, Rick," he said, wrapping his strong, leathery hands around Rick's.

"Hank, this is Alexa," said Rick, putting his hand back on Buddy's nudging head.

Hank turned to Alexa and acted like he expected her. "Rick's dad has talked about you quite a lot."

"How's he doing?" asked Rick, sounding concerned.

"He's resting right now." The older man, slightly stooped with thinning gray hair, led the way through the sunny front room to the kitchen, Buddy following at his heels. "How about a beer or iced tea?"

"A beer would be great," said Rick. "Alexa?"

"I'd love an iced tea," she answered.

Hank handed Rick a can of beer and took one for himself. He got the iced tea pitcher out of the refrigerator and poured some in a tall glass for Alexa.

The three of them sat down at the long-planked table in the country-style kitchen, Buddy curled up underneath at Rick's feet.

"You're kind of famous," said Hank, looking at Rick over his bifocals.

"Yeah, I guess I am." Unsmiling, he tipped back the can and drank several swallows.

"I'm real sorry about your wife." Hank shook his head.

"Thanks," said Rick, staring at the beer can he'd set down on the table.

"Your dad was real glad to see you the other night," said Hank.

"I should have been out to visit sooner."

"I think it was the right time." He nodded, white froth clinging to his gray moustache.

"Yeah, I do too," said Rick. He turned to Alexa. "I came out to see my dad last Friday night. After the reunion."

"But you didn't tell Chief Hastings where you were." She looked at Rick, puzzled. "Why didn't you?"

"I didn't want him bothering my dad. And Hastings has his mind made up anyway."

Alexa didn't know what to say. She could only look at Rick and love him for the man he'd become. He'd visited his father that night, the night of the terrible scene at the reunion, and didn't feel he had to explain to anyone where he'd been. She was so happy to be part of Rick's life again, on any terms. She'd never loved him more than she did at that moment.

73

Alexa looked up as Rick's dad came into the kitchen. He was an older version of Rick, just as handsome, only stockier, with creases at the corners of his blue eyes and his once-dark hair mostly gray and cropped short. He was wearing a red button-down shirt, blue jeans that were worn at the knees, and Western-style boots.

"Hey, sorry. I was taking a nap when you kids got here." He smiled at the threesome in the kitchen.

Rick got up and gave his dad a quick hug and pat on the back. "You feeling all right, Dad?"

"I'm fine. Hank and I were up early, arranging for the trucks and equipment for the harvesting," he answered, looking over at his friend.

"The trees look ready," said Rick, returning to the table, Buddy settling back down at his feet.

"The pickers are coming the end of the week," said Hank.

"I'll be out to help, Dad."

"Thanks. I appreciate the offer, but you take care of yourself right now. You've got enough on your plate." Mr. Young turned his attention to Alexa. "I've been worried about you, son. But I see you brought your moral support with you." He smiled at her.

"Yes, sir, I did. Alexa, you remember my dad?"

"Yes, hello, Mr. Young." She stood up.

"Alexa, honey, good to see you again." He embraced her, then held her at arm's length. "You're just as pretty as ever."

"Thanks, Mr. Young. I'm glad you see you too."

"And call me Rich. 'Mr. Young' makes me sound so old," he said, chuckling.

"I will, Rich," she answered, smiling.

"How's that little grandbaby of mine, Rick?" he asked, turning to his son.

"Healthy, Dad."

"She'll be fine—don't you worry." He poured himself some leftover coffee and joined them at the table. "What are the police saying?"

"They aren't," he said. "I guess they still think I'm a suspect."

"Everyone knows you could never do anything like that." His dad didn't say the word that she knew they were all thinking: *murder.* "But I sure wish they'd find whoever did this terrible thing. Who could do something like this?"

It wasn't really a question, and Alexa could see the worry in the older man's face. The room became very still.

Hank broke the silence. "I heard about some girl being attacked at one of the resorts earlier today. They locked up Josh Logan."

"What are you talking about?" Rick looked stunned. "You're sure it was Josh?"

"Yes, I heard on the news that he was in jail. He assaulted someone, but they aren't releasing the name."

Alexa decided she'd better open up about what happened. She didn't want to talk about it, especially to Rick, but she knew he was going to find out about it anyway.

"I'm the one who Josh attacked."

The three men turned and stared at Alexa.

74

Rick hadn't spoken since they'd left his dad's house. He was accelerating, shifting fast, and without warning, he pulled off onto the side of the road, gravel and dirt swirling around the truck as the tires dug into the berm.

"What the hell happened to you, goddammit? Why didn't you tell me?" He turned to look at her, grabbing both of her hands in his.

He looked at her wrists and saw the dark-purple bruises. Then his eyes trailed to her neck, and he slowly began untying the scarf. Alexa tried to hold it in place, but Rick wouldn't stop. When he saw the red blotches on her throat, he stared at her in disbelief.

"Jesus, Alexa. What the hell did he do to you?" His eyes narrowed, his facial muscles tightening.

"I didn't want to upset you, Rick," she said. "You have enough going on. You don't need this."

"When were you going to tell me? That bastard! Goddamn him!" Rick was ready to explode.

"Stop, Rick. It's OK. He's in jail now," she said, trying to calm him down.

"Seriously, are you really OK?" He looked at her, worry clouding his face.

"I'm fine. Really." She tried to reassure him. "I got checked out at the hospital. Nothing's wrong. It was scary, but I'm OK."

"I need you; don't you get it?" He held her hands and looked into her blue eyes, wet with tears that had formed. "If anything had happened to you…" His voice trailed off.

"I know, Rick," she said. "I just couldn't tell you."

"Even before she…" His voice broke. "Before Friday, she wasn't with me. Kim hasn't been with me. Just understand that."

"I know," she said. "I'm so sad about the ways things turned out for you. And for us."

"That was a long time ago. Now you're back. I can't let anything happen to you. Now that I've found you again."

He was still holding her hands in his. He leaned toward her, gently pulling her to him, and kissed her lightly on the lips. Her mouth felt warm and soft. He leaned back, his eyes locked on her lips, and he kissed her again, harder this time. He pulled away and held her hands tighter in his, his strong hands surrounding hers.

"I'm not letting you go this time. You're not running away from me ever again." It was a statement.

"I don't want to run away. I couldn't. I love you too much," she said, tears glistening on her cheeks.

He brought her hands up to his mouth and kissed her wrists before releasing his hold on her.

"I better get you back to the hotel."

He drove back to the resort, parked near the entrance, and turned off the engine.

"Can you come in, Rick? We could have dinner," she said.

"No, I need to get home and check on Bethany," he answered. "And I don't want you in trouble because of me."

"I love you, Rick. I don't care about me. But I don't want to add to your problems," she said.

He looked away, shaking his head. "You're not adding to my problems. Do you understand?"

"Yes."

"I love you, Alexa, and I don't want to leave." He turned his gaze to her.

"I know." She didn't move. "But I know you have to."

He got out, walked around the front of the truck, and opened the door for her. He held her hand as she stepped down onto the pavement, and he pulled her against him, his arms wrapped around her, and bent down and kissed her, long and slow. He pulled his mouth from hers, his face buried in her hair, and held her tight, taking a deep breath before letting go. She looked up at him and touched the roughness of his face, gazing intently into his eyes.

"I'll call you when I can." His voice was low. "You better go inside now."

He stood by the truck, watching her walk to the hotel entrance. She turned and waved goodbye before disappearing inside. He got into the truck and drove back to his baby girl, thinking about the nightmare he was living, praying it would be over soon. At least he had Alexa back in his life again. She had given him a reason to believe in something. A future with her. But he had to get through the present. Until the person who'd killed Kim was found, he couldn't move on with his life. No matter what Kim had done, she'd been his wife, the mother of their child. Whoever had hurt her had to be found. The longer it took, the harder it would be on everyone he loved. He was still in shock about what had happened to Alexa. At least that bastard Josh Logan was locked up. He wouldn't be able to hurt anyone else. Ever again. And he'd get what he deserved.

75

As Alexa entered the lobby, she thought about everything that had occurred. The week was going by so quickly. She needed to talk to Meghan and tell her what had happened. Thank goodness she had such a good friend. They could always share everything with each other. But she didn't want Meghan to worry. She wouldn't tell her about the attack. She'd fill her in on all the details when she got back to Chicago, and right now, Alexa didn't know when that would be. So many things were unresolved.

The only meaning in her life was now crystal clear. It was Rick. What was going to happen to him? When would the police find Kim's killer? She prayed it would happen soon. After Josh had attacked her, she thought he might be the one responsible for Kim's death. He'd looked crazed and capable of anything. But what if it wasn't Josh?

She entered her suite and locked the door, checking every room to make certain she was alone. She felt anxious and very frightened. The thought of a killer still out there terrified her.

Maybe Alexa was overlooking the one person who might know more than she was letting on. What was Katie hiding? She loved her friend and couldn't believe she'd ever do anything wrong. Unless she was in trouble. Katie had secrets, and Alexa hoped she'd soon find out exactly what they were.

76

Alexa saw the incoming text when she plugged in her phone. All it said was, "Please meet me in the parking lot." It was from Katie.

Alexa didn't know what to think. Why would Katie want to talk to her now? It must be about the anonymous phone call involving her and Rick that was made to the police. She hesitated, but Katie had been a lifelong friend. She should at least give her a chance to explain. Maybe she was wrong. Maybe Katie hadn't made the call. But she had reacted with so much anger when Alexa wouldn't provide her with an alibi the night Kim was killed. Alexa shouldn't judge Katie until she heard all the facts. If Katie had made the call, maybe there was a good reason. There had to be.

Alexa went down to the lobby and stood just outside the entrance and scanned the parking lot. It didn't take long to spot her, dressed in a bright-yellow skirt and white blouse, standing next to her car that was parked in a visitor's space. Alexa walked over to her, and Katie started talking without even saying hello.

"I want to try to explain and to tell you that I'm so sorry," said Katie, her voice unsteady.

"What's going on, Katie?"

"I don't know why I did it." Katie was babbling, wringing her hands. "I called the police and said you were with Rick the night of the reunion."

Alexa was truly puzzled. "Why would you do that?"

Katie looked away, staring into the distance, as though she wasn't sure herself why she'd tried to get Alexa in trouble. "I made some mistakes. And I was wrong." Her voice dropped so that Alexa barely heard her. "My life is so screwed up."

"Why would you try to hurt me? I thought we were friends."

Alexa was in shock now that she knew for certain that Katie made the call to the police. It was more than just a little white lie. Katie had tried to implicate her in a murder.

"I am your friend," said Katie, trying to explain. "Please believe me. I was upset because you wouldn't help me."

"Help you by lying for you? You misled the police. You lied about me, and you lied about Rick. You're not my friend." Alexa was furious. "How could you do it?"

"I don't know. I was so confused and didn't know where to turn." She tried to grab Alexa's hand. "I want to tell you where I was last Friday night and why—"

Alexa pulled her hand away and took several steps back. "I don't want to know. Whatever is wrong, I hope you get some help. But don't ever call me again."

Katie was crying. "I hope one day you can forgive me. My life is messed up, and I struck out at you."

"I'll try to forgive you, Katie. But this isn't a game where you can play with people's lives. I was your friend, but I realize that you're not mine."

Alexa walked away without saying goodbye. Her heart was broken by the betrayal and the loss. Her lifelong friend was gone. Alexa started to cry when she got in the elevator. Everything was falling apart. Rick was in trouble, and she was still reeling from Josh's attack.

She needed Rick's arms around her. She loved him so much that it hurt. But she had to stay strong for him. She prayed that all this would be over soon, for his sake.

77

Dan took a sip of his coffee and lit another cigarette. The sun was down, but it was light enough that he could see the backyard. He sat in the aluminum chair on the screened-in porch and stared at the uneven patches of grass growing out of the sandy soil. He'd been too busy to work on the modest square of lawn and overgrown shrubs. He heard the next-door neighbor's kids splashing in their above-ground pool, their happy squeals floating over the fence. When he and Lynn had gotten married six years ago, she'd told him that she wanted a baby. But it hadn't happened. Maybe they would have been happier if it had. But it was no excuse for what he'd done. To her or to them.

He wondered how long the undeclared stalemate would last. He didn't blame Lynn for the barrier between them. But the case was getting to him. It wasn't making sense, and it was too personal. He thought about the pivotal moments that could have made things turn out differently. But looking back, he couldn't see how he could have changed anything. He took a deep drag of his cigarette, exhaled, and thought about that day, about a year ago, when he'd stopped by Kim's apartment.

⯅

They'd made love, and afterward, Dan had pulled her on top of him, their skin slick with their sweat blended together. He'd closed his eyes, and she put her head down on his chest as though she was listening to his heartbeat while he gently traced circles on her back with his fingertips. They stayed like that, dozing, the air from the ceiling fan cooling their damp skin.

She woke up first, unwrapping herself from his arms, and got out of bed. She'd gone into the bathroom, come out a little while later in a short silk robe, and stood in front of the bureau mirror combing her long, wet hair. He'd pulled the sheet up to his waist, put his arm behind his head, and watched her.

"You're beautiful," he said, feeling himself getting turned on again.

"You're so sweet, Danny." She smiled back at his reflection.

He got out of bed naked and walked over to her, wrapping his arms around her and pulling her against him so that she could feel his erection through the flimsy robe. He laughed a low growl into her neck.

"Stop it." Her laughter was playful and sexy.

"Why?" he asked. "We don't have to stop."

He turned her around, his mouth found hers, and their kiss was long and slow. He reached inside the robe, cupping his hands around her hips, and pulled her even closer.

"Really, I can't. I have to be somewhere," she said. She'd pushed him away and turned back to the mirror.

"Where?" He'd stood behind her, watching as she began combing her hair again.

"You know I'm seeing someone."

He hadn't answered her. He'd gotten dressed, fastened his holster around his waist, and put on his cap.

He'd stood at the end of the bed and looked at her. "Are you serious about him?"

"Look, Dan, you need to know something."

Kim turned to face him, throwing the comb down on the bureau. Her hair was wet, in long ringlets, and the robe was tied, but he could see the curve of her breasts through the opening.

He glared at her. "What is it?"

She hesitated, averting her eyes. "I'm pregnant."

Dan felt as though he'd been struck. "How far along are you?"

"Three months."

"Is the baby mine?"

"I don't have to tell you anything." Her voice was cold.

"Yes, you do. It's mine, isn't it?" He wanted an answer. She turned back to the mirror and picked up the comb. Dan walked over and grabbed it out of her hand. "Stop and look at me. What do you want to do, Kim?"

"I'm going to tell Rick," she said. "Tonight."

"Fuck!" He'd looked away, then turned back and confronted her. "Goddammit!" he said. "So you're going to tell Rick it's his?"

"Maybe it is his baby," she said, defiant.

"I'll get a divorce and marry you, Kim," he said. "You have to wait for me." His voice was pleading.

"No. Rick can marry me now. You can't."

He walked to her bedroom door and turned around.

"And he can give you everything I can't. Isn't that it?"

"You said it; I didn't." She had a pleased look on her face. "Look, Dan, we always said no strings."

"Yeah, no strings."

He'd left the bedroom and stormed out of her apartment. He'd sat in the car in front of her apartment complex for a long time, thinking about the bomb Kim had dropped on him. Maybe it was Rick's baby, but maybe it was his. It didn't matter to her. And he didn't matter to her either. She'd always made that clear. But it hadn't sunk in until then.

▲

He'd been a fool to get involved with her. He'd met her late one night when he'd pulled her over for a broken taillight on her car. She'd been flirtatious, and on impulse he'd bought her a cup of coffee. The friendly encounter quickly evolved into more than that. He began to look for her, making excuses when he drove by her apartment, telling himself that he was checking on her car. Then she became a distraction that had turned into a love even he couldn't explain. He hadn't stopped seeing her, even after she married Rick. Dan hadn't mentioned the baby again, as though the conversation had never taken place. But Dan still thought about it, especially now that Kim was gone. He felt a lump form in his throat.

He heard Lynn moving around in the kitchen. He should go inside and try to talk to her. He wished he could make things right between them again, but he didn't know how. He needed her now, but he knew he didn't deserve anything from her. He couldn't expect her to understand. Now or maybe ever.

He took a deep drag of his cigarette. He heard the voice of the woman next door yelling for her kids to get out of the pool, and after a few more splashes, it got quiet. Suddenly Dan's cell phone rang. He picked it up and looked at the caller ID. It was the station; the dispatcher told him they had an urgent call and to hold on until they patched it through.

"Chief Hastings here."

Dan stood up so fast that his chair moved backward several inches. He stuck the phone in his pocket, hurried into the kitchen, and put on his holster and baseball cap. Lynn was loading dishes into the dishwasher, but she stopped to look at Dan.

"What's wrong?" she asked.

"I've gotta go. I'll call you."

"What's happened?" She followed him to the door.

Dan didn't answer. He slammed the kitchen door and ran to the squad car. The tires squealed as he backed the car out of the driveway, turned on the siren and lights, and sped down the street.

78

Rick was surprised to see that Patrice's car wasn't in its usual spot. He pulled into the driveway, ignored the few reporters who were standing on the sidewalk, and unlocked the front door. He went into the too-quiet house. He took the stairs two at a time and looked in Bethany's room. The crib was empty. He walked down the stairs and into the kitchen. He saw the paper stuck under a place mat on the kitchen table. The handwriting was hard to read, but he recognized it as Patrice's. The words weren't sinking in, and the more he read it, the more it didn't make sense.

He ran to the phone sitting on the counter and called the police station.

"I need to speak to Dan Hastings. It's urgent."

"Who's calling?" the dispatcher asked.

"Rick Young. Just get him on the phone! My baby's been kidnapped!"

"Hold on while I patch you through."

Rick heard a few clicks. "Chief Hastings here."

"Dan, this is Rick. Kim's mom took the baby. She left a note that doesn't make any sense. I'm going to look for her."

"You stay there, Rick. I'll put an APB on her car. It's the tan Camry, right?"

"Yes, it's a 2010, I think."

"I'll check the registration. Are you sure she took the baby with her?"

"Yes, she's gone! Maybe she took Bethany to her house." He couldn't believe this was happening. "Jesus, Dan. She's lost her mind."

"I'll be right there. Don't leave. Do you understand?"

"Hurry up, or I'm out of here."

Rick hung up. He reread the note. It couldn't be true. It just couldn't be.

79

"Let me see it." Dan followed Rick into the kitchen.

Rick handed the piece of paper to Dan. He put on his reading glasses and studied the words.

"You're sure this is her handwriting?"

"For Christ's sake, yes!" His jaw muscles clenched, and he began stalking around the room.

"Take it easy, Rick. How long ago did you see her?"

"She was here with Bethany when I left at three thirty." He stood there thinking. "Maybe three hours?"

"She couldn't have gone far." He pulled Rick's phone out of his pocket and handed it to him. "You have a recent photo of Patrice and Bethany?"

Rick didn't answer but instead started scrolling through his phone's photo gallery. He stopped on a photo of Patrice holding Bethany. Patrice was smiling at the camera, and Bethany was drooling, her baby hands trying to grab the stuffed animal that Patrice was holding. He showed the screen to Dan. "This one."

"Send it here," said Dan, pointing to Betsy's contact number on his cell phone. She would forward it to the state police and the NCIC.

Rick sent the photo while Dan reread the cryptic message that Patrice had left. He didn't want to, but he had to ask Rick.

"Do you know if this is true?" asked Dan, holding Patrice's note in the air.

He looked at the note, then at Dan. "How the hell would I know? She's been acting so strangely." He stopped. "But Kim's dead, for God's sake. Now she's gone with the baby! Patrice must be delusional. Who knows where the hell she's gone?"

"Hang on, Rick. We'll find her."

Rick walked over to the kitchen counter and opened one of the drawers while Dan was on the phone. Rick closed the drawer as Dan hung up.

"Let me read the note again," asked Rick.

Dan handed it to him, and Rick carried the piece of notepaper with Patrice's hurried, uneven scrawl to the window overlooking the sunlit kitchen sink. His back was to Dan, and as soon as Dan smelled the smoke, he ran to the sink and grabbed Rick's arm, knocking the burning match out of his hand. The ashy black remnants floated in the air before falling into the standing water in the bottom of the sink. The note was gone and Patrice's words with it.

"What the fuck?" yelled Dan, shoving Rick with both hands, knocking him hard against the edge of the granite counter, so hard that he almost fell down. "You just destroyed evidence in a fucking murder case!"

"You read the note. We have to find Patrice. That's all you need to know. She has my daughter." Rick steadied himself against the physical assault and glared at Dan in defiance.

"You know what you just did." Dan face was expressionless.

"Yes, I know what I just did. Now go find my little girl."

80

Dan kept thinking of Patrice's note. The words were written clearly enough, but he wasn't sure whether they were true. Or exactly what they meant. Rick had his own reasons for destroying it. Dan would have to deal with Rick later. But Dan knew that he'd made a mistake. A big one. When they'd searched Rick's house, he hadn't gone into Patrice's room because she was sleeping. She was the victim's mother. He hadn't wanted to bother her. Now he regretted his monumental error in judgment.

"Did you try calling her?" asked Dan.

Rick nodded. "No answer."

"I'm going to have a look in Patrice's room. You check the baby's room. See what's missing."

Dan headed toward the foyer, took the stairs two at a time, crossed the landing, and pushed open the door to Patrice's room. Rick was right behind him, and he disappeared into Bethany's nursery. Dan started with the closet; two knit tops, a pair of jeans, and several empty hangers were all that was left, except for a bathrobe hanging on the back of the door. He opened the drawer in the oak night table—nothing stuck out as unusual, just a tissue box, hand cream, and a few magazines. The white bed coverlet was rumpled and unmade. One blue slipper was sticking out from under the dust ruffle. Dan leaned down, looked underneath, and saw the matching slipper. A tall oak dresser stood against one wall. He looked through the drawers: a few pairs of white cotton panties, a nightgown, and several pairs of socks, the contents in disarray. The countertop in the bathroom was bare except for a bar of soap in a white ceramic dish. He slid open the medicine cabinet's mirrored doors. Both sides had empty spaces, as though items had been removed.

As Dan turned to leave the bathroom, he noticed the white wicker laundry hamper in the corner. He dug into his pocket for latex gloves, slipped them on, and began sifting through the damp towels, socks, and underclothing. Then he spotted it. Grabbing a single corner between his thumb and forefinger, he lifted the white pillowcase off the bottom and held it up. Red lipstick was smeared across the wrinkled fabric, as though someone had tried to wipe it off, using back-and-forth strokes.

"Jesus." Dan swore in a whisper under his breath as he dropped the pillowcase back into the hamper and tore off the gloves. *Goddammit,* he thought, falling back against the sink, his eyes closed in disbelief. He closed the bathroom door, stepped out of the room, and met Rick on the landing just as he was coming out of Bethany's room.

"What'd you find?" asked Dan, still shaken by the discovery but trying to regain his composure.

"Some of her clothes are missing. The diaper bag is gone and a few stuffed animals," answered Rick, his breathing ragged.

Dan started down the steps, stopped in the entry hall, and pulled out his cell phone, Rick at his heels.

He punched in the number. "Are you at the Langston residence?" he asked the person who answered.

Dan listened to the response. "Yeah, break into the house. Search everything, even the trash. And send Jimmy over here. I've found something, and I need to secure the house. Now! And call me if you find anything." Dan hung up, dialed the county forensics lab, explained what he needed, gave the address, and ended the call.

Rick stared at Dan. "What is it?"

Dan ignored Rick's question. "Where would she go? Does she have any family anywhere? Brothers or sisters?" He looked at Rick, waiting for an answer.

Rick shook his head. "I don't know of any family. Kim was all she had."

"Give me her cell phone number. We'll get her carrier to locate her."

Rick wrote Patrice's number on a scrap of paper and handed it to Dan. Dan called the station and asked the officer on duty to call the carrier and track the phone's location. Before he hung up, he told the officer to call him back ASAP.

"Did she own a gun?" Dan turned to Rick.

"She hated guns. But I gave her one of my revolvers to keep in her room. I think she kept it in the nightstand next to her bed."

"It's not there now."

81

While waiting for Dan to arrive, Rick had reread Patrice's note.

Dear Rick,

Bethany and I are leaving. I'm going to do what Kimmie would want. She'd want me to take the baby and raise her as my own. Kimmie told me that Josh Logan is Bethany's real father. I don't want him to try to take her away, now that Kimmie is gone. If she asks, I'll make certain that Bethany always thinks of you as her real father. I know you'll understand that this is the only way.

You're a good man, Rick. I loved my beautiful girl, but she didn't deserve you or Bethany. I took care of everything so you could be free. I hope you can forgive me.

Patrice

Rick had gone into his office and placed Patrice's handwritten note facedown on the copier. He'd placed the photocopy in an envelope, addressed it to Donna Pratt, and then locked it in his office safe. If he was arrested for Kim's murder, he'd have evidence that might be convincing enough to prove his innocence.

Rick had always been close to his dad, especially since his mom had died a few years ago. But he hadn't talked to his dad about his worries over Kim's excessive drinking until the night of the reunion. It was late when he'd gotten to his dad's place. His dad was still awake, but he was getting ready for bed. He hadn't wanted to upset his dad by telling him the graphic details about finding Kim with Josh, but he needed to talk about what Kim's drinking had done to their marriage and how it was affecting Bethany.

Rick had told his dad that he'd seen Alexa again and that he still loved her—that he'd never stopped loving her. He realized what he and Kim had wasn't a real marriage, and he knew after seeing Alexa that he wanted more. He also believed that Alexa still loved him, and if there was a chance for them to be happy together, he wanted to take that chance. His father had told him that he understood, and that he knew Rick hadn't been happy with Kim. Rich knew Alexa, and he was glad that Alexa had come back into Rick's life. Rick's dad had reassured him that Bethany would be better off in a happy home, not in an unstable home with a mother who had a drinking problem. Rick was grateful that he had a father in whom he could confide and who believed in him.

Before Rick had married Kim, his dad had expressed his misgivings, but Rick told him about the baby; he told Rick he was proud of him for doing the right thing by taking responsibility. He'd been supportive of Rick, and he wished Rick and Kim every happiness when they were married in a small church wedding ceremony with only immediate family present. Rick knew his dad had wanted them both to be happy. But that wasn't the way things had turned out.

The police might not believe that Rick had been with his dad the night Kim was murdered. Patrice's note might be the only insurance policy he had to keep him out of prison, but it also raised the possibility that he wasn't Bethany's birth father—if Kim had told her mother the truth. Rick didn't know the truth, but he couldn't risk losing his daughter, especially to someone like Josh. He had to protect her at all costs. Bethany had lost her mother. She was not going to lose the only father she'd ever known. A father who would love her and protect her always. Rick was going to make certain she would never know the identity of her real father. He loved her too much to ever let that happen.

82

"Are you going to tell me what you found, or am I going to have to look for myself?" asked Rick.

"I found something—it may be the evidence that Patrice did what she said in her note." Dan paused. "But I'm not sure yet. We'll have to wait for the forensics lab to check it out."

"What is it? Tell me, goddammit!"

Dan didn't want to tell Rick until he was certain, but he had to tell him something. "I found a pillowcase that looks like it has lipstick on it. It was at the bottom of the hamper in Patrice's bathroom."

Rick went into the living room and sat down in one of the armchairs. He put his head down, pressed his fingers into his forehead, and closed his eyes. Dan followed him and stood quietly next to him.

"You mean Patrice may have actually suffocated Kim?" He could barely say the words.

"We can't be certain until the lab checks it out," said Dan, trying to keep his voice calm. "Maybe it isn't what I think it is. But we have to be sure."

"It can't be," he whispered, shaking his head before looking up at Dan. "And she has Bethany."

"We're doing everything we can. Just hang on, Rick," said Dan. "We'll hear something very soon."

Rick got up and started pacing back and forth in the living room. "Do you believe her? That Josh is Bethany's father?" Rick looked confused and upset.

"I know that Kim was a mixed-up girl, Rick."

"Kim was anything but discreet, and I'm not stupid. You know I didn't kill her, Dan." Rick looked at the police chief with a knowing expression on his face.

"I don't think you did, Rick. Let's just concentrate on finding Patrice and getting Bethany back."

Dan didn't know what Rick knew or didn't know, but Dan had been trying to help Kim. He'd slept with her, and it was a mistake. He'd been foolish, and he'd fallen for Kim while trying to get her to stop drinking. At least, that was what he'd told himself. He'd made lots of mistakes, and this was a big one. It had caused him to lose his judgment and objectivity. It had jeopardized the safety of an innocent baby. *Not to mention what I've done to my own wife*, Dan thought, remembering the scene at breakfast on Sunday morning. He had a lot to make up for, and he hoped somehow, he could convince Lynn to forgive him. But he couldn't indulge himself in thinking about his screwups. Now he had to concentrate on finding Patrice and Bethany.

Dan couldn't believe the turn of events. Would Patrice have been crazy enough to kill her own daughter? Was she sick enough to commit such a despicable act? She'd spelled it out pretty clearly in the note, and the pillowcase would be the definitive proof—Dan was fairly certain it was. If she'd known that Josh was the baby's father, she might have gone completely over the edge when she found out he was in jail. Kim's out-of-control behavior could have been more than Patrice could bear. With Kim out of the way, Patrice could raise Bethany by herself. Kim must have told her mother about Alexa. Patrice took care of everything for Rick too. First, she'd gotten rid of

Kim. By taking the baby, she'd set it up so that Rick would be free to be with Alexa.

Dan hoped he'd hear something soon. Every minute that ticked by meant a greater risk to Bethany. Patrice was on the edge, and she must be feeling desperate. Dan kept thinking of the note Patrice had left: *"I took care of everything so you could be free."* That could mean only one thing. And if she'd killed once, she'd have nothing to lose by killing again.

83

Patrice put the handset down as quietly as possible. She'd heard Rick talking to that girl, Alexa. They were going to meet at the resort where she was staying. Before he'd left the house, Rick reminded Patrice to keep the security alarm turned on, that he'd be back soon. She didn't let on that she knew where he was going. She'd hugged him goodbye and told him to be careful and not to worry. That she'd take good care of Bethany. That was precisely what she was going to do.

She'd packed quickly, putting the .38 revolver in her purse. She didn't like touching it; it felt heavy and cold in her hand, but she might need it, especially if she and Bethany had to spend the night in a strange motel or sleep in the car. She couldn't take any chances with Bethany's safety. She pulled the cash-filled envelope out of her bottom dresser drawer and shoved it deep into her oversize leather tote. The last time she'd counted, she had about $4,000 in fifties and twenties. She'd always been careful with money, especially after Kim's father had left them when Kim was just a baby. Patrice had learned to be frugal. She grabbed handfuls of clothing from her dresser and closet and threw them in a large canvas tote, along with a jacket and an extra pair of tennis shoes.

Bethany's clothing didn't take up much room, but Patrice also took the diapers and some of the toys that the baby loved and stuffed them in a white plastic trash bag. She packed several grocery bags with fruit, bottles of water, baby food, formula and bottles, a six-pack of Diet Coke, and plastic utensils. She carried everything to the car and placed it in the trunk. She went back in the house, looked in the kitchen drawer, and found the writing tablet that she and Kimmie had used for grocery lists. She tore out a piece of the paper and grabbed the ballpoint pen from the same drawer. She wrote as fast as she could, then folded the paper in half and stuck it under one of the place mats.

Then she went upstairs and picked up the sleeping infant. Bethany didn't stir as Patrice strapped her in the carrier in the back seat of the compact car. A few moments later, Patrice climbed into the driver's seat and backed out of the driveway. She'd drive north for as long as she could and find a safe place to spend the night, then make her way to the coast. She'd stay off the interstate, but Rick wouldn't be home for a while, so she'd have a good head start.

She knew Rick would understand about everything. She loved Rick so much, and she was so sad about the way Kimmie had treated him. If Patrice had had a good husband like Rick, she would have cherished each moment they had together and thanked God every day for putting a good man in her life. Kimmie hadn't deserved Rick. But that was in the past. Bethany was the future, and Patrice would make certain that her grandbaby was safe and that no one would ever take her away. No one.

84

Jimmy was upstairs, securing Patrice's room, when the doorbell rang. Dan looked out the front window.

"The reporters are here, Rick," he said. "I'd better talk to them. You stay inside."

Dan went outside and spoke into the microphones as the reporters circled him and the cameras zoomed in for the live broadcast. He gave a brief summary, asking that anyone who might know Patrice Langston's whereabouts to please call the police department. After answering a few questions, he went back inside the house. He walked back toward the kitchen, looking for Rick. He wasn't there. He checked Rick's office and found him standing behind his desk, his baseball cap on, sticking his Kimber in the waistband of his jeans.

"Hold on, Rick. Where do you think you're going?" asked Dan, standing in the doorway of Rick's office.

"I'm going to look for her."

He picked up his truck key from the desk and put it in his pocket.

"Wait a minute." Dan's two-way radio beeped, and he picked it up. "Yes, thanks. Let me know what you hear. I'll stay here with Rick." He turned to Rick. "They didn't find anything at Patrice's.

The house is empty, and it looks like no one's been there for days. Probably since last Friday."

He didn't say, "Since the night Kim had been murdered."

Rick started to walk out of his office, but Dan stopped him, grabbing him by the arm. Rick jerked his arm out of Dan's tight grip. "Leave me alone. Bethany's my little girl. I have to try to find her."

"Where are you going to go? You don't have a clue where Patrice went, and she's been on the road at least three hours. It's not smart, Rick. The state police will spot her car. The whole state is on the lookout for her." Dan was convincing. "She won't get far; you know that."

Rick didn't say anything, letting Dan's words sink in. He exhaled, closed his eyes, and tightened his fists. "They'd better find her soon." He looked at Dan.

Dan recognized the look on Rick's face. It was fear. "They will, Rick." Dan's phone rang. "Yeah, where is she? Shit!" He hung up. "The carrier tracked the phone to this location." His finger pointed to the spot where they were standing.

"What do you mean?"

"Call her number."

Dan walked back to the entry hall and stood quietly, listening.

Jimmy called down to him. "Up here!"

He ran upstairs, past Jimmy, and into Patrice's room. He heard the ringtone coming from the closet. He opened the door and stuck his hand in the pocket of the bathrobe hanging on the back of the door. He pulled out Patrice's cell phone.

"Fuck!"

85

Bethany had slept most of the drive. *Thank goodness,* thought Patrice. But she was getting tired. It was dark now, and the drive had been slow. She'd had to fill her tank on the way out of town. And she'd been driving steady, Highway 27 North past Clermont, then she'd caught Route 19 North, a two-lane road heading toward Claysville. The baby was starting to fuss, making hungry noises, and she was probably wet. But Patrice didn't want to stop. Not yet. She knew they would start looking for her soon. Rick would be home by now, realize she and the baby were gone, and he'd read her note. But he'd understand. He might call the police, but maybe he wouldn't. She couldn't count on that. Rick loved Bethany. She knew he'd want her back.

She kept driving north, trying to ignore the baby's whimpering. Patrice made soothing noises, trying to keep her still for just a little while longer. Patrice was driving through the middle of Ocala National Forest. It was normally scenic, but not in the dark, and especially not when she was trying to spot police cars. She was on the outskirts of Claysville when she saw it. The sign for the Pines Motel was white with bright-green letters and *Vacancy* lit up in red. She pulled the compact car under the narrow carport next to the office and turned off the motor. Bethany was wailing now.

"Just a few more minutes, sweetie," said Patrice, putting the pacifier that had fallen onto the seat back into the baby's mouth. Bethany's mouth clutched on to it, and she quieted, but her eyes were mottled and red from crying.

Patrice didn't want to take the baby into the office with her, in case the news might have spread about her taking Bethany. She locked the car and stepped out into the warm night. Moths fluttered around the dim yellow light above the door. A bell rang when she went into the air-conditioned lobby. It was clean looking but rundown. A thin, elderly man, deeply tanned and wrinkled from years in the sun, was sitting on a chair behind a tall desk. He put down the newspaper and looked at her.

"Yes, ma'am, can I help you?" He stood up slowly.

"Do you have a room for the night?"

"A single?" He turned his head and looked through the smeared glass windowpane, trying to see if anyone else was in her car.

"Yes," she said. "How much?"

Satisfied, he looked back at her. "Sixty-five for the night."

"OK," said Patrice. She started digging in her wallet, pulled out four twenties, and placed them on the counter. He looked at the bills, picked them up, and studied her for a moment. He opened a drawer, pulled out a ten and a five, and handed them to her. He took a key from one of twenty wooden pegs mounted on the wall behind him.

"Room 108. It's at that end." He pointed toward the left, at the long, flat-roofed, white strip of rooms. "Checkout's eleven a.m."

"Thanks," she said, taking the key from his hand.

"Wait a minute. Sign here. And I need to see your driver's license." He slid an open black leather registration book toward her.

She found her license, handed it to him, and scribbled her name and address on the guest registration sheet. He turned it around and looked at her name.

"Thanks, Mrs. Langston." He handed the license back to her.

Patrice felt his eyes on her. She must have seemed nervous, and she wondered if he had seen the baby in the car. She said good night, trying to act calm, and got back into the car, driving slowly through the nearly empty lot until she found room 108. She grabbed Bethany first, gave her a comforting hug, put the diaper bag over her shoulder, and unlocked the door to the room. She looked around at the double bed with the thin green bedspread and dull-brown carpet. There was a television on the dresser across from the bed. She set the diaper bag on the bed and looked at the bathroom. It smelled like mold, with two dingy white towels hung over a chipped towel bar and a miniature bar of soap wrapped in paper on the sink. It would have to do. The air conditioner mounted under the window was chugging cool air, but the room felt humid.

She had Bethany balanced on her hip when she caught a glimpse of herself in the black speckled mirror over the dresser. She didn't recognize the gaunt face and blonde, unkempt hair. She touched her straw-like hair, not remembering when she'd last combed it. Or washed her face. Black mascara was caked under her eyes. No wonder the man in the office had stared at her. She looked frightful, even to herself. But that didn't matter now.

First things first. Get the baby changed and fed, unpack what she needed for the night's stay, and then decide her next move. Jacksonville wasn't too much farther. She'd stay off the main roads, then look for a room to rent on a side street. Staying out of sight for a while made sense, and she and Bethany would plan their life together. So far, so good.

While Patrice was unpacking the car, she didn't see the older man step out of the motel office. His eyes were fixed on the end unit, on the Toyota Camry parked in front of it and the nervous movements of the blonde woman who was lifting a white trash bag out of the back seat. She carried it into the room and slammed the door. The man's hearing wasn't very good anymore, but he was sure he could hear the sound of a baby's cries coming through the darkness.

He stepped back inside, into the narrow room behind the front office, and plopped down onto the saggy sofa. He went back to the newspaper he'd been reading when Patrice came in. While he'd been outside, his cell phone had made a series of piercing tones followed by a bright-yellow banner signaling an Amber Alert. The details were all there, including the make of the car, Patrice's description, and a description of Bethany Young, the abducted baby. But several hours would pass before the night-shift clerk checked his cell phone and called 911 to report that the missing baby and her kidnapper, Mrs. Patrice Langston, had been at the Pines Motel in room 108.

86

Dan went into the kitchen, leaving Rick in his office watching local news on the television set on the credenza behind his desk. Dan stared out the back door into the darkness and pulled out his cell phone. He dialed the number, hoping she'd talk to him. He was relieved when he heard her voice.

"Hey," he said.

There was a long silence before she spoke. "What is it?" Her words were crisp and cold.

"I'm sorry, Lynn." He waited for her to say something. Anything.

"So am I."

"I never meant to hurt you." His voice was filled with deep regret.

"What do you want me to say? That everything's OK?" Her tone was angry.

He knew she didn't want to talk to him, now or maybe ever. "I don't know. I just wanted to talk to you."

He heard her take a deep breath. How could he tell her everything he was feeling? He had so much to make up for. He wanted to tell her he loved her and didn't want to lose her. He didn't even know how to begin.

"How's the investigation going?" Thankfully, she'd changed the subject to a safe topic.

"Not good. Have you seen the news?"

"No, what's happened?"

"Patrice Langston, Kim's mother, took the baby. The whole state is looking for her."

"Oh, no, Dan. Why would she take the baby?"

"I can't go into it now, but it's bad."

There was a long silence. "When will you be home?"

"Not until we find her."

"Will you call me when you know anything?"

"I will," he said.

Lynn hung up. At least she was talking to him, which was a start. He hoped she'd forgive him. He hoped he could forgive himself. Sadness about Kim and the baby engulfed him, and he squeezed the inner corners of his eyes, stopping the tears. He would never understand why she couldn't accept his love or even love herself. She'd thrown her life away. But for it to end the way it had wasn't fair. And if her mother had killed her, it was incomprehensible.

He stood there, looking through the sliding doors, into the darkness, the faintest glimmer of moonlight reflecting off the lake. He wondered how often Kim had seen the moonlight from this very spot. He turned away and pulled out his phone again. Dan needed to get updates, check on possible leads. Patrice wouldn't get far before someone spotted her. Especially because she was traveling with a baby. But finding her was one thing. What would happen after that was the big question.

87

"Dad, try not to worry," said Rick. He'd wanted to tell his dad before he'd heard it on the news.

"Rick, what can I do? Should I come over?" he asked his son.

"No. Stay there."

Rick didn't want to tell his dad that he might not be there. If something didn't break soon, he would have to try to find Patrice on his own. He couldn't sit and do nothing. His mind was racing, trying to think of where Patrice might take Bethany. Where would an older woman go, alone, with an infant, someone who wasn't thinking clearly? Where would Patrice take her granddaughter?

"I'll be here, son. Call me when you hear anything."

"I will, Dad." He hung up.

Rick dialed another number, and her businesslike voice answered. He told Donna about the note and that the photocopy was in the safe. He told her about Patrice and the baby, but he didn't mention the other possible evidence. Donna had seen the news and had been getting ready to call him. She expressed her shock at the turn of events, but she said that it sounded as if Patrice's note had cleared him. She asked Rick to call her when he'd found Bethany or had any news. Rick said he would and hung up.

He stared at the television, not listening or seeing what was on the screen. His thoughts were drifting to the past. Suddenly he remembered something. Something Kim had told him. Maybe that's where Patrice would go. It was a long shot, but it was the only place he could think of where she might take the baby. If she was delusional, it might make sense to her. It was a place that had meant something to her. Once. A long time ago.

Rick texted Alexa that she could reach him on his cell and that he would call her as soon as he could. He grabbed his hat, gun, and car key and went into the kitchen, where Dan was talking on his phone.

Dan hung up as soon as he saw Rick. "What the hell are you doing, Rick?"

"I think I know where she might have gone."

"Where?"

"Patrice and Kim's dad lived in Jacksonville when they were first married. She was a baby when he took off, and Patrice never heard from him after that."

"Is her dad still in Jacksonville?" Dan looked surprised.

"No one knows where he is."

"Shit." Dan looked at Rick, puzzled. "So why would she want to go back there?"

"It's a hunch, but Kim said her mom always talked about how happy she'd been when she lived there with her dad, especially right after she was born." Rick was searching his memory. "Maybe she'd want to go back. I don't know." He shook his head and shrugged his shoulders.

Dan stared at Rick for a long time, thinking.

"Maybe."

"You got something better?"

"I'll call the state police and give them a heads-up." Dan made the call and then went upstairs to tell Jimmy what was going on and what instructions to give to the forensics team.

Rick looked out of the front window. The streetlights were on, and he could see some reporters still hanging around in front of the house, several vans parked along the curb. He and Dan ignored the shouted questions as they climbed into the patrol car. Dan took off, headed toward the interstate, lights flashing.

"I hope we're not on a wild goose chase." Dan stared at the road and then glanced down at the speedometer. The digital readout was 82 mph.

Rick didn't answer. His gut told him that Patrice was on her way to Jacksonville. He hoped someone would spot her car and call the police. It had been over four hours since he'd last seen his daughter. He was barely holding it together, especially since reading Patrice's note. It was one thing for her to take off with the baby. But knowing Patrice had killed her own daughter made Rick sick to his stomach. She had his baby girl with him. He hoped to God that when they finally caught up with her, it wouldn't be too late.

88

Bethany drank the bottle down fast, and when all the formula was gone, she started crying. Patrice changed her, held her against her shoulder, and patted her back gently while walking around the room until Bethany had calmed down. She finally fell asleep, and Patrice placed her on her back in the bed, covered her with a pink blanket, and surrounded her with three of the lumpy bed pillows. All the crying had made Patrice edgy. *Thank God she finally shut up,* she thought.

Patrice needed food too. But she felt too tired to eat. She pulled a can of Diet Coke out of the plastic bag, popped the tab, and drank until the bubbles burned the back of her throat. She set the can on the nightstand, took her shoes off, and stretched out her legs, leaning back against the thin wooden headboard. She tried not to shake the bed. She looked over at the baby, sound asleep, her thumb in her mouth. She looked just like Kimberly had when she was a baby. Exactly like her.

Patrice finished the Coke and decided she'd better check her phone. She hadn't looked at it since she'd left Cypress Lake. She got out of the bed, opened her purse, and searched through the clutter. No cell phone. *Where is it?* she wondered. Then she realized she'd forgotten it. "Shit!" She looked around the room until she found the television remote. She turned it on and flipped through the channels until she found a local station. There it was. She saw the photo of her and Bethany.

Dammit! she thought. She'd have to pack the car, load the baby back into her car seat, and start driving again. She was tired, but thankfully the Coke had given her a lift. She dug another one out of the bag and drank it down as fast as she could. She felt awake now, and her stomach was full. She went into the bathroom, splashed cold water on her face, and stared at herself. "Everything's going to be all right. You and Bethany will be home soon," she said to the face in the mirror, the eyes staring back at her glazed and bloodshot.

She put on her tennis shoes and tossed the package of diapers back in the garbage bag. She was glad she hadn't had time to unpack. She left the baby asleep on the bed while she loaded the car. The gnats and moths were flitting around the light mounted outside the door, and they kept buzzing near her head. She swatted at them, annoyed, but managed to get everything packed into the car within ten minutes. She picked the baby up gently while singing Kimberly's favorite lullaby and placed her in the car seat, tucking the pink blanket snugly around her.

Patrice got behind the wheel, took a last look at the motel office, and backed out. *The old guy must be asleep,* she thought. The caffeine buzz still at work, she pulled onto the two-lane road and started driving. Hopefully she'd get to Jacksonville without being spotted. It wouldn't take long to get there, to their two-bedroom furnished apartment only a few blocks from the beach. She and Jack and Kimmie. They'd all be together again. Patrice was going home at last.

A few large drops of water began to splatter against the windshield before the light rain turned into a downpour. Patrice had to strain to see the dotted center line on the blacktop. She could barely see through the rain-streaked window; the wipers were on high speed, but they couldn't keep up with the pounding spray. She could see a few stores and gas stations along the side of the road. The lights blurred as she passed, but she didn't want to stop. She couldn't risk getting caught now. She had to keep going until she got home. She was getting tired, but she couldn't stop now. Jack would be home, and he'd be waiting for her and Kimmie.

Patrice pressed harder on the accelerator, and the small car raced through the deluge, the rain mixing with the thin slick of motor oil that coated the surface of the blacktop. The headlights illuminated the yellow triangular-shaped sign with the curved black arrow, but Patrice didn't see it until it was too late. The worn tires lost traction as she hit the brakes, and the tan Camry slid into the left lane, then off the steep edge of the road, the front end plowing into the deep drainage ditch. Patrice screamed just before her head hit the driver's-side window, breaking the glass and cutting a deep gash in her temple. She slumped in the seat, unconscious, the car no longer visible from the road. The wipers kept their steady rhythm as the rain pounded the car in the darkness. Bethany felt the sudden jolt, startled into near consciousness, but she quieted herself, falling into a deep and oblivious sleep.

89

Alexa tried to fall asleep, but her body ached all over from Josh's brutal attack. She hadn't realized how much he'd hurt her. She'd never forget his face and the crazed look in his eyes or how vulnerable and helpless she'd felt. Thank God he hadn't raped her. Or worse. He might have killed her if Chief Hastings hadn't stopped him.

She'd lived with Meghan after she'd moved to Chicago and was often alone in their apartment when Meghan was away on a flight. Now she lived alone in her condo, and she'd spent many nights alone in hotel rooms when she was on layovers. But she'd never had a close call like the one she'd had with Josh Logan. Men had come on to her, and she'd had to push a few away, but she'd learned to handle herself. She'd never really been afraid, and she was determined not to let this one traumatic experience affect her life.

But Alexa found it hard to put her worries aside, especially about Rick and everything he was going through. She missed him so much, and she was grateful she'd gotten to spend time alone with him. Alexa's last thoughts before falling asleep were about Rick and how his lips felt on hers and the way his strong arms felt when he was holding her. She longed for him, to be near him, to hear him whisper her name in the dark. She prayed that somehow this nightmare would soon be over, but she knew his life and Bethany's would never be the same because of what had happened to Kim. If it was meant for them to be together, that's what she wanted—more than anything in the world.

Alexa's sleep was unsettled, and she woke up disoriented as well as very hungry and thirsty. She looked at the clock. It was 9:00 p.m., and she realized she'd missed dinner. She checked her phone for messages before calling room service. The blinking green light signaled an unread text message. She was surprised to see it was from Rick, saying he'd call her later. She knew something must have happened. She dialed his number.

"Rick, are you OK?"

"Patrice has taken Bethany. Dan Hastings and...for her." She had trouble understanding what he was saying because the call was breaking up.

"Is Bethany all right?"

"I don't know."

"Oh, my God. Where are you?"

"We're heading north. I'll call you"—his words were unintelligible—"know anything." He hung up.

She heard enough to understand that he was with the police chief and that they were looking for Patrice and Bethany. Rick sounded frantic. Alexa grabbed the remote and turned on the local station. The program had been interrupted with a special news bulletin. The reporter was talking about the Amber Alert, and a photo of Patrice and Bethany appeared on the screen. Alexa was stunned. How could all this be happening? She sat on the bed, listening to the details, unable to believe what she was hearing. They were implying something about Patrice being a suspect. She didn't understand what that meant, but Alexa prayed for Patrice and the baby, for their safety. And for Rick.

90

The Pines Motel parking lot was lit up with flashing lights from a mix of state and local police cars. Dan parked near the office, in the section of the lot not blocked off by yellow tape, and he and Rick walked under the overhang until they got to room 108. The rain was coming down in sheets, flashes of lightning adding to the eerie scene. They were stopped by a local police detective, Devon Anderson, who asked to see identification. Dan pulled out his badge and introduced Rick as the baby's father. The detective stared at Dan's ID and then looked at Rick and nodded.

"What'd you find?" asked Dan.

"The woman who registered as Patrice Langston and the baby are gone. We're looking for her car now. Doubt she's gone too far. The clerk saw the Amber Alert around eleven p.m., and by then, she was out of here."

Dan had a partial view of the room, empty except for two officers wearing rubber gloves and searching for evidence. He looked at his watch; it was 11:30 p.m.

"How did the room look?"

"We've found a used disposable infant diaper in the trash can. The bed was disturbed, the pillows thrown off the bed, and only one wet towel was found in the bathroom." He looked at his notes. "Mrs. Langston checked in around eight, and it looks like she had a few Cokes. Maybe took a nap. She must have seen the news, gotten scared, then packed up fast and left."

"That's it?" asked Rick, trying to go through the doorway into the motel room.

"I'm sorry, sir. You'll have to stay out of the room." He held his arm in front of the door, blocking it.

"She has my little girl," said Rick, his eyes boring into the detective's.

"I understand, sir. We're looking for her car right now," he said, his voice reassuring.

"No sign of any disturbance?" asked Dan.

"No, sir. No drugs, no blood, just a woman and a baby in the room for a short time." He looked back into the room.

"Did anyone see Bethany?" asked Rick.

"No, sir. But there's no indication that your little girl has come to any harm."

Rick turned his back to the police detective. "Let's go, Dan. We'll look for her car."

Detective Anderson interrupted him. "Sir, I understand how you feel. I have a little girl too. But we have the local police searching, and we have all units looking for her car. We'll find her."

"Is there a place we can get some coffee?" asked Dan.

"There's a diner on the right, about a half mile north. It's open twenty-four seven."

Dan handed his card to the trooper. "Thanks, Detective Anderson."

"I'll call you as soon as I hear anything."

Dan and Rick walked back to Dan's cruiser and climbed in. Rain was pelting against the roof of the car, the thunderclaps loud.

"Let's keep driving and look for her," said Rick.

"We need to do what the detective said," said Dan, starting the car.

Rick had been right, thought Dan, looking both ways before he pulled the car slowly onto the wet two-lane road. Patrice was heading toward Jacksonville. It wouldn't be long until they found her and the baby. And from what the detective said, it sounded like Patrice was taking good care of Bethany. But Patrice was trying to get away, and she might be getting desperate. However, Dan knew there was nothing to do. They'd have to wait. And hope that someone spotted her car—before it was too late.

91

Wednesday

They sat in the booth by the window, drinking coffee, watching the rain blowing sideways, the wind bending the palm trees nearly in half. Two men in soiled work shirts sat on stools at the counter, locals on their way home after working the second shift. The workers exchanged a few words between bites, concentrating on the meatloaf special and chatting up the young waitress.

"What do you want to do? We can't sit here all night," asked Rick, frustrated that they weren't searching for Patrice.

"I say we sit tight," said the chief.

Rick didn't say anything. He got up and walked toward the men's room, pulling out his phone. He dialed Alexa's number.

She answered right away. "Rick, I hoped you'd call."

"I'm sorry if I woke you up. I just needed to hear your voice."

"I wasn't asleep. I've been watching the news. Have you found Patrice and Bethany?" she asked.

"Not yet."

"The police will find her, Rick. I know they will."

"I'm worried, Alexa. Patrice isn't thinking straight."

"It must have been too much for her, losing Kim."

"I think it was more than that," said Rick. How could he explain something that he himself didn't fully understand? "I need to go, Alexa. I'll call you as soon as I hear anything."

"Rick, wait a minute."

"What is it?"

"It's not the right time, but I have to say it. I'm sorry for everything. Can you ever forgive me?" she said.

"I'm the one who messed up, not you."

"I promise I'll never leave you again, no matter what."

He heard her crying. "I'll never let you leave me again." His voice broke. "I have to go. I'll call you when we find them."

He hung up and stood alone, staring out into the blackness of the night and the rain that wouldn't let up. He'd been through so much. The shock of finding Kim dead. He'd never wanted her hurt, even though she'd hurt him so many times, destroying whatever marriage they'd had with her lies. The years of feeling alone. Now the possibility of losing his daughter was beyond his comprehension. He wouldn't be able to bear it. She was all he'd ever had to live for. He loved her so much, his beautiful baby girl. Even if she was Josh's baby, which he doubted, he'd make certain she never knew. He was her father in every sense of the word, and if there was one thing in the world she could count on, it would be him. He prayed to God that they'd find Patrice soon. And that Bethany would be safe. He wasn't sure how much longer he could hold himself together. But he had to. For Bethany's sake.

Rick walked back to the booth and looked down at Dan. "Let's start checking the motels between here and Jacksonville." Rick looked outside. "She couldn't have gotten far in this storm."

Dan stood up and threw some bills on the table. "Let's go."

The two men walked out into the heavy rain, hunkered down, climbed into the patrol car, and began their search.

92

Dan kept the car close to the center line, the headlights casting dim shadows on the wet, almost invisible roadway. "Shit!"

The road disappeared in front of him as he missed the sharp curve. He jerked the steering wheel hard to the right, and the back end of the car skidded to the left before the tires caught, the car fish-tailing back into the right lane.

"Jesus Christ!" Rick gripped the door handle as the car lurched, almost sliding off the road before Dan regained control.

Dan was leaning forward over the steering wheel, straining to see through the heavy downpour. "Patrice must have stopped somewhere. No one could drive for long in these conditions."

"How about letting me drive for a while?" Rick looked over at Dan, worried.

"No, I'm fine," he answered, eyes glued to the road ahead.

He was going about twenty miles per hour when Rick spotted the diffused bluish light of the Best Western sign.

"Dan, turn right here!"

Dan almost missed the entrance, but he managed to make the turn, driving slowly through the blacktop parking lot that wrapped around the three-story hotel. Patrice's car wasn't there. Dan pulled out of the lot, back onto the road, and kept driving. They were about five miles outside Claysville, with more motels lined up along the outskirts. They repeated the process, driving through one motel lot after another, looking for any sign of Patrice's car. No luck.

They finally got to the small town, exhausted from the long night of searching, as well as the treacherous driving conditions. Dan pulled into an all-night convenience store with two gas pumps and parked in one of the spaces in front of the nearly empty store.

"Let's get some coffee," Dan said. He glanced over at Rick, who was slumped down in the seat, staring out of the window.

"OK," answered Rick.

"We'll head to the local police station and wait there until we hear something."

Rick nodded in agreement. They were worn out and needed to take a breather. The rain was tapering off, and the sun would be up within the hour. Dan knew she couldn't just disappear. She must be holed up somewhere. But where? He also knew that every minute she remained missing was another minute that the baby was in possible danger. Patrice didn't want to be found.

93

Kristin and her BFF, Shawney Lynn, were walking along the rain-soaked berm of the road, trying to avoid stepping in the mud puddles. The storm had lasted most of the night, but now the sun was up, and the heat was starting to build. The girls walked to the bus stop each school day, about a quarter mile from their neighborhood. They lived next door to each other and had played together since they were in kindergarten. Their moms were best friends, too, and they took turns driving the girls to school when the weather was bad. On sunny days, the girls had to ride the bus, which was so uncool.

Shawney Lynn heard the beep and pulled her phone out of the back pocket of her jeans. She stared at the screen. "Hey, Kristin, look at this. Can you believe it?"

She handed the phone to Kristin so that she could read the text from her boyfriend. At least, she wished he was her boyfriend.

"He wants to ask you out," said Kristin, handing the phone back to her friend.

"No, he doesn't." She looked disappointed. "He just wants to know what's on the math quiz."

"Maybe you can help him study."

Shawney rolled her eyes. She held the phone in front of her, her thumbs flying over the small keypad. "I told him I'd sit next to him in study hall."

"I think I know what he wants to study," said Kristin, her laughter sounding more like a squeal.

Shawney had stopped listening to her friend and walked over to the edge of the embankment. The grass was high, and the rolled-up cuffs of her jeans were getting wet, but she didn't seem to notice. She looked down and saw the tan car, wedged, nose first, into the deep ditch. The rear end of the car was sticking up, and the taillights were still on but dim.

"Hey, look at this, Kristin."

"What is it?" Kristin stepped through the tall grass to stand next to her friend.

"Listen." Shawney put her right index finger over her lips.

The girls stood in silence looking down at the car, listening. A truck rumbled past, and they waited for the noise to fade away.

"There it is. Did you hear it?"

"I heard something," said Kristin, her eyes widening as she nodded.

The noise got louder. It sounded like a mewing cat or maybe a person crying.

"Someone's in that car," said Shawney, excitement rising in her voice. "I'm going down."

"No. Wait!"

"Maybe they're hurt," she said. "Here, hold my backpack."

"Don't go down there! You could get bitten by an animal or something!" exclaimed Kristin.

Shawney started making her way slowly down the steep slope, turning sideways, her sandals sliding in the wet grass and weeds. She had to catch herself several times before she reached the car. She walked around the car, her feet sinking into deep mud. She stood on her tiptoes and looked into the right-side passenger window.

"Oh, my God!" she called up to Kristin. "Call 911!"

"Are you sure?"

"Hurry!"

She walked around the rear of the car and saw a baby in the back, strapped in a car seat. The baby was whimpering, eyes closed, barely moving. She tried to open the car door, struggling with the door handle, and finally it fell open. Shawney unfastened the restraining strap, pulled the baby out, and held her against her chest.

"It's OK, it's OK," she said, trying to comfort the warm but unmoving infant.

Kristin yelled down. "They're on their way!"

Shawney cradled the very still baby in her arms and walked toward the front of the car. She looked at the woman slumped against the broken window in the drivers' seat, her head bent at an odd angle. She felt sick to her stomach and had to look away when she saw all the blood. She'd never seen a dead person before, but the teenager was certain that the lady in this car was dead.

94

Dan dropped Rick off at the emergency room entrance of the Claysville County Hospital and looked for a place to park. Rick ran through the emergency doors and stopped to speak to the nurse at the triage desk.

He was out of breath and struggled to get the words out. "The ambulance brought my daughter here. Can you tell me where she is?"

"Are you Mr. Young?" asked the young woman in the blue scrubs.

"Yes, ma'am," answered Rick, his hands on his hips, chest heaving.

"She's on the third floor, pediatrics. The elevator is down the hall." The young woman pointed to the right.

Rick ran down the hall and punched the silver up arrow. He started pacing and then saw the door indicating the stairwell. He opened the door and ran up the stairs to the third floor.

"Bethany Young," he said to a nurse walking down the hall.

"You're her dad," she smiled. "She's going to be fine, Mr. Young. She was just a little dehydrated, so don't be concerned when you see the IV." She stopped at the desk and talked to the clerk, explaining that the baby's father was here, then turned back to Rick. "Let me take you to her."

The nurse talked to Rick while they walked down the quiet hallway, stopping him before they went into the pediatric intensive care unit.

She guided him to a changing room outside of the unit. "Wash your hands and put this mask and gown on; then you can hold Bethany."

The nurse was waiting for him when he was ready. When he saw her in the infant crib, tears welled in his eyes. She was sleeping and looked so fragile. The nurse nodded that it was OK, and he picked her up. Bethany's eyes opened as soon as she felt the familiar arms, and she smiled up at Rick, her blue eyes locked on his. The nurse led him to a lounge chair and handed him a bottle. Holding her gently, he fed her, talking softly to his baby girl.

When she fell asleep again, Rick was overcome with relief, the tension in his body falling away. He leaned his head back against the headrest, closed his eyes, and said a silent prayer of gratitude for the tiny blessing he was holding in his arms. Tears of exhaustion and sadness streaked down his face. He also wept for the mother Bethany would never know, sad that Kim's life was taken away so tragically. He made a promise that Bethany would always be safe and would know how much her mother loved her and didn't want to leave her. He would be both mother and father to her and provide all the love she ever needed. Now and forever.

95

The nurse stood next to Rick and touched his arm. He stirred awake.

"Let me take her now. There's someone here who wants to talk to you." She picked up Bethany and gestured to the police officer standing in the hallway.

When Rick walked out, Dan smiled at him. "You got good news."

"Yes, good news." Rick nodded, jaw muscles flexed as he held back tears.

"Let's go down the hall."

The men walked down the hallway until they came to a sunny room decorated with colorful murals of rainbows, balloons, and unicorns, complete with a play area with toys, games, strollers, and small tables and chairs. Two little girls were playing with baby dolls in a far corner.

Dan spoke quietly so that only Rick could hear. "Patrice didn't make it."

Rick was numb, the news not sinking in.

"She was driving too fast, missed a turn, and the car slid off the road. She hit her head." He paused. "It's a miracle the baby survived. Two teenage girls walking along spotted the car in the ditch, and they heard Bethany crying."

The two men stood there, both shaken and worn out. Rick had tears in his eyes. "Thanks for helping me find my daughter."

"I think we both need something to eat," said Dan.

He and Rick walked in silence, side by side, down the hall to the bank of elevators.

96

Saturday

Bethany balled up her fist and tried to put it into her mouth while resting her cheek on her dad's shoulder. Nestled in his arms, her thumb in her mouth, her eyelids fluttered before her she fell into a deep, contented sleep. The organ began to play, and Rick stared straight ahead, listening to the choir singing his mother's favorite hymn, "Amazing Grace."

Rick and his dad had sat in this very same front row pew once before—when his mother had passed away. He was sure his dad had sat here when Rick's grandmother had left them too. Rick was too young to remember that day. He was glad that Bethany wouldn't remember this day either. No one should have to lose their mother, and this way was the worst. But Rick would never let her feel any hurt from it. Not if he could help it.

The service ended, and Rick, his dad, and Hank stood up as the congregation filed out. Rick had arranged an informal reception in the church hall for anyone who wanted to visit with the family after Kim's funeral service. Rick looked around the empty church and saw

333

her. He handed the sleeping baby to his dad and said he'd be right back.

Alexa was standing in one of the last rows near the atrium. Rick walked down the crimson-carpeted aisle and stood next to her.

"Can you stay for the reception?" he asked.

"I don't think I should, Rick."

He looked toward the altar. His dad was standing next to a table filled with arrangements of carnations, lilies, and roses. Bouquets surrounded the gold-framed photos of Kim. His dad was talking to Bethany, pointing toward the photo of her mother. Bethany was quiet, her head on his shoulder, sucking her thumb.

Rick turned back to Alexa and said, with a catch in his voice, "Dad would love to see you again."

"I'd love to see him too. But it's not the right time," she answered. "And I can't miss my flight."

"I know." He looked around the empty church. "This is a tough place to say goodbye."

"You need some time. Everything has been so difficult for you."

"It will be harder with you gone."

"I don't want to leave you, but if I stay, it might feel wrong." Her eyes began to glisten with tears.

"Nothing with us has ever been wrong. You've been the only right thing in my life." His voice was low as he grabbed her hand and held on to it as though willing her not to leave.

"I'll come back soon, Rick," she said. "I promise."

He glanced at the necklace he'd given her. "I love you, Alexa." His jaw was clenched as he tried to keep firm control of his emotions.

"I love you, too, Rick." She was crying now. "Will you kiss Bethany for me?"

He nodded.

They walked out together, side by side, down the wide steps, and stood on the sidewalk. Everyone had left or was already at the reception. The morning felt strangely cool, the sky overcast with the promise of rain in the air. The palm fronds rustled above their heads as the wind blew in from the lake.

"I'd better go," she said.

Rick let go of Alexa's hand and watched as she walked away. He went back into the church and made his way to the reception hall. He said hello to a few friendly faces as he looked around for his dad. The older man was standing near one of the windows, Bethany comfortable in his arms. She was giggling, her cheeks flushed to match her pink baby dress, her soft blonde curls resting against his dad's face. She saw Rick and reached out for him.

He pulled his little girl into his arms, kissed the top of her head gently, and whispered, "That's from Alexa."

She gazed up at him and smiled, her small fingers gently touching his mouth.

97

October

Why hasn't he answered? Alexa picked her phone up off the night table, hoping to see the green blinking light telling her that she had a new text message, but there wasn't one. She checked for missed calls. Nothing. Rick had called her on his way to work that morning and said he'd call her at lunchtime. But he hadn't. She'd texted him that afternoon from the airport when she'd gotten back to Chicago, but he hadn't responded. *That isn't like him*, she thought. He'd always returned her texts within an hour, or two at the most. It had now been over twelve hours since she'd heard from him. She hoped he was all right. *Maybe something has happened to the baby!* Alexa had to stop "going there" every time she didn't hear from Rick. The kidnapping, Josh's brutal attack, and Kim's murder had affected her deeply. She had to stop thinking the worst, but it was easier said than done.

Alexa and Rick had been in almost-daily contact since she'd left Cypress Lake the day of Kim's funeral. It had been so hard to leave him that day, even though she knew it was the right thing, and she felt he knew it too. They'd drawn closer with each phone call, their bond stronger than ever before. Rick and Bethany had lost everything in many ways. He'd undergone so much stress and was making every effort to rebuild their lives. He'd made it clear to Alexa that he wanted her to be part of his world and part of his future. She hadn't wanted to intrude in his life or push him as he coped with the terrible tragedy he'd had to face. But she loved him and missed him. And she couldn't understand why he hadn't called her—she was really beginning to worry that something was wrong.

Alexa was upstairs, propped up in bed trying to concentrate on the book she was reading, when she heard the doorbell. She didn't have to check the clock to know it was too late for someone to be at her door. Every alarm bell in her head went off. The security system was armed, but she felt a cold chill, hairs prickling on the back of her neck. *Who would be ringing my doorbell at this time of night?* She grabbed her cell phone and pulled up the security app, and the video feed appeared. The wide-angle lens mounted high above the front door picked up the porch and most of the manicured lawn and street in front of her colonial townhouse. An unfamiliar SUV was parked in the shadows alongside the curb.

Her stomach knotted in fear when a dark figure standing on the front porch came into view. His back was to the door, jacket collar turned up, and his hands were in his pockets. He was wearing a baseball cap. He turned around, faced the door, and rang the bell again. Alexa stared at the figure, not believing her eyes. *Oh, my God! It's Rick!*

Alexa's heart felt as though it was going to burst out of her chest. She didn't care that she was dressed in her oldest college T-shirt and pajama pants, and her hair was pulled up in a messy ponytail. She punched in the code to disarm the security system, raced down the stairs, and opened the front door. A gust of frigid air swept into the townhouse. Rick had his back to her, his broad shoulders hunched against the early cold October wind. When he turned around, a flood of emotions swept through her. Before she could catch her breath,

Rick stepped into the entry hall, wrapped her in his arms, and pressed his lips against hers, his face cold against her warm skin. He pushed the door closed with one hand, never taking his mouth from hers. He finally pulled away long enough to look at her but kept her locked in his embrace, and she melted into him, his coat cold against her chest.

"I had to come," he exhaled, his voice low and gravelly.

"I must be dreaming," she whispered, overwhelmed at being in his arms again and at how natural and right it felt.

"This is no dream; this is real," he answered, kissing her again, pulling her against him.

"I love you so much." Alexa was breathless as he tightened his embrace, his face pressed against hers.

He pulled away, holding onto her hand as he looked around the well-decorated foyer with its framed mirror and antique table with fresh flowers. Then he turned back to look at her. He smiled the half smile she'd known since they were in high school, but his eyes weren't smiling. He looked worn out and serious. Even in the dim light, she could see the flecks of gray at his temples. She reached up, took his cap off, and brushed his hair lightly with her fingertips.

He grabbed her hand and pressed his lips against her palm. He gazed down into her eyes, which were pooling with tears. "I love you, too, Alexa, and I had to see you." He released her hand, his arms falling to his sides as he stepped back, his eyes locked on hers. "I need you to start your life with me." It was a statement.

"Are you sure it's the right time? What will people think?" Her voice was full of uncertainty.

"I don't give a damn what anyone thinks," he said, his eyes narrowing. "If you meant everything you said to me."

"I meant everything, Rick. With all my heart," she answered, her voice quivering as tears slid down her cheeks.

"That's all I needed to know."

He reached for her and pulled her against him, as though he'd never let go. She looked up into his deep blue eyes, and his arms engulfed her, his mouth locked on hers, his kisses wet and forceful and demanding. Alexa arched into his body, grasped his hair, any part of him that she could touch, her mouth open to his, their desire and need exquisite, full of longing and waiting. Out of breath, Alexa pulled away, took Rick by the hand, and led him up the stairs.

EPILOGUE

November

Alexa took her eyes off the country road for only a second to glance at the colorfully wrapped package sitting on the passenger seat of the rental. She hoped Bethany liked the doll that the sales clerk had recommended as the perfect gift for a one-year-old girl—soft, washable, and vanilla scented. Alexa had held the soft toy and inhaled the scent, imagining how Bethany would react when she saw the cuddly doll. *Perfect.* Alexa smiled as she thought of Rick and his daughter. Her heart was overflowing with so many emotions, wondering how she'd gotten to this place in her life. *Could all of this really be happening?* she wondered, shaking her head in disbelief. *Maybe Meghan had been right all along—things do work out the way they're supposed to.*

Alexa turned her attention back to the two-lane blacktop, straining in the gray light of early dusk to see the sign that marked the cutoff. The GPS indicted that she was approaching the turn just as she spotted the almost-invisible road. She made a right turn, driving slowly on the narrow dirt road that tracked through the groves. She maneuvered the car through the open steel gate and drove about a half mile farther until she saw the two-story white-frame house tucked under the tall oaks, its porch light on. She pulled onto the gravel drive and parked next to Rick's truck. As she shut off the engine, she saw the screen door open. Her heart skipped a beat, and she felt the warmth of desire spread through her body. Every time she saw him was like the first time. She watched as Rick crossed the porch, wearing jeans, boots, and a flannel shirt, sleeves rolled up, holding Bethany in the crook of one arm. Buddy ran down the three wooden steps ahead of them and raced up to the car, placing two paws on the door, his tail wagging in a quick rhythm.

Alexa grabbed the present, opened the car door, and stepped out, greeting the big dog with a hug and affectionate pats on his head.

"Hey, boy," she spoke softly, rubbing his ears. "I missed you too."

He did a few spins as she walked to the front of the car where Rick and Bethany were waiting. Bethany was smiling, looking into her dad's face, and Alexa heard him say, "Alexa's here for your birthday party." Alexa studied Rick's face in that brief exchange, the delight and love in his eyes for his daughter. Alexa loved him so much at that moment.

Alexa gave Bethany a kiss on her chubby cheek. "Happy birthday, Bethany."

Rick wrapped his free arm around Alexa, pulled her into him, and kissed her lightly on the lips. "I'm so glad you're here," he said, a catch in his voice as he looked into her eyes.

"So am I," she said, looking up at him, his face inches from hers. "I wouldn't miss this day for anything in the world."

"You're just in time for *cake*." He emphasized the word, smiling at his little girl, who began to bounce in his arm with excitement.

Rick kept his arm around Alexa as they walked across the driveway and up onto the porch, Buddy at their heels. Bethany kept trying to grab strands of Alexa's hair, and as she did, Alexa grabbed the little hand and kissed it, making Bethany giggle and repeat the game. Rich and Hank came out onto the porch to greet her, both men taking turns giving her big hugs, telling her they were glad she could come. Alexa told them she couldn't be anywhere else on this special day. She'd thought about this day, a day that marked new beginnings, as well as the unspoken feelings and sadness that they all felt, as they remembered the end of a young mother's life. Alexa fought back tears, knowing how painful that loss was.

"Come to Poppa," said Rich, taking Bethany from Rick, holding her above his head as she squealed with delight, kicking her legs in the air.

He lowered the baby into his arms, opened the screen door, and led the way into the house. Rich carried her into the kitchen, snuggling Bethany against him and talking in a high-pitched singsong voice, telling her that she was the prettiest baby girl he'd ever seen in his life. Bethany giggled and wriggled in his arms, her eyes widening when she noticed the dancing flame from the single candle on her birthday cake.

The kitchen was dark, except for the candlelight that cast soft light on the round two-layered cake, frosted white with a ribbon of pink icing around the border. Four purple-and-pink edible butterflies were perched on top of the cake, with HAPPY BIRTHDAY, BETHANY spelled out in pink frosting. Rick, Alexa, and Hank followed Rich into the kitchen, all taking their places at the planked table. Alexa placed Bethany's present on the table next to the other gifts.

Rich handed Bethany to Rick, who was sitting across from Alexa.

"I think we better hurry before the candle melts down," said Hank, watching as dripping white wax began sliding onto the cake.

The chubby-cheeked baby girl was staring at the cake and smiling, showing two-brand new bottom teeth and clapping her tiny hands as they all began to sing "Happy Birthday." When the song ended, everyone laughed as Rick tried to get Bethany to blow out the half-melted candle. She blew tiny spit bubbles as Alexa, Rich, Hank, and Rick leaned in, and in unison, blew out the flame. Rick looked over at Alexa, stared into her eyes that were beginning to fill with tears. Rick stood and handed Bethany to his dad.

"Hank, are you going to cut the cake?" he asked.

"I sure am," he answered as he began cutting big slices of the festive cake, placing them on pink paper plates.

Rick walked around the table and took Alexa's hand. "We'll be right back."

Buddy jumped out from under the table, panting with excitement, but Rick told him to stay. The dog dropped his ears, curled up on the floor, and leaned affectionately against Rich's legs. Rich rubbed Buddy's head, saying, "Good boy."

Rick led Alexa out of the kitchen and through the living room and held the screen door open. It was cool on the porch but not cold for early November. It was almost nightfall, a sliver of the moon just becoming visible in the clear sky. The crickets were chirping, but it was mostly quiet except for the sounds of the deep voices of Hank and Rich that drifted outside from the kitchen.

Rick was still holding tight to Alexa's hand. "Are you okay?" He searched her blue eyes.

She smiled at him, but tears began to fill her eyes. She was tired; the long day and the long months of anticipation were catching up with her. Rick held her close against him. She nuzzled her face into his neck, her body pressed against his warm chest, her arms around his neck.

"Are you cold?" he asked.

"Not now," she whispered.

He wrapped her in his arms and held her as tight as he could. She never wanted this feeling to end. She was so grateful that Rick was back in her life, and at this moment, she understood that everything happened for a reason and that a plan had been in place for her. For them both.

She looked up, searching his eyes. "I can't believe that I'm really here. That this is really happening."

He bent down and kissed her tenderly, his lips warm and lingering on hers before pulling away. He pulled her close again, exhaling. It was a while before he spoke.

"This is real, Alexa. I love you, and nothing has changed, except I love you more than I can ever tell you."

She stepped away and stood a few feet from him, trying to figure out how to say the words. "I love you, Rick. You're the only man I've ever loved, from the instant I first saw you." Alexa began to cry. "Everything that happened is my fault. I couldn't bring myself to forgive you. I should have understood." She paused. "We would never have been apart."

"Alexa, we were both young." His face got very serious. "Nothing is your fault. And we're here now. That's all that matters. And we're never going to be apart again. Ever."

He wiped the tears off her face with his fingertips. Alexa watched as he reached into his pocket and pulled out a small blue-velvet box. He held it tight in his hand, his mouth set as he looked at her.

"I wish I could have given this to you a long time ago," he said. "I remember the first time I held you in my arms at the dance after the game. My life changed that night." He took a deep breath; his voice was husky.

She looked down at the box and then up at Rick. She didn't move. He opened the box, took out the ring, and reached for her left hand.

"Will you marry me?" It was a second before she nodded, tears of happiness streaming down her face.

He slipped the sparkling solitaire diamond ring on her finger, and Alexa didn't even look at it, but wrapped her arms around him and kissed him. They were locked in an embrace; his arms enveloped her, and when he released her, he grabbed her hand and stared at the ring, then into her eyes. "I'll never leave you. I promise." His face was streaked with tears.

"I love you so much, Rick."

She reached up, put her arms around Rick's neck, and kissed him with passion and longing. She would never forget their first kiss—how his lips felt, the taste of his skin, their whispers in the night when they were young and making love and promises of forever. Nothing had changed. He was still that boy who had become the man she would love forever. She thought of the love she saw in his eyes for Bethany, and she felt an overwhelming love for him—and thankfulness, as she thought of all he'd been through to get to this day. It was the beginning of a new year for Bethany and for her and Rick, and a celebration of the life they would share together as a family.

They turned at the sound of a baby squealing, and Rick smiled at her. "Let's go celebrate."

Rick took her hand and led her through the open screen door. Hank and Rich looked up as they returned to the kitchen.

"I let her open your present, Alexa," said Rich. Bethany was on his lap, bouncing the baby doll up and down and giving it wet kisses.

Alexa smiled down at Bethany. "Do you like your birthday present?"

Bethany smiled at Alexa and gave the soft doll a tight squeeze.

"May I hold your baby doll?" asked Alexa in a playful voice, reaching toward the toy.

Bethany dropped the doll and reached for Alexa. Alexa picked up the little girl, drew her close against her, and sat down at the table across from Rick.

"You're the perfect baby doll," said Alexa warmly, cuddling the little girl before giving her a gentle kiss on her forehead.

"You two almost missed the cake," said Hank. He handed Rick a paper plate with an ample serving, along with a plastic fork. "Would you like some cake, Alexa?"

"I'd love a piece, thank you," she answered. "Wouldn't we?" She looked down at Bethany.

Hank set the rich dessert with extra pink frosting in front of them both. Alexa stuck her fork into the cake, broke off a small bite, and offered it to Bethany; she ate it quickly and gestured for more. After several more bites, she reached for her sippy cup. She tipped the cup so she could finish every drop of the milk.

"You've had a big day, baby girl," said Rick, his eyes misting as he looked at his daughter.

"I think we've worn her out," said Rich, patting his son's arm.

Bethany was sucking her thumb, her head resting against Alexa's chest, when she noticed the gold heart necklace that Alexa was wearing. Bethany grasped it with her delicate fingers and began playing with it. Alexa smiled down at her, spoke in soft whispers, telling her that her daddy had given her the necklace many years ago. They all lingered around the kitchen table, drank coffee, and talked late into the night while Bethany slept peacefully in Alexa's arms.

ABOUT THE AUTHOR

Linda Wells brings her own background to her latest novel, *Cypress Lake: A Romance Thriller.* Like her heroine, Wells grew up in Florida and went on to travel the world as a flight attendant.

Before taking to the skies, Wells attended the University of South Florida in Tampa. Through her work, she has lived in Atlanta and Chicago. She now makes her home in the Midwest, where she enjoys both reading and writing mysteries. She is the author of three thrillers: *Dead Love, Dead Promise, and Cypress Lake: A Romance Thriller.* She is hard at work on her fourth. Find out more by visiting Linda at lindawellsbooks.com.

Made in the USA
Coppell, TX
31 December 2020

47362919R00208